THE WOODPECKER ALWAYS PECKS TWICE

Being alone in the woods was a lot spookier than I'd imagined it would be. It was something I did not plan on doing again.

A flash of red appeared in the distance, then disappeared just as quickly. Was that a man's shirt? My arms grew cold. Maybe I wasn't so alone after all.

That was an even scarier thought.

I stood still a moment, my eyes scanning the trees and coming up empty. I turned as silently as I could and reversed course.

I came across a small leaf-clotted stream and followed it. Funny, I didn't remember crossing a stream yesterday. Had I missed it? Had I missed a turn?

Worse, was I lost? I looked at the treetops, hoping for a sign of the McKutcheon house, but was disappointed to see only the trees.

The sound of a woodpecker drew me. There was a red-bellied woodpecker midway up the trunk of an old sycamore. It looked like my old pal, Drummy. There was no way to be certain. But it wasn't the bird that interested me.

It was the body of Bessie Hammond propped up against the base of the sycamore.

Books by J.R. Ripley

DIE, DIE BIRDIE

TOWHEE GET YOUR GUN

THE WOODPECKER ALWAYS PECKS TWICE

TO KILL A HUMMINGBIRD

CHICKADEE CHICKADEE BANG BANG

HOW THE FINCH STOLE CHRISTMAS

FOWL OF THE HOUSE OF USHER

A BIRDER'S GUIDE TO MURDER

CARDINAL SIN

Published by Kensington Publishing Corp.

The Woodpecker
Always Pecks Twice

J.R. Ripley

KENSINGTON BOOKS
www.kensingtonbooks.com

KENSINGTON BOOKS are published by

Kensington Publishing Corp.
119 West 40th Street
New York, NY 10018

All Kensington titles, imprints, and distributed lines are available at special quantity discounts for bulk purchases for sales promotion, premiums, fund-raising, educational, or institutional use.

Special book excerpts or customized printings can also be created to fit specific needs. For details, write or phone the office of the Kensington Sales Manager: Attn.: Sales Department. Kensington Publishing Corp., 119 West 40th Street, New York, NY 10018. Phone: 1-800-221-2647.

Kensington and the K logo Reg. U.S. Pat. & TM Off.

First Lyrical e-book edition: May 2017

First printing: September 2019
ISBN-13: 978-1-4967-1972-0
ISBN-10: 1-4967-1972-7

ISBN-13: 978-1-4967-1973-7 (ebook)
ISBN-10: 1-4967-1973-5 (ebook)

10 9 8 7 6 5 4 3 2 1

Printed in the United States of America

For Dodu. Shut the door.

1

R*at-a-tat-tat-brrr.*
I peeked at the clock on the bedside table: 6:30 a.m. As usual. "Good morning to you, too," I said with a groan. I sat up. My feet bounced around on the pine floor in search of my pink slippers.

Rat-a-tat-tat-brrr. The sound was loud and dissonant—hardly the stuff of "Peachum's Morning Hymn" from *The Threepenny Opera.*

I came to my feet and rubbed my fists into my eyes. "You're killing me, bird." It had been a late night. I'd had a real, honest to goodness date with Derek Harlan. Dinner and a movie, the whole nine yards. Now, if I could have only followed it up with nine hours' sleep. Heck, I'd have settled for six, but it wasn't in the cards.

Rat-a-tat-tat-brrr. The bird could've used a music lesson from Kurt Weill.

Nonetheless, I crossed to the dresser and picked up my binoculars, determined to get a better look at him. I removed the tethered lens covers, pulled the curtains and brought the binocs to eye level. There he was, a beautiful red-bellied woodpecker, clinging to the gray bark of the big bitternut hickory outside my bedroom window, tapping away at the twisted hollow branch hanging closest to the house.

Waking me up, like he did every morning lately, the relentless pounding reverberating across my skull as if he were perched on my head and not in the tree. The woodpecker wasn't tapping to drive me crazy. He—and this was a he because I recognized the bird as a male by the intense red coloration on the back of its neck and top of the head; a female only has the red coloration adorning its neck—was tapping to drive out carpenter ants and other insects. In other words, breakfast.

I moved the binoculars out over the street toward Ruby Lake. There was a doozy of a storm brewing. The sky was the color of lead with streaks of black running like watercolor down a page. Jagged bolts of lightning streaked across the distant sky.

The woodpecker went about its business, oblivious to the storm. When a bird's got to eat, a bird's got to eat. Don't ask me why it is named a red-bellied woodpecker when it is the bird's head that is the most clearly and visibly colored red. A small patch of red is distinguishable on a red-bellied woodpecker's lower belly but that's all. Perhaps it was because the scientists had already proclaimed another woodpecker to be the red-headed woodpecker. First come, first served. I'm no ornithologist. I was an English major in college and now run a small-town store selling bird-watching and bird-feeding supplies.

I scanned the distant treetops, wondering if I might spot any other interesting or unusual bird species this morning. There was no avian activity to be seen along the shoreline. Generally, I would spot ducks, kingbirds, swamp sparrows, and the occasional swallow flying low across Ruby Lake.

A small motor-powered fishing boat sat alone in the lake, bobbing side to side in the windblown water. I searched the woods for signs of bird life. With the heavy clouds blocking the sun, there was little to see besides shadows. Lately, a pair of red-shouldered hawks had spent early mornings settled on the broad limbs of a tall oak whose branches loomed over the water. But not this morning. They seemed to have taken the day off. I suddenly wished I could do the same.

I was about to retreat in search of my own breakfast—I smelled fresh-ground coffee brewing—when my eyes fell on the old McKutcheon house across the lake. The McKutcheons had been one of the Town of Ruby Lake's first families, having settled in our small North Carolina town back in the early 1800s. The house was nearly that old—even older than the late nineteenth-century home that now housed both me and my business, Birds & Bees. Though much of the original McKutcheon house had burned to the ground in the 1890s, family members had rebuilt the house and barn and added various other outbuildings around the turn of the twentieth century.

Then, fortunes failing, the McKutcheon house had sat empty for decades, when the last members of the family moved to Boston, or so I seemed to remember hearing. But there was a light on in one of the upstairs windows now. Wisps of smoke fought to rise from the central chimney against the onslaught of rain falling in heavy sheets.

I heard a flutter and turned. My woodpecker friend shook himself to rid his feathers of raindrops, then returned to digging into the hickory bark.

I trained my eyes once more on the McKutcheon house. The light coming from the upstairs window danced like flame, but I knew this to be a trick of the rain, which blurred and bent the light until it looked almost alive. I was about to turn away, when a man stepped into view. At least, I thought it was a man. It was really too dark to be certain at first. I was too far away. The rain was falling too hard.

A second, smaller shape stepped into view. He, if it was a he, moved quickly, arms flailing. The larger figure threw up his arms as if to ward off an impending blow.

It wasn't a blow that came next. It was a full-scale attack. The smaller man launched himself at the larger one as if to tackle him. Both fell in a heap. I gasped. What were the two fighting about?

They disappeared from sight, the window ledge blocking my view. A moment later, one of the men's heads came into view. He crossed the floor on his knees, stood, and opened the window.

What on earth was he up to?

My hands were shaking as I tried to see what would happen next. The binocs were bouncing so much, the room jumped in and out of my sight. I squeezed my elbows against my ribs to steady the binoculars and narrowed in on the room once more.

The smaller man threw open the window and hoisted something up over the sill. I fiddled with the focus, trying to get a sharper look. I now realized what I was seeing. A pair of legs dangled over the window ledge, nothing more distinguishable than a pair of dark trousers with two bare feet protruding.

Rat-a-tat-tat-brrr! My heart skipped a beat.

The smaller man stooped and lifted the other man, pushing him up. The larger man put up no struggle. Was he unconscious? Was he dead?

A moment later, the smaller man heaved. His victim fell silently, tumbling like a sack filled with wet straw, from the upstairs window to the ground below. If he wasn't dead before, he most certainly was now.

I gasped. The startled red-bellied woodpecker took flight. I ran to the phone.

2

"What on earth?" my mother exclaimed as I came running into the kitchen.

"Phone!" I cried. "Where's the phone?"

Mom set the coffee carafe back on the warming plate. "Right here." She lifted the portable phone from the base on the corner of the counter and handed it to me.

The landline doubled as the Birds & Bees business line. I punched in 911 and reported what I'd seen. Mom gaped at me.

I dropped the phone on the counter and pressed my face against the cool window. The rain was letting up. If I turned my head just right, I could make out the McKutcheon house from this vantage.

Mom poured two cups of coffee and handed one to me. She cinched her robe around her waist, sat, and motioned for me to do the same. "You saw some man throw another man out a window?" There was shock, surprise, and maybe a smidgen of disbelief in her voice.

My hand trembled as I lifted the cup to my lips and sipped. "Yes. I mean, at first I wasn't sure what I was seeing. But it was definitely a couple of people fighting." I took a steadying drink. The coffee was black and unsweetened, but I didn't mind for a change.

Mom broke off a piece of her breakfast cookie. "At the McKutcheon house? Across the lake?"

I nodded and glanced out the window. How long would it take the police to reach the house?

"I thought the old place was empty," Mom said. "What were you doing looking at the McKutcheon house?"

I turned back to my mother. I felt terrible to be causing her any concern or alarm. Mom's got muscular dystrophy and, though it is still very manageable, I was concerned for her health and didn't want to say or do anything that might cause her undue stress.

Unfortunately, in practice, I seemed to be doing the opposite despite my good intentions. "I'm sure it's nothing." I patted Mom's hand. "Jerry will get it all sorted out." Jerry Kennedy is Ruby Lake's chief of police. I don't exactly have the highest opinion of him, but then, his opinion of me isn't exactly the stuff upon which friendships are formed.

I explained to Mom how I had picked up the binoculars to watch our resident alarm clock, then happened to be perusing Ruby Lake for further bird sightings. I keep a chalkboard behind the counter in the store where I and anyone else can post local bird sightings on a weekly basis.

"Ah, Drummy." Mom smiled. Drummy was the name we'd given to what we had come to think of as *our* woodpecker. After all, if he was going to come around every morning, noon, and night giving us a solo drum performance, he might as well have a name.

Curses are much more personal if you can attach a name to them.

Mom slid the package of breakfast cookies my way. She'd begun eating one of the prepackaged oatmeal-raisin cookies each morning with her coffee since discovering them in the cereal aisle in the market a month ago.

I declined. "I don't think I could eat a thing." My stomach was churning. I thrummed my fingers against the kitchen table as I glanced at the clock on the wall. "How long do you think before we hear something?"

"You need to be patient, Amy." Mom is a retired high school teacher and still knows how to talk to me, when necessary, like I'm a troubled teenage student in need of a calming, steadying, grown-up influence, instead of the mature, thirty-four-year-old woman my driver's license claims I am. Dad passed away awhile back and Mom and I share the third-floor apartment above Birds & Bees. "I'm sure Jerry will call us the minute he has the situation under control."

I stood and began pacing. "I don't think I can stand to wait."

Mom grinned. "I can call Anita, if you like." Anita Brown is one of my mother's best friends, pinochle partner, and more importantly in this case, part-time dispatcher for the Ruby Lake Police Department. If anybody else knew what was happening, Anita would.

The doorbell interrupted my answer. I opened the door. "Esther?" Esther Pilaster, or "Esther the Pester" and "Esther Pester" as I sometimes interchangeably refer to her, is a renter of mine. She came with the house when I bought it and, until her lease is up, I am stuck with her. Her apartment is on the second floor of Birds & Bees.

"You've got company downstairs," snapped Esther. "I let him in and told him to wait." Esther is a long-in-the-tooth spinster in her seventies. Narrow shoulders only barely supported the flowery dress she wore. She's a small woman with a hawkish nose, sagging eyelids, and a silver ponytail. Wispy white eyebrows topped off a pair of rheumy gray-blue eyes that looked at me funny. "Hey! What's that? Kittens?"

"What?"

She pointed a crooked finger at my pajama top. "Your jammies are covered in kittens." She squinted at me. "I thought you said you didn't like cats."

I tugged at my pj's and blushed. "I'm allergic to cats, Esther. I never said I didn't like them."

Footsteps pounded up the steps from the shop below. "What the devil is going on up here?" Chief Kennedy's head appeared at the top of the stairs. His cap was damp and dripping.

"Jerry—Chief Kennedy." I pulled my collar closed.

He took off his cap and thumped it against the side of his thigh. "If you're not coming down, I'm coming up." The chief pushed past me and into my apartment. "You got coffee?"

"Please"—I cleared my throat—"come on in," I said, hoping the sarcasm wasn't too heavily laced. I wanted to learn what he'd discovered at the McKutcheon house, so this wasn't the time to start sparring with the man.

"Thank you, Esther," I said, turning to my renter. "Shouldn't you be prepping the store for opening? Thank you." I shut the door on her before she could object.

Not only was I stuck with Esther the Pester as a tenant, I was now stuck with her as an employee of Birds & Bees. That was Mom's fault. Mom figured I needed more help around the store, as if she and my best friend and business partner, Kim Christy, weren't enough assistance.

To tell the truth, Mom was right. Somehow, I seemed to be spending as much time out of Birds & Bees as I did within. Mom had made the executive decision to hire Esther part-time. As much as it irritated me, it made sense. And, so far, Esther had been a pretty decent employee. Sales were up. I was pretty sure that was because customers were afraid of her. But, hey, a sale's a sale.

"Dammit, Mrs. Simms," I heard Jerry say as I crossed the living room to the kitchen. "I mean, no disrespect, but that daughter of yours is daft as a brush and half as useful!"

"What's that supposed to mean?" I shot back, feeling my pulse quicken. Jerry has a way of making my blood boil faster than most—dropping me in a cauldron of boiling oil wouldn't heat me up any faster than Jerry did. "Name-calling? That's the thanks I get for reporting a crime?"

Jerry snorted. "Crime?" His two-tone brown uniform was sodden, especially around the shoulders and cuffs. He'd left a trail of wet footprints across the floor. That meant there'd be mopping in my future today. Oh, joy.

Mom handed Jerry a steaming coffee mug. "Drink this. You'll feel better." Mom had been one of Jerry's teachers in high school. Neither of us would have suspected he'd grow up to be Ruby Lake's chief of police one day. Personally, I wasn't so sure Jerry would ever grow up mentally.

"The only crime is that you wasted a perfectly good morning sending me out on a wild-goose chase, Amy Simms!"

I threw out my chest. "Wild-goose chase? That's what you call reporting a murder, Jerry?"

Jerry twisted one of the kitchen chairs around and

straddled it. He thumped his mug against the table. "There is no crime, Simms."

Mom slid the plate of cellophane-wrapped breakfast cookies the chief's way. She's become a real proponent of them. Jerry wasted no time peeling one out of its wrapper and wolfing it down.

He slapped at his trousers. "My squad car's filthy. I'm filthy. It's storming out, in case you didn't realize. And it's a dirt road out around the lake to the McKutcheon homestead."

Mom took a seat and said calmly, "Tell us what you found, Jerry."

Jerry huffed. "The place is a hostel of some sort."

"Hostile?" I jumped in. "You see? I told you there was something nefarious going on over there."

"I didn't say they were *hostile*." The chief growled. "I said they're running a hostel. H-O-S-T-E-L. All sorts of foreigners and such running around over there."

"You mean like a bed and breakfast?" Mom inquired.

Jerry shrugged. "Young fellow at the door called it a hostel, so hostel it is. Guster McKutcheon is running it. He wasn't home."

"Guster McKutcheon," Mom said thoughtfully. "I'm not sure I remember him. Who were his folks?"

"I've no idea," answered Chief Kennedy. "Apparently he works out at the diner. Nobody at the house knew anything about a murder. And there was no body!"

"But—"

Jerry's hand chopped through the air between us. "Not on the ground, not in the house, not in the air circling the property like a freaking pigeon! Do you have any idea how big a fool you made me look, Amy?"

I was pretty sure Jerry didn't need my help in that department but knew better than to say so. Mom shot me a warning look just in case. "I know what I saw, Jerry."

"Maybe you were hallucinating." He stuck his nose in my face. "Your eyes are red. Are you hungover?"

"Of course not!" I backed away. I may have had the teeniest bit too much to drink last night and I may have had a teeny bit too little sleep, but still, I knew what I saw.

Jerry leaned across the table toward me. "Explain to me how you happened to see anything at all." He shook his arm at the window. "The McKutcheon place must be a mile away from here."

I looked at my mother for support. "We were bird-watching," Mom said.

"Bird-watching!" Jerry chuckled. "Lord, I had no idea what this town was getting into when you came back and opened that silly store of yours." I refrained from protesting because no good could come of it.

He thumped his fist and the table jumped an inch. "Sorry, Mrs. Simms," the chief said, grabbing a paper napkin from the vintage brass holder on the table and wiping up the few drops of coffee that had spilled from his cup. He squinted at my mother. "Do you mean you saw this so-called murder, too?"

Oh, sure, if my mother, his former history teacher, says she saw a murder, he'd be all over that.

"Actually, no," admitted Mom. "You see, Amy was holding the binoculars." Oh, well. She tried.

Jerry nodded as if everything was now clear as day, though not this rainy morning.

"Then what was that I saw being tossed down, if not a man?"

"Junk," replied Jerry Kennedy. "Plain and simple. Nothing but junk. At the time of your so-called fight, a couple of the youngsters were cleaning out that upstairs room the fastest way possible—tossing garbage out the window. The roof's got a leak and water was getting in. Same thing in the barn. Several others were out there in the barn covering some boxes of supplies with plastic.

"There was a whole pile of trash on the ground outside the window when I arrived. Bits of furniture, piles of newspapers, clothes, and"—he screwed up his eyes at me—"even an old dressmaker dummy."

"But I saw—"

Jerry interrupted. "The kid at the house explained that the room had been used to store all kinds of stuff. They're turning the room back into a bedroom so one of the boys doesn't have to keep sleeping on the sofa."

He turned to my mother as if she was the only one even worth trying to explain anything to. "You should see the place, Mrs. Simms. There are a bunch of young foreigners staying there. Some of them barely speak English."

Mom rose and started a fresh pot of coffee. "I had no idea one of the McKutcheons had come back to town. It will be nice to see the house come alive again."

"Come alive?" I couldn't help quipping. "Mom, somebody only this morning got defenestrated there."

Jerry looked nonplussed.

"It means thrown out a window, Jerry," I filled in.

Jerry's only reply was an eye roll.

"Look, I don't know what you saw." Jerry stood and shoved a couple packs of breakfast cookies in his trousers. I waited eagerly for Mom to berate him, but she didn't. She's way too nice to the man.

"Maybe you saw a big old bird," Jerry said. "Maybe you saw the wind shaking the branches." He wiggled his arms for effect. "It was storming out pretty good. Hell, maybe you saw the widow in the lake!"

Everyone in town knew the story of the widow in the lake. The story goes that she'd drowned herself after her husband was murdered by marauders around the time of the Civil War. She'd laid a curse on the men and they had died one by one, each death more hideous than the previous.

After the last man died, she walked into the lake and disappeared. Some say she still rises from the center of the lake once a year, on the anniversary of her husband's death. Today was not that day. I pursed my lips. At least, I didn't think today was the day.

"All I do know is that you did not see one man throw another man out that window." Chief Kennedy was pointing across Ruby Lake at the McKutcheon house. He headed for the apartment door and threw it open. "Nice jammies, by the way!"

My cheeks burned as I slammed the door and turned the lock in case Jerry decided to come back. Mom offered me a third cup of coffee and I didn't refuse it. I carried my steaming mug to the kitchen window and looked out. The sky was brightening now. In a couple of hours, we might actually get some sunshine.

"Maybe Jerry's right," Mom said, coming up behind me. "Maybe your eyes were playing tricks on you. It was early. You were tired. The storm."

I exhaled deeply, turned and smiled. "You know, I hate it when you're right."

"I know."

"And I doubly hate to even think that Jerry Kennedy could be right."

Mom chuckled. "You don't have to tell me that, Amy. How was your date last night?"

"Great." I couldn't resist smiling at the memory. "How was yours?" I knew she'd had a date of her own with Ben Harlan last night. It was a little funny and maybe a little weird that she happened to be dating Ben and I happened to be dating his son.

Mom deftly evaded the question and fingered my lapel. "Shouldn't you be getting dressed and down to the store? I hate to think of Esther being stuck down there opening up all alone."

I handed Mom my mug. Thoughts of Esther running around the store unsupervised took precedence over nearly everything else, including dating gossip. "Me too." Who knew what trouble the Pester might get into?

I took a quick shower, then brushed my teeth and hair—puzzling at the frazzled brown-haired, blue-eyed woman in the mirror as I did so. Were Jerry and Mom right? Had my imagination run away with me? I threw on a comfortable pair of slacks and a red Birds & Bees–logoed polo shirt.

Before leaving the bedroom, I picked up the binoculars from the bed, where I'd dropped them in my hurry to telephone the police. I retrained them on the house across the lake. There was nothing out of the ordinary going on. A couple of lights were on upstairs and down. The rain had diminished to nothing more than a fine drizzle that created a gloomy pall over the lake.

Somewhere deep in those waters, the bones of the widow in the lake were said to be stirring restlessly. I could picture her white skeleton rolling along the lake floor in search of a peace that would never come.

The storm had quieted, the wind had died. As I laid the binocs back atop the dresser, I couldn't help wondering if someone else had died this morning, too.

3

"Amy, dear, before you go, I was hoping we could have a little talk." Mom sat in the big chair next to the sofa, a copy of the *Ruby Lake Weekender*, our town's small local paper, in her lap. She was yet in her robe. Mom had been letting her unnaturally blond hair grow out. Soon it would be a similar shade of chestnut to my own hair. I could see a lot of myself in her as she reverted to her natural color.

"Can it wait, Mom?" I said. "Esther's probably opened by now. Plus, there's a delivery truck due."

Mom opened her mouth, tapped the thin newspaper against her leg. There's not a lot of news in Ruby Lake—not that that's a bad thing. "Of course, dear. I'll be down a little later myself."

"Tell me, do you believe in this whole widow-in-the-lake thing that Jerry was blathering about?"

Mom shook her head. "A town like Ruby Lake has a lot of local stories. I'm not that familiar with this one, though the story has cropped up now and again." She pointed a finger at me. "I'm a historian, remember, so I believe in facts, not fairy tales. If I'm remembering correctly, anecdotal evidence does suggest that a crime was committed, a woman's husband brutally murdered.

"Perhaps she even committed suicide afterward. I doubt we'll ever know the entire story. There was no one around to tweet then or post the news on Facebook or in some blog." Mom leaned forward. "Why? You didn't see the widow in the lake, too, did you?"

"No!" Thank heavens.

"Then I'd worry about the lady running around downstairs in Birds and Bees and not the widow in the lake," Mom said with a big grin.

Esther. "Thanks." I planted a kiss on her warm cheek and headed downstairs.

In the shop there's a small kitchenette and seating area where customers can have a drink or a snack and peruse some of the bird literature—books and magazines—I keep available on a built-in wooden bookshelf between a pair of rocking chairs. I found Esther hovering over the kitchen sink. She'd added a green Birds & Bees–logoed apron to her ensemble.

"Trouble with the cops again?" Esther asked, her eyes flashing with delight. She had a pot of coffee going and was filling a jar with tap water for iced tea.

I smothered a yawn. My stomach grumbled. I should have taken Mom up on the breakfast cookies. The only food on hand downstairs this morning was a plate of Danish butter cookies, the remains of a tin I'd bought a couple of days before at the Lakeside Market up the street. Hardly the breakfast of champions. Or shopkeepers. "Not exactly." I helped myself to a small stack of cookies, then glanced at the front door. "Have you opened up?"

"Five minutes ago." She stared at me like a dog waiting for a juicy treat. "So what did Chief Kennedy want, busting in here all wet and covered in mud first thing in the morning?"

I sighed. Esther was obviously not going to let go of this figurative bone. "Look, Esther," I began, "you've lived here a long time—"

"My whole life."

"Yes," I said, "your whole life. What do you know about the McKutcheons? Do you remember them?"

Her wispy white eyebrows formed a V above her nose. "Them from the farm on the other side of the lake?"

"Yes," I said, nibbling at my final cookie. After this, I'd look for some real nutrition. Maybe a candy bar.

"What do you want to know about them for?"

The corners of my mouth turned down. Why did she seem to answer every question with a question? "If you must know, I—" I hesitated. Did I really want to tell Esther the Pester what I'd seen? Or thought I saw? Finally, I began again. "If you must know," I said quickly, before I could come to my senses and change my mind, "I saw a man throw another man out the window this morning." I folded my arms across my chest and stared her down.

"At the McKutcheon house?!" Esther hooted.

"Yes," I said sharply. "At the McKutcheon house."

Esther had finished filling the tea jar. She added a half dozen tea bags, sugar, and lemon, and set it in the window to warm in the sun. Not that I was certain we'd see any sun today. No matter. We could always warm the water in the microwave if it came to that.

"What were you doing at the McKutcheon house?" demanded Esther.

"I wasn't *at* the McKutcheon house."

"Then how did you see what you say you saw?"

I explained how I had been bird-watching and happened to glance across the lake.

"And you just happened to see a murder?" Esther pulled the plate of cookies out of my reach as I extended my hand for a second helping. "These are for the customers."

As if waiting for their cue, a pair of women walked through the front door and Esther followed me as I went to greet them. I inquired if they were looking for something specific, but they said they wanted to take a look around. I retreated to the cash register and checked to make sure I had sufficient change to get through the day. If not, I'd need a trip to the bank.

"Nobody has lived in the McKutcheon house for some years," Esther said from the other side of the sales counter. "Last McKutcheon moved out before you were born."

"Well, according to Jerry Kennedy, there's one living there now."

Esther was clearly surprised. She scratched at her ear. "You don't say?"

"Apparently a Guster McKutcheon has come back to Ruby Lake. He's opened the house up as a hostel."

"You mean like a hotel?"

"Something like that." I gazed across the street to Ruby's Diner. "Apparently Mr. McKutcheon also has a job over at the diner."

"I never thought we'd see a McKutcheon living in that old place again." Esther cackled.

"Why not?" I pushed the cash register closed. Esther was interrupted from answering by the approach of our two customers. One carried a birdhouse constructed of recycled material.

The blonde held the birdhouse aloft. "Will I get robins to nest with a birdhouse like this?"

I took the birdhouse from her hands. "This house would be perfect for chickadees and wrens," I explained. "See this opening?" I ran my fingers around the edges of the hole. "It's an inch and a quarter. It's designed for cavity nesters, like the wrens and black-capped chickadees, but too small for others like house sparrows and bluebirds."

The woman looked disappointed. "So, no robins?"

I smiled to lessen the blow. "Sorry. In addition to using branches, robins build their nests on shelves and ledges. You can build them a nesting platform yourself." The two women looked at each other dubiously.

"We do sell a selection of nesting platforms. I can show you, if you like?"

The women agreed and followed me over to a wall where I had different types of birdhouses and nesting boxes arranged by the bird species they were best suited for. I helped them select a simple cedar nesting platform. The platforms look like a typical birdhouse with the front removed, except for a low border along the front to keep the nesting material from spilling out.

"I'll take it," the customer said.

"And I'll take the other birdhouse, Claire," added her friend. "The one for wrens and such."

"Perfect, Eden." The woman named Claire explained that the two were next-door neighbors. "We can share."

I gave them instructions on how to mount the birdhouses—they'd both opted for pole mounts rather than affixing them to trees—and rang up the sale.

I caught up to Esther, who was ordering around the deliveryman as he rolled boxes of supplies in through the back door using his red hand truck. I pulled her aside. "About what you were saying before, Esther," I said out of the side of my mouth.

"About what?" Esther cocked her head. "Do you want the seed back here or out front?"

"Out front, like always," I said, struggling to maintain my calm. We always keep the twenty-five-pound bags of unshelled black oil sunflower seeds up front in the corner beside the bins. There was no point lugging them from back to front one at a time when there was such a nice, compliant worker who'd move them all at once for us.

I chased after Esther as she directed Ralph, our young deliveryman, out to the sales side of Birds & Bees. Of course, he'd been delivering here for six weeks or more already, so he knew perfectly well where everything went.

He was too nice to point that out to Esther. "Thank you, Ms. Pilaster," he said with a nod of his head. "Anything else I can do for you, ma'am?"

"Well"—Esther tapped her foot against the hardwood—"there is that pile of pallets in the storeroom doing nothing but collecting dust and cobwebs. An old lady like me can't just pluck the lot of 'em up and toss 'em in the dumpster alone, can she?"

Ralph grinned. "Yes, ma'am. I'll get right on it." Ralph has short red hair, green eyes, and an arc of light freckles running across his face. He looks all of eighteen, but I know for a fact he is twenty-four. I'd asked to see his driver's license.

"Ralph," I said, "you'll do no such thing. Kim and I can handle that." I turned to my employee—though sometimes I felt it was the other way around and I was working for Esther. "I'm sure Ralph has a lot of other important deliveries to make today." Ralph has a route running from Charlotte in the south to Asheville in the north and all points in between.

"Harrumph," snorted Esther.

Ralph grinned. "It's no problem at all, Miss Simms." He rubbed his hands together. "I'll get on those pallets and be on my way."

I thanked Ralph and held Esther in place by clamping my arms on her shoulders. The woman was harder to keep still than a nervous chicken. "Okay, Esther." I resisted shaking the woman—just barely. "Tell me why you said what you said."

She squinted in puzzlement.

"About the McKutcheon place." I nudged her some more when an answer wasn't forthcoming. "You said you didn't think you would ever see a McKutcheon living there again. What did you mean by that?"

The door chimed and Esther swiveled—a shark catching the scent of fresh blood in the water.

"Oh, no you don't," I whispered. Over Esther's shoulder, I called to the gentleman as he marched toward the book section. "Be with you in a minute!" I turned my attention back to Esther. "So?"

Esther removed my hands from her shoulders. "The McKutcheons never had much luck on that homestead. The ground's no good for growing. It's evil. Haunted. Old Indian burial grounds, too."

I chuckled. "Please, next you'll be telling me Ruby Lake has its own Loch Ness Monster."

Esther smirked. "We sort of do, don't we? We've got the widow in the lake."

I waved a disparaging hand. "An old wives' tale." I was trying hard to believe the story was as phony as a three-dollar bill.

"Mary McKutcheon was no old wives' tale," Esther shot back. "She was a real life, flesh and blood, saliva-spitting pioneer woman."

"The widow in the lake was a McKutcheon?" Why had I never heard that before?

"Of course." Esther folded her arms across her chest. "After she passed, the life just sort of went out of the place. Family tried to keep the farm going for years and years. But trouble always followed. My grandpappy, rest his soul, said that nobody was safe living there, not a McKutcheon or anybody else."

She twisted her head toward our customer, who was working his way back toward the door and his escape. "Can I go now?"

A few more steps and the man would have made his escape. "Fine, go."

Esther called out to the sitting-duck-slash-customer, then turned back to me. "I'd stay away from the McKutcheon house, if you know what's good for you!"

Sadly, I rarely did.

4

Things got busy at the store, not that I was complaining. I forgot all about the widow in the lake and the body I'd seen, or thought I'd seen, being thrown out of the upstairs window of the McKutcheon house.

The day passed quickly and uneventfully. Kim came in around noon to help out and Esther took off for parts unknown. Probably upstairs to watch TV, smoke the cigarettes she claimed she didn't have, and talk to the cat she swore she didn't own.

Mom was going to handle the store that evening. The hours between dinner and closing are the quietest. "Aunt Betty will be here, too. The girls and I are going to play cards after closing." Aunt Betty, Mom, and their friends Anita and Luann participate in a weekly four-handed pinochle match. Occasionally, Mom hosted and they set up the card table in our apartment.

"Have fun!" I called with a wave.

"Don't lose more than you can afford, Mrs. S," Kim added.

"Not much fear of that," Mom quipped. Mom has little more than her pension and Social Security checks.

Most everything else went to cover Dad's medical expenses. What little she'd had left in savings, she'd loaned to me to help get Birds & Bees off the ground. I wasn't worried about her betting the bank. I was worried about paying her back one day though.

My aunt Betty is Mom's fraternal twin. At least, so they and the medical records declared. I'd never seen two women more different, personality-wise. Mom was steadfastly married to my dad until his passing, and I'm her only child. Aunt Betty is on her third husband, Sterling, and has a pair of twins of her own from her first marriage. My two cousins, Rhonda and Riley, are a couple years older than me.

Mom shooed us off after I promised to come back with a fresh apple pie from the diner, for her and her friends.

Kim and I dodged traffic—Lake Shore Drive is a bustling thoroughfare in the summer—and walked into Ruby's Diner. I inhaled the mingled scents of fresh savory dishes coming from the kitchen.

The diner was nearly full. Kim and I waited up front for a table.

"Be with you in a minute," promised Tiffany, one of the waitresses, looking harried at the moment. She blew a strand of blond hair from her eyes. "Busy tonight." Tiffany's a buxom, green-eyed blonde a few years my senior. She's practically as popular as the food.

The busboy finished wiping and resetting a window booth and Tiffany led us to it. She dropped a couple of laminated menus on the tabletop. "Good to see you both. What can I get you to drink?"

I ordered the tea and Kim a root beer with a dollop of whipped cream on top. If I ate as much junk food and sugar as Kim did, I'd gain two pounds a day.

The diner, once a gas station, still maintained that charming old 1940s petrol station ambience, with a couple of antique gas pumps in the lobby and original neon signage and décor. Staff wear khaki pants and Kelly green shirts with white name patches, like old-time gas station attendants. Tiffany looks like a demure 1940s pinup girl in hers.

We chatted over our beverages and a big appetizer basket of deep-fried onion rings—a diner specialty. The onion rings were disappearing fast. I was starving, having nibbled on nothing but bird food all day—peanuts and sunflower seeds. Eating the inventory was proving to be something of a problem. The crunchy golden rings were delectable. The only downside was that they were especially good at adding rings of fat to my waistline.

Kim shot me a look. "Not that it matters to me, but I thought you were watching your weight now that you've got a man in your life."

Kim's a long-legged blonde with devilish blue eyes. She's never had to worry about having a man in her life. They follow her around like flies on a wedge of ripe watermelon.

I frowned. "I'll walk it off this weekend." I'd be leading a two-hour bird-watching expedition through the state park the next day. Surely that would more than make up for a few lousy onion rings?

Nonetheless, I threw a half-eaten ring back in the wax paper–lined basket. "And I don't exactly have a man in my life. Derek and I have only dated a couple of times."

Kim plucked the half-eaten onion ring from the basket and polished it off. "If you ask me, there's love in the air."

I snorted. "Please, what do you know about love?

What do either of us know, for that matter?" We are the same age and grew up together. There isn't much we don't know about each other.

I've never been married and have had only one serious long-term relationship. At least, I'd thought it was serious—my then-boyfriend, not so much.

Kim leaned back as Tiffany dropped our burgers in front of us. "Refill on the onion rings?" Tiffany asked.

"Not a chance," I said. "And please," I added, scooting the basket toward the edge of the table, "take the rest of these away before somebody gets hurt."

Kim laughed.

I glanced toward the glass display case on the corner of the front counter. A row of polished chrome stools with red vinyl seats runs the length of the counter along the rear of the diner. The cash register's up near the door. A half dozen pies rested inside the round display case. "I promised Mom I'd bring back an apple pie."

Tiffany looked toward the display. "It looks like we've got a couple whole ones left. I'll save you one," she said with a wink, before leaving.

"You know," said Kim, picking up the thread of our earlier conversation, "just because I've never been married, doesn't mean I don't know what love is. Look at me and Randy. We've been together six months."

Randy Vincent is a local property manager. He owns a number of rental cabins, some at Ruby Lake and others around town. He's been separated for over a year from his wife, Lynda, who shares the business. Kim swore the divorce was going to be final anytime now. I only hoped for her sake that she was right.

"Where is he, by the way?"

"He's got a quarterly meeting with Lynda," she said matter-of-factly. "Business stuff."

"Doesn't it ever bother you that—" I couldn't figure out how to end my sentence in a way that wouldn't cause hurt feelings or insecurity.

Kim understood anyway. "The man's got baggage," she said with a shrug. "Who doesn't?"

I liked her attitude and said so.

Kim stuffed several French fries in a glob of mayo—a taste she'd acquired on a vacation to the Netherlands—and practically inhaled them. Disgusting.

I grabbed the ketchup bottle and smothered my burger. Unfortunately, it reminded me of blood, and blood reminded me of death, and death reminded me of what I'd seen that morning.

"What's wrong?" Kim bit into her sandwich. "Is there something wrong with your burger? You look like you've seen a ghost."

I told Kim about what I'd seen at the old McKutcheon house. I'd refrained from bringing it up in the store, not wanting to get into it with customers around.

"You really think you saw a murder?" Kim sat back. Her plate was wiped clean. She dabbed her lips with a napkin, then reapplied red lip gloss.

"To tell you the truth, I'm not so sure anymore. Jerry thinks I'm crazy."

"Nothing new there."

"Do you suppose that's him?" I pointed with my chin to the man visible through the kitchen's long order window.

"Him who?" Kim swiveled to look.

"That one there." I pointed my fork toward a squat, bristly haired man standing at the edge of the grill in a soiled white apron. "Could that be Guster McKutcheon?"

"Beats me. I've never seen him before." I said I hadn't

either. Tiffany laid the bill between us and removed our dishes. "Why don't you go ask him?"

I opened my wallet and pulled out enough money to cover my share of dinner and the tip. "There's Moire," I said. "Let's go pay at the register." We could ask her about Guster McKutcheon. As we approached, a swarthy, dark-haired man approached Moire from behind. He wrapped his arms around her and pulled her close. The diner owner turned with a smile, rose on her tiptoes, and kissed him on the lips.

"Wow," Kim whispered in my ear. "I'll have what she's having."

The man turned his hazel eyes on me. Moire caught his look and turned. "Hi, Amy, Kim." She took the check from my hand. "How was everything?"

The man she'd been smooching with smiled seductively and stepped back, leaning against the counter. He stood more than a head taller than Moire and, unlike everybody working in the diner, he wore a crisp, white, button-down shirt and charcoal trousers.

I wondered who the new man in her life was and where she'd found him. "Irresistible, as always," I quipped, patting my tummy.

"Yeah," added Kim, "like your friend here."

Moire giggled and adjusted her blouse.

The man touched her shoulder and said he'd be back in a minute. He left to talk with one of the waitresses working the counter, a recent hire named Lana Potter, a smoldering raven-haired beauty who'd been turning Ruby Lake heads since the day she arrived.

"Sure," Moire said. Her full name is Moire Leora Breeder. Moire's husband was killed in a U.S. Marines training accident some years ago. Plump in all the right places, Moire's a blue-eyed blonde. She lives in the apartment upstairs.

"Who's the new guy in the kitchen?" Kim demanded, not one to waste time.

"Which one?" Moire asked.

I described the man at the grill.

"That's the new prep cook. He's working part-time. Emmanuel quit."

I nodded. "I heard Guster McKutcheon is working at the diner now, too."

Moire tilted her head and pushed the register drawer slowly shut. "Who told you about Gus working here? It's only been about a week."

I explained how I'd called Jerry Kennedy to investigate a possible murder I'd seen.

"It was at the old McKutcheon house," Kim put in. "Amy saw some guy toss another one out the upstairs window!"

Moire's eyes grew. "Are you certain?" She turned toward the kitchen. "I didn't hear a thing about it."

"Well, if I were you," I said, "I'd be very careful with this Guster McKutcheon, Moire. Jerry might not have found anything, but there's something funny going on across the lake. I can feel it. Murder or no." I pocketed my change. "Did you run a background check on McKutcheon before you hired him?"

Moire pursed her lips. "Well . . ."

"I mean, because this is Guster McKutcheon's house, whatever is going on, I'm guessing he's at the center of it." I turned my eyes pointedly on the man at the grill as he fired up a couple of burgers.

Moire chewed her lower lip. Mr. Swarthy headed our way, running a well-groomed hand along the side of his head as he did.

"Hey, babe." He draped an arm possessively around Moire's waist. "Who are your friends?" His white teeth gleamed like they'd come straight from the film set of a toothpaste commercial.

Moire squeezed his hand. The look she gave me was inscrutable. "Gus, I'd like you to meet Amy Simms and Kim Christy."

My mouth fell open. "Gus?" I felt my face heat up. "As in Guster?" I rasped.

Behind me, I heard Kim suck in a breath.

The man held out his hand and I shook it. "That's right," he said, easily. "Gus McKutcheon. Pleased to meet you, ladies." His fingers were cool to the touch.

I trembled and stuttered a goodbye. I went for the door. Kim caught up with me outside. "Are you okay?" she asked.

"Yeah." I inhaled lungfuls of fresh mountain air. "Just confused."

"Tell me about it," said Kim, shifting her purse up over her shoulder. "Moire's been holding out on us. I had no idea she was seeing someone." Kim's eyes skirted to the diner. "Let alone someone so sexy."

"Sexy?" I replied. "The man could be a murderer."

Kim rolled her eyes. "You said yourself that Jerry didn't find anything at his house. Besides, you also said that Guster McKutcheon wasn't home when Jerry got there."

"That doesn't mean he wasn't home when the murder was committed." My eyes widened. "Quiet!" I whispered. "Here he comes."

Gus McKutcheon loped toward where we stood at the edge of the street. He seemed taller than the one man I'd seen in the window of the McKutcheon house, and not as heavyset as the other. But it had been dark and stormy, and I'd been watching from afar, so there was no way to be sure one way or the other.

Gus held out a white cardboard box. "You forgot this." His voice was deep and rich. "Moire asked me to run it out to you."

I nodded and relieved him of the apple pie. "Thanks," I said, my mouth dry as sawdust. "I forgot."

"No problem. We all forget things one time or another." He placed his hand on my upper arm. "Sometimes forgetting is the best thing we can do."

McKutcheon impaled me with his eyes and I hurried across the street, oblivious to the honking cars and Kim's plea to be careful and slow down.

5

Rat-a-tat-tat-brrr.

Drummy the woodpecker woke me at the crack of dawn. I rose, stretched, and picked up the binoculars. "Okay, okay. I'm up, I'm up."

There he was, in his usual spot on the gray hickory. "I'd have thought you'd have run out of bugs by now," I muttered. Maybe if I hung some suet cakes in the backyard, I could get him to change his habit. It was definitely worth a try. Suet cakes are quiet eating compared to hollowed-out tree limbs.

"You know, Drummy, it's not like I'm a night owl, but I'm no morning lark. Do you suppose you could take a morning off now and again?"

His only reply was to bang out a beat reminiscent of the overture to *My Fair Lady*. Maybe I should be flattered. Maybe he was serenading me.

Maybe I needed to stop talking to birds.

The sun was coming up and the sky was nearly cloudless. As much as I knew I shouldn't, I couldn't resist another look across the lake. A lazy wisp of smoke came from the brownstone chimney. Two men were visible in the yard, one pushing a wheelbarrow. It was too far away for me to determine if either was the house's new owner, Guster McKutcheon.

Several boats bobbed in the water. An early morning kayaking tour was already underway. Four blue kayaks followed the red one belonging to the tour's owner and guide. I still hadn't had the chance to seek out the skipper of the boat that I'd seen on the water the morning I'd been watching the McKutcheon house. The watercraft had a distinct orange top and had been on the small side, maybe a thirty-footer.

I dressed quickly and beat Mom to the kitchen. "Scrambled eggs are ready!" I beckoned my mother to the table.

She carried the toast over on a plate and we dug in while going over the morning's plan. I'd be leading our fledgling bird-watching group on a tour of the state park while Mom and Esther ran things at Birds & Bees.

Kim was spending the day with her boyfriend, Randy. A property he was rehabbing was taking longer than usual and she was providing design assistance. I wasn't sure what that meant exactly. Prior to working with me, Kim had worked as a real estate agent. That was how she'd met Randy. She'd sold him a property or two.

Kim still has her real estate license and dabbled in real estate the way she dabbled in birds—lots of enthusiasm, not so many hours at the grindstone, or, perhaps it would be more appropriate to say, cuttlebone.

After breakfast, I opened up the store. Several budding birders were waiting outside, eager to get started. I had hopes that offering the monthly bird-watching hikes would be good for business, get more folks interested in the benefits of bird-watching and bird feeding.

Mrs. Bessie Hammond extended her arm and held her gold watch under my nose. "You're late."

"Sorry, come on in." I waved Bessie and her fellow early arrivers inside and told them to help themselves to coffee and tea. Within minutes, everyone I'd been expecting had appeared.

"Good morning, John," I said, as John Moytoy, the last of the ten people on the list, showed up and signed in. "I'm glad to see you could make it." John Moytoy works at the Ruby Lake Town Library and is a good friend.

"I wouldn't miss it," John replied, pushing his thick black glasses up the bridge of his nose. John is of Cherokee heritage. He's also a history and nature buff. "Thanks for putting this together." A heavy-looking pair of binoculars dangled across his chest.

"Where'd you get the antique glasses?" I quipped.

John grinned. "They were my dad's." He rubbed his sternum. "I may have a bruise or two before the day is done."

I gathered them all together near the front entrance. "Does everyone have everything they need?"

"Shouldn't we get started?" snapped Bessie Hammond, a sixty-something brunette with a stick-like figure and a know-it-all personality.

"Of course, Mrs. Hammond. As I explained, I can take half of you in my van. The rest of you will have to drive in separate cars." There were several elderly residents in our small group, too, including four from Rolling Acres, a senior living facility at the edge of town. I was pleased to see my friends Floyd Withers, a retired banker, and Karl Vogel, former Ruby Lake chief of police, among them. The two other Rolling Acres residents introduced themselves as Clara and Walter Kimmel. Clara had shopped at the store a time or two. They spoke softly and dressed in identical khaki shorts, calf-length white socks, and pistachio-green National Audubon Society shirts.

"I don't drive," snapped Mrs. Hammond. "I rode the bus."

"You can ride with us!" Ed Quince hollered. Ed's a roly-poly retired grocer and might know more about birds than any of us. He certainly knows how to dress a turkey for Thanksgiving dinner. "The Caddy's got plenty of room!"

Ed and Abby Quince had brought their own vehicle and had offered to chauffeur. Several others talked among themselves and worked out who would drive with whom. It appeared the van and Ed's car would suffice to get us all there.

"I am not riding with them!" Bessie exclaimed, clutching her knapsack close to her chest.

"I'll ride with Ed and Abby," offered a fiftyish brunette named Otelia Newsome, who had a beehive hairdo. "You can have my seat in Amy's van." Otelia was single and owned a chocolate shop on Lake Shore Drive.

"Works for me," said Abby, a retired Lakeside Market cashier, with a moon face and red-tinted hair. My cousin Rhonda, a hair stylist-slash-colorist, does her personal best to keep Abby's gray at bay.

"There you go, see? Problem solved." I had no idea what Bessie had against Ed and Abby. They had all worked in the same grocery market at one time or another. The Quinces were a lovely couple, always upbeat and friendly. Perhaps that was her problem—she preferred her company to be as ill-disposed as herself. Or maybe she had something against plush, comfortable

Cadillacs. I'd have gladly traded the tired old minivan for a sweet, leather-trimmed luxury car. I'll bet Ed's AC worked.

I led Bessie to the door, wondering what had compelled her to go on a bird walk with a group of folks she had nothing in common with and little patience for. "Let's get started, shall we?" As we shuffled outdoors, I said, "By the way, there has been a slight change of plans."

"Oh?" said Mr. Withers. His mustache flapped in the light breeze coming from the lake. Floyd and Karl are constantly bickering over whose mustache was the more dashing. I gave up taking sides long ago. Who knew elderly men could be so vain about their facial hair?

"Yes," I explained, "an itinerary change. Instead of going to the state park, we are going to explore the area on the far side of Ruby Lake."

"Ruby Lake?" Bessie eyed me narrowly. "You promised we'd go bird-watching at the state park!"

"Yes, but several interesting sightings at the lake have been reported to me." I looked at my small but dedicated group. "Possibly even a magnolia warbler and a bobolink." My ears caught several oohs and one snort. I scanned the crowd for the troublemaker but no one had *guilty* clearly stenciled to their forehead in red letters, so I had no choice but to ignore the affront. "We wouldn't want to miss that now, would we?"

Everyone agreed and Bessie had no alternative but to go along. I crossed my fingers that we'd find some interesting birds to watch, hopefully not only common crows and sparrows. Whether we'd spot a magnolia warbler or a bobolink was anybody's guess. I'd be happy if Drummy, my cranium-splitting woodpecker friend, showed up. We could use all the birds we could get.

Our walk to the curb was interrupted by a fortyish femme fatale in tight blue jeans who came bouncing across the street from the direction of the diner. Certain parts of her bounced more than others. A fact of which the men in attendance were not remiss to note.

She waved a manicured hand with brilliant red fingernails. "Do you have room for one more?" She had neither a daypack nor a pair of binoculars but she had a decent pair of white sneakers on her feet. Not the best color for a hike in the woods, but that would be her problem. The shoes matched the white cotton shirt with the rolled-up sleeves that she'd knotted up at her waist front.

"Good morning. Sure. You can ride in the van with us. I've got room."

"That would be wonderful."

"Lana, isn't it?" I said. I sniffed. Was that a hint of cigarette smoke mingled in with that undercurrent of rose perfume?

"That's right, Lana Potter."

I nodded. "I've seen you around the diner."

Karl winked at Floyd and whispered something in his ear. Probably something lecherous. Harmless, but lecherous, I was sure. Karl Vogel is the lady-killer of Rolling Acres, or so he claims. I was afraid that Lana was out of his league—not to mention, half his age.

As I helped my passengers into the van, I plotted a plan of attack. There is a city-owned park along the edge of the lake. We'd park there and hike out, taking the trail along the far side of the lake that turned away about midpoint. Toward the McKutcheon homestead.

My ultimate destination.

"Say, Amy!" Karl shouted from the rear seat. "I hear tell you saw another murder!"

"Another murder?" I heard from directly behind me. That was Bessie.

"Yep," said Karl, in a loud but friendly voice. "This one over at the old McKutcheon house." He chuckled.

"Give Amy a break, Karl." Via the rearview mirror, I saw Floyd give his friend the elbow.

"Aw," Karl said with a scowl, "Amy knows I'm only joshing." He cupped his hands and yelled, like I couldn't hear him anyway. "Right, Amy?"

I grinned and waved. "Right, Karl! Don't tell me," I said, while I waited for the stoplight to turn green. "You heard from Jerry."

"That's right."

I sighed. The current and former chiefs of police were on friendly terms. Sometimes, that was useful. Other times, I wished Jerry would keep his big yap shut.

"A murder. Wow," said Lana. She occupied the front passenger seat. Her teal eyes were on the lake.

"Is that correct, Miss Simms?" asked Bessie, tapping the back of my seat. "You witnessed a murder?"

"No, I mean, I don't know. The chief says not."

Karl continued. "He says you saw a dummy being thrown out the window."

"I'd like to throw a certain dummy out the window," I muttered, turning the wheel at the next right, and reveling in the accompanying titters I'd elicited.

"Our Amy is aces at catching killers," Karl boasted. "Heck, I'll bet she's already caught as many killers in her short time here as I did my entire tenure as chief of police."

"I don't know if I'd go so far as to say that." I found myself blushing.

"Does that mean you're investigating another mystery?" John asked with a smile.

"There's nothing to investigate," I said, my eyes on the road ahead.

Karl scratched his ear. "Of course, we didn't have so many murders then as we do now."

My eyebrows shot up. That was an unsettling thought.

"Not a murder at all then," Bessie said matter-of-factly. "Of course, if there ever was a murder, I'll bet I could solve it." She snapped her fingers. "Like that."

"You don't say?" Lana turned to look back at Bessie.

"Like that." Bessie snapped her fingers a second time. "I'm quite the whiz at crossword puzzles, too. I can do them in ink, you know."

"Is that so?" Lana managed to sound impressed.

"Shouldn't we talk about birds?" suggested Floyd, bless his heart.

"Good idea," I replied quickly. "Anybody care to tell us what favorites you're hoping to spot?"

"I'm hoping to see a roc or two," answered John.

"Very funny, John." I glanced at his cherubic face in the rearview mirror.

"A roc?" Lana swiveled her head around.

"John's joking. Rocs are mythological birds of prey."

"Oh." Lana sounded disappointed.

"I'd like to add the hooded warbler to my life list," Bessie said, flipping through a small notebook.

"Possible. Possible." A life list is a list that many bird enthusiasts keep, identifying every bird species and sub-species that they have spotted in the wild. The hooded warbler is a striking yellow bird with a black bib and hood. They're known to be active in the Carolinas in the summer. "Keep your eyes on the understory." Warblers are mostly ground foragers.

We continued this way, pleasantly immersed in idle bird chatter, until I pulled into the public parking lot that serves the Ruby Lake Park and Marina. The town holds title to the land the marina sits on but leases the running of it to a local firm. That management company, in turn, rents out space to other local business owners for such enterprises as boat rentals and storage, a restaurant and an ice cream parlor.

The lot was only half-full, but I took a space nearer the road—and the restrooms, should anybody need a pit stop before we got underway. The Quinces slid into the space beside me.

Ed and Abby had clearly been arguing and Abby's face was bright red. Their passengers jumped out and quickly separated themselves from the ex-grocer and his wife.

We gathered our essentials and I reminded everyone that this was our last chance for a pit stop. "I suggest you top off your water bottles, if you need to. It's going to be a hot one."

Several took me up on my suggestion and filled their bottles from the drinking fountain outside the restroom. "Okay, follow me!" I waved. "Keep your binoculars and your cameras ready!"

I felt a tap on my shoulder and turned to find Lana Potter at my heels.

"I'm afraid I didn't bring a pair of binoculars."

"No problem." I fished in my day pack and brought out a spare compact pair of glasses. "You're in luck. I always bring an extra pair. They aren't the most powerful pair in the world, but they'll do in a pinch."

"Luck of the Irish!" Lana took the small pair from my hands and expressed her thanks.

We quietly followed the trail along the lakeshore, each of us whispering and pointing whenever a species of interest came into sight. I pointed out four ruby-throated hummingbirds zipping through a wild patch of bee balm.

We admired their aerial antics for several minutes. Bessie took several photos using the expensive-looking camera she carried. Others settled for cell phone shots.

"Nice camera," admired Ed.

Abby looped her arm through the crook of her husband's elbow. "A camera's a camera."

"This one is state-of-the-art," bragged Bessie, holding the camera out at the end of its tether. "It's capable of high-speed, ultra-close-up and panoramic photography."

Using her own little digital camera, Clara Kimmel shot a picture of her husband, Walter, posing beside a fallen oak. Otelia then offered to take a picture of the two of them together. Clara told her that wouldn't be necessary.

We left the hummingbirds behind. A half mile in, a smaller trail led inland, toward the McKutcheon homestead.

"Listen!" I said, stopping once more. I cupped my ear. "I believe that's a whip-poor-will." Once common to the area, this would be a rare find indeed—if we could spot and confirm its appearance. The medium-sized bird's gray and brown coloring camouflages them nearly perfectly amongst bark and leaves.

"I thought whip-poor-wills were nocturnal?" Bessie said, apparently unconvinced of my identification.

"Tell him that!" Floyd said as the bird sang once more.

All eyes turned to the treetops as the bird's distinctive whistling *whip-poor-will, whip-poor-will* call rang out. "Anybody got a backache?" I asked. "Because if you do, according to folklore, if you do a backflip while the whip-poor-will sings its song, you'll be cured."

Ed guffawed. "Why don't you try it, Karl?"

"You first!" urged the ex–chief of police.

We marched on, following a narrow dirt trail winding among a tall stand of pines. A crumbling dry-stack stone wall loomed ahead. I stopped and inhaled deeply. I love the earthy scent of the woods.

"I don't believe this is part of the public trail," complained Bessie, assiduously poring over a free trail map she'd picked up at the trailhead.

"I'm sure it is," I said softly from the front of the line. "Besides, it's along these quiet routes that an alert birder can more often encounter a rare species or two."

"Yeah, be quiet and let Amy lead," wheezed Karl. The old gent wasn't in the fittest condition. Then again, neither were the majority of my fellow bird-watchers.

We spotted several birds, but nothing out of the ordinary. Somehow, Lana managed to get her right shoelace tangled up in a bramble of wild blueberries. Ed came to her rescue, extracting a multi-tool knife from his front trouser pocket and cutting her loose. "I call it my centipede," he quipped, "because it's got a hundred uses." His wife clearly didn't like the attention he was showing Lana.

After fifteen minutes of walking, I saw the top of the McKutcheon house peeking up out of the trees.

"Hey," whispered Ed, "that's the McKutcheon house."

"That's where Amy saw that guy get thrown out the window," Karl just had to say.

"*Thought* she saw," corrected Bessie. She aimed her high-powered binocs at the house.

"I've never seen the McKutcheon house up close before." Ed sounded a little awed.

"I heard one of the McKutcheons had moved back to town." John Moytoy trained his ancient binoculars on the house.

"Who cares about a stupid old house?" complained Lana. "I thought we hiked out here to look at birds."

"Is that an owl?" Floyd pointed a wavering finger up into a tall, skinny pine fighting for its share of sunshine.

"That's a squirrel's nest," snapped Karl.

Floyd's eyesight isn't so good. "I'm afraid Karl's right, Floyd." I crouched under a low branch and held it aloft for the others. "Come on." I wanted to get closer to the house.

An eerie silence hung over the woods. The forest absorbed our voices and our footsteps. Where had all the birds gone?

"Good Lord!"

I spun around. Abby was clutching her husband's arm. Her binocs dangled from her concave chest.

"What's wrong?" Ed said, looking startled and not a little annoyed.

His wife pointed toward a clearing about twenty yards up. "That's a cemetery!"

Sure enough, a black iron fence, fallen in places, kept watch over a half dozen or so gray tombstones looming up from a patch of tall weeds. I took several steps nearer and raised my binoculars.

Ed frowned and removed his wife's fingers from his arm. "So what?"

Abby visibly shook. "It gives me the creeps is so what." She spun around. "I'm not going any closer."

"A grave can't hurt you!" snapped Bessie. She shot Abby the evil eye. "You'll end up in one, one day." She raised her camera and snapped a couple long-distance photos of the cemetery. "We all will."

"The family plot," I heard John whisper.

"Creepy, isn't it?" whispered Lana, who'd crept up beside me.

"A little," I had to admit. I forced a smile and faced my group. "Perhaps we should go back." I looked at my watch and was surprised to see how long we'd been gone. "Who's ready for lunch?"

Otelia Newsome was the first to agree.

With Karl leading the rearward charge, we said good-bye to our inaugural bird walk. I stood for a moment, steadying my binoculars on the gravesite before turning to catch up with the others.

One of those mounds looked fresh.

6

"Why don't you simply tell Chief Kennedy?" Kim said for the umpteenth time. She'd pinned her hair atop her head and her blond locks spilled forward.

For the umpteenth time, I answered her. "Because, number one, he won't believe me." If I called him to report a fresh grave at the McKutcheon house, it would only make him mad. "Number two, I want to check it out first before I go making a fool of myself." I seemed to be doing a lot of that lately and this seemed to be a good time to put an end to the habit.

We were alone in my kitchen. Mom was out, and Birds & Bees doesn't open until one on Sundays. Kim had come early to take inventory. It was best done when there were no customers about, confusing the process with their purchases. We'd learned that lesson the hard way.

I laced up my hiking shoes and hefted my binoculars. "Are you sure you won't come with me?"

"Not a chance. Sunday is a day of rest." Kim wrapped her fingers around her coffee mug. "And rest is exactly what I'm going to do." She studied her fingertips. "Maybe I'll run downtown for a manicure later."

I looked down my nose at her. Sometimes Kim's lack of focus amazed me. "What about the inventory?"

Kim's brow went up. "Oh, yeah." She giggled. "I almost forgot."

After extracting my best friend's promise that she'd get the inventory done, I headed off. I ran into my other temporary renter, Paul Anderson, as he stomped down to the shop from the second floor. His apartment is next door to Esther Pilaster's.

"Hey, good morning, Amy!" Paul called. "Got a minute?" He's about my age, with wavy brown hair and a pair of close-set hazel eyes that always seem to be containing a joke.

"Not now. Sorry, Paul. Big plans." I lifted the binocs.

"Ah, bird-watching, eh?" He ran his finger along the barrel of the binoculars. "Ever do any peeping with these things?"

I pulled the glasses away. "No." My ears were burning.

His hand fell to my shoulder as I scurried down the last flight of steps. "There's something I'd really like to talk to you about. I think you'll like it."

I swiveled. "Are you moving out?" I asked, hopefully.

Paul barked out a laugh. "Nope. Sorry. Still working on getting things at the house in order."

Paul Anderson's house seemed to be plagued with problems that prevented his moving out of my house and into his. My real problem with Paul Anderson ran deeper. He and my ex-boyfriend, Craig Bigelow, owned the recently opened Brewer's Biergarten directly next door. Seeing Paul only reminded me of Craig.

And Craig reminded me of hurt and pain.

"Then it will have to wait!" I hollered, turning the

key in the lock and leaving him standing alone inside.
Things could have been worse. At least Craig was not an
active partner in the pub. He lived in Raleigh and I
hoped he stayed there.

The day was sunny and warm. I left the van parked
behind the store, determined to hike to the lake. The trek
would do me and my waistline good.

My stomach rumbled as I cut across the Ruby's Diner
parking lot. The smells of eggs, bacon, and biscuits
called my name, but I kept on walking. After my hike,
I'd reward myself with a nice Sunday brunch.

Following the greenway out to the lake and marina, I
spotted what appeared to be the same boat I'd seen in
the water on that now infamous stormy morning that the
McKutcheon house had come into my world. The small
boat was one of dozens tied up along several finger
piers that jutted out into the lake. The roof of the motor-
boat was orange. Across the stern, the name *Sunset Sally*
was spelled out in matching orange letters. I stepped
onto on the pier and called out. There was no reply.

I didn't know who owned the boat, but I was certain
the marina manager could tell me. Whether he *would*
tell me was a whole other issue. I decided to leave the
motorboat for later and linked up with the same trail my
bird-watching group had taken the day before.

A light fog had settled on the lake overnight and the
sun worked to slowly burn it off. I unzipped my jacket
and moved inland, into the cooler shadows of the trees.

A rustling caught my ears and I followed the sound to
find a gray squirrel foraging through the undergrowth
for seeds and nuts. We eyed each other warily. A titmouse flew past my nose and disappeared among the

dense branches. The squirrel went one way and I went the other.

Being alone in the woods was a lot spookier than I'd imagined it would be. It was something I did not plan on doing again.

A flash of red appeared in the distance, then disappeared just as quickly. Was that a man's shirt? My arms grew cold. Maybe I wasn't so alone after all.

That was an even scarier thought.

I stood still a moment, my eyes scanning the trees and coming up empty. I turned as silently as I could and reversed course.

I came across a small leaf-clotted stream and followed it. Funny, I didn't remember crossing a stream yesterday. Had I missed it? Had I missed a turn?

Worse, was I lost? I looked at the treetops, hoping for a sign of the McKutcheon house, but was disappointed to see only the trees.

The sound of a woodpecker drew me. There was a red-bellied woodpecker midway up the trunk of an old sycamore. It looked like my old pal, Drummy. There was no way to be certain. But it wasn't the bird that interested me.

It was the body of Bessie Hammond propped up against the base of the sycamore.

7

Bessie Hammond sat on the ground, propped against the bole of the tree, shoulders slumped, hands at her sides. Bessie's head lolled to my right, her sagging chin on her chest. She was dressed in a pair of khaki pocket shorts, a blue popover top with a tiny white flower pattern, brown hiking shoes, and white socks. This was not the outfit I'd seen her in the day before.

The leather strap of her binoculars hung around her pale white neck. The glasses rested against her breasts, two lenses staring at the cold hard earth between her outstretched legs. No matter, her eyes were shut.

I turned and ran. I thrashed through the brush, ignoring the beating my bare legs were taking as the branches whipped relentlessly at my thighs and calves. The heavy binoculars around my neck slammed mercilessly against my chest with each step. I grabbed at the strap in an attempt to stop the pain.

A hundred yards away, I stopped, out of breath. I'd veered off the trail and was hopelessly lost.

I doubled over, supporting myself with my hands on my knees. I gulped mouthfuls of air. Rivers of sweat ran from my forehead, stinging my eyes. I felt frigid and scared. I had that prickly sensation at the nape of my neck, of being watched. I did a three-sixty. Nothing but trees and more trees.

Then I remembered I had my cell phone in my day pack. I unzipped the side pouch where I'd secured it and punched in 911. I waited impatiently for the operator to pick up.

And waited. And waited. I pulled back the phone and looked at the screen. No reception.

Now what?

I did another 360-degree turn, not that it made any difference. I still had no idea where I was and not a single bar of signal. I pushed the useless phone down into the front pocket of my shorts. Okay, this called for some rational thinking. I was alone in the woods with a dead woman.

And maybe her killer.

Oh, this was so not good.

I heard a muffled shot. Were there hunters about?

I glanced skyward. *Think, think, think.* From the angle of the sun, I reasoned that the lake would be to my left. So that was the direction I took.

After about fifteen minutes of speed walking—and I feared ten of those minutes had been spent running in circles—I came upon a narrow, hard-packed trail sloping uphill, maybe nothing more than a deer trail. But at this point, if it was good enough for Bambi, it was good enough for me.

An arch of yellow sunlight soon came into view and I quickened my steps.

Until I saw where the trail led. I stood at the edge of the woods staring up at the McKutcheon house.

The rambling two-story house had a broad wraparound porch. A couple of dusty rockers sat on either side of the solid front door. All the curtains were pulled shut. The chimney was cold and smokeless.

There was a barn to my right with a lean-to against it that contained bales of hay. A gray goat peered at me from within a wood-fenced pen. Several others huddled at the far end, their snouts grazing the ground. I told myself that it was just a house like countless other houses in countless other towns. Still, it frightened me.

I cautiously approached the McKutcheon place. I angled closer until I was standing pretty much directly below the window I'd been looking in the other morning. I ran my toe over the patchy grass and earthen ground. A few scraps of paper, a bit of wood, and a torn and stained white rag were the only signs of whatever had lain here before—body or otherwise.

I thought long and hard about what to do next. Now that I knew roughly where I was, should I turn and run back to Ruby Lake? Or should I knock on the door?

I didn't think time was of the essence. After all, there was little to be done for poor Bessie now. But still, it would seem disrespectful to the woman to leave her lying alone any longer than necessary out in those woods.

Besides, the sooner the police were called, the sooner they could catch her killer.

Despite my reservations, I approached the front porch. The wooden steps creaked and groaned as I put my weight upon them. I held my breath, made a fist, and knocked.

A moment later, I heard the patter of feet. It sounded like someone was bounding down a flight of stairs. The front door was thrown open quickly and I took a surprised step back.

"*Oui?*" A young man stood looming over me. His

shirt was unbuttoned and hanging loose over a pair of skinny jeans. He was barefoot. "I can help you?"

He eyed me without fear, which I thought was kind of funny for two reasons. Number one, I was up to my eyeballs in fear. And, number two, I'd be wary, at the very least, if I lived out in the woods and a stranger suddenly appeared knocking at my door.

"I'm Amy Simms," I blurted. "Can I use your phone? Do you have a landline?" I couldn't imagine how I looked to this guy. My legs were crisscrossed with cuts, my hair was wild, my clothing torn and smudged and, though he couldn't see it, my chest was bruised from the beating I'd gotten from the pounding of the binoculars against my sternum and ribs.

"Who is it?" I heard a second male's voice call from somewhere deep in the house.

"Phone?" His green eyes blinked as if he was trying to comprehend my meaning.

"Yes, I need to use your phone." I looked back the way I'd come. Bessie Hammond was out there somewhere. "It's an emergency."

He stepped aside. "Come." He waved me inside. I followed. The house was dimly lit. There was a musty quality to the air as if the house and its occupants had an aversion to fresh air and sunlight.

"I said, who's at the door?" A young man came sauntering in from what must have been the kitchen. An old white stove was framed by the doorway. He carried a plate containing a half-eaten slice of toast and two runny eggs. "Oh!" He came to a stop. Egg yolk oozed over the lip of his plate. He cursed and wiped at it with his fingers, then licked them clean.

The two young men looked at one another. The young man who'd opened the door was the taller of the two, with wavy brown hair. His companion's hair was blond and his skin pale in comparison. Though he did sport a well-groomed goatee.

"Madam she needs to use the telephone," said the first man.

"Mine's in the other room," replied the man with the eggs. His accent was foreign and Germanic sounding, but I couldn't yet place it exactly. "Come on." He waved for me to follow him back to the kitchen. "I'm Dominik Lueger."

He twisted his thumb toward his companion. "That's Jean Rabin. I don't suppose he bothered to introduce himself?" I shook my head no. Dominik set his plate down on the tattered seafoam-green laminate kitchen countertop. "Who are you exactly?"

"Amy," I said. "Amy Simms."

He propped himself against the counter with his elbows. "So what brings you to our forest, Amy Simms?" His steel-gray eyes washed inquisitively over me. A curious tabby cat sat on its haunches gazing out the French door at a pair of cardinals playing in a lopsided birdbath at the edge of a little patio laid out with slate tiles.

I lifted the binoculars. "I was bird-watching." It was sort of the truth, or at least close enough to it.

"See anything interesting?" inquired Jean.

"That's just it," I said. "There's been, well, there's been a murder!"

The two young men exchanged an indecipherable look. All of a sudden, Jean laughed, catching me by surprise. "Ha!" He slapped his thigh. "Yes, your police were here yesterday. The man in charge said some, how did he say, fool woman, reported seeing somebody thrown out the window!" He laughed again and mimicked tossing a body out a window.

I winced. That fool woman was me, of course. Had Jerry no discretion at all?

"Are you a reporter?" asked Dominik. "If so, I am afraid there is no story." He held up a French press coffee-maker. "Coffee, madame?"

"No!" I stamped my foot against the linoleum and shook my head vigorously. I'd spooked the cat. It meowed a high-pitched complaint and left the kitchen with its tail high. "You don't understand." I pointed outside. "There's a dead woman out there. In your woods."

Dominik settled the French press on the counter. "No!"

"Yes," I said. "We have to call the police."

"You are certain, madame?" Jean asked.

"Yes, please," I said, growing more and more exasperated. "We have to get help." The two men shared yet another look. Dominik nodded and picked up his cell phone from the small kitchen table tucked close to the fridge.

"Don't you have a landline?" I asked. "You won't get any signal."

Dominik ignored my warning and slid his finger across the screen of his phone. "What do I dial, 112? 147?"

Jean shrugged.

"It's 911," I replied. "Dial 911."

Dominik explained to the operator the nature of the emergency and our location. His English, though heavily accented, was quite good. "That's right, the woman tells us she sees a dead woman in the forest." He angled his eyes at me and Jean. "The operator is putting me through to the Ruby Lake Police Department." This being Sunday, emergency calls were first directed to the county emergency response center.

I gulped.

"Hello?" Dominik said. "Yes." He repeated his story.

I could hear a tumble of words coming from the receiver but couldn't make them out. It sounded like Anita at the other end. "Yes." He nodded, looking my way. "Amy Simms. She is right here beside me." He pushed the phone at me. "She wants to talk to you."

I took a deep breath and put the phone to my ear. It was Anita. "Yes, Anita. Everything Dominik said is true. Yes," I said in reply to her unprofessional response. "A dead woman."

"Do you know who it is?" Anita inquired.

"Bessie Hammond. Please, Anita, get Jerry out here right away!" Anita promised that help was on the way and I cut the connection. I handed Dominik his cell phone.

"The police will be here soon," I explained.

"Maybe we should go take a look at this body," Jean suggested.

"I don't know if that's such a good idea," I replied. "We don't want to disturb the scene." And the scene consisting of Bessie sitting with a snapped neck under a sycamore tree was disturbing enough. "Besides, we should wait here so we can show the police where the body is."

Dominik rolled the now cold toast through his runny eggs and took a bite. "Maybe. But perhaps someone should be there to be certain no one disturbs the body." Yellow yolk hung at the corners of his lips.

Jean nodded. "*Oui.* Perhaps even a bear or wolf."

I wasn't so sure we had wolves and bears, and would rather think we didn't, but realized the boys could be right.

"Besides, Channing, Annika, and Ross are here." Dominik ran his tongue over his lips.

"Who are they?"

"More of our roommates," Jean answered. "I believe they are tending the vegetable garden at the minute."

Dominik shoved his feet into a pair of leather sandals.

"Is Guster McKutcheon home?" I asked.

More looks passed between the young men. Jean answered that Mr. McKutcheon was out and they weren't expecting him until later in the day.

"We are never certain when he comes," added Dominik, throwing open the back door. He hollered and waved to several young people tending a large garden about a hundred yards away.

A lithe young woman with long dark hair set down a long-handled hoe and jogged to the house. "Yes?" She looked at me with searching blue eyes. A pair of jean shorts showed off an excellent pair of suntanned legs. Her flimsy silver-and-black tank top shimmered in the sun.

Dominik and Jean took turns explaining the situation. Jean asked Channing to stay put until the police arrived and then tell them where they could find us—and the body.

"Sure," Channing said, quickly. "Where will that be exactly?" She had a lovely accent. Dirt from the garden had insinuated itself under her short fingernails.

I turned to the woods, half blocked by the house. That was a good question.

8

I was lost when I found Bessie. In my haste to get away from there and go get help, I'd become even more lost.

"We have a conundrum, *non*?" Jean said, recognizing the confusion on my face.

"I'm afraid so," I admitted, glumly. We walked to the front of the house and I pointed out the path I had come in on. "It's down that way. So, I think if we—"

I was saved from having to come up with a suggestion I was pretty certain would only get us all lost, by the sound of approaching sirens. Sure enough, two police cars and the town ambulance came screaming to a halt on the gravel drive.

Part of me wanted to disappear rather than face Jerry Kennedy. But I held my ground. I owed it to Bessie.

Chief Kennedy flew from his squad car, heading straight for me. "What's going on here, Amy?"

"That was fast, Jerry."

"I was at the marina having coffee, if you must know. What is it now?" He looked at the two young men. "Is this woman making a pest of herself?"

Jean and Dominik looked amused. "Hello, Chief Kennedy, sir." Jean bowed ever so slightly. "She is no pest. She found a murder."

"Found a what?" Jerry removed his cap and scratched the top of his head.

I stepped in front of Jean. "He means found a body. I found a body, Jerry."

Jerry's mouth fell open. "Come on. You are not going to start that again?" He spun on his heels. By now we'd drawn a crowd. Channing and her two gardening companions, Officer Sutton, and the two EMTs watched with interest.

"What is it this time, Simms? You saw another body pushed out a window?" He played to his audience. "Or maybe this one was in their storeroom—" I winced at the image of something I'd seen once and wished I could forget.

"Maybe," Jerry drawled on, a big stupid grin on his face, "this one came flying out that chimney!" He pointed and we all followed the imaginary line from his finger to the chimney top. "Like Santa Claus making his rounds."

I tried my best to avoid the snickering of the two EMTs. Even Officer Sutton was smiling. The kids stood mutely and seemed curious rather than skeptical. I fought down my anger. "Bessie Hammond is lying dead out in that woods!" I practically shouted. "I think her neck's been broken!"

Dominik said something to Jean in French, which I couldn't understand, but from the way he mimed a pair of hands squeezing viselike around a neck, I got the gist of it.

"If you'll stop hamming it up and start acting like the

chief of police you claim to be, you'll see soon enough yourself."

Jerry opened his mouth, then closed it again. His fingers drummed the grip of his pistol. I wondered for a moment if I'd crossed a line—and that line led to handcuffs or, worse, bullets flying. Finally, he plopped his hat back on his head and spoke. "Okay, so you're telling me Bessie Hammond is lying out there dead?"

"That's exactly what I'm telling you."

He turned to the small crowd. "Anybody else here see the body?"

I answered for them. "Only me, Jerry. And when I found her, I raced to the house to get help." I explained how I'd had no cell phone reception out in the woods.

"Fine," he huffed. "Show me." He ordered Sutton and the EMTs to tag along and for everyone else to remain there. The medics grabbed a portable stretcher and a red EMT trauma bag from the back of the ambulance before joining us.

I led him confidently to the trailhead. After that, I was less certain. I followed the winding trail as far as possible. When it spilled out into a small glen, I paused to get my bearings.

"Well?" Chief Kennedy grumbled, impatiently.

"Give me a minute." I tapped my index finger to my lips and thought out loud. "This looks familiar." Recognition came to me as if a lens had been wiped clean. "Yes, I remember we came this way yesterday."

I pointed to a bare beech tree branch that stood out like a gnarled finger. "We had stopped to look at a female titmouse, when I noticed the mound." Jerry gave me a funny look. It took me a minute to figure out why. "I said titmouse, Jerry. Titmouse." The man still lived in the middle school of his mind.

I thought hard. I caught a muffled *rat-a-tat-tat* coming from about a hundred yards to the north. "This way." I hurried through the brush. Jerry alternated between wheezing and cursing as he pushed to keep pace. I shoved a low hanging branch from my face and stumbled down a small incline. I'd reached my goal. "There!"

And there she was. Bessie hadn't moved. Not that I had expected her to. I'd have been more than a little freaked if she had. The only thing different now was that I was seeing her in profile, having come on the tree from another angle.

I craned my neck, scouring the sycamore's limbs and trunk. The solitary woodpecker hammered once more, flapped its wings and flew off.

The two EMTs grunted and hurried forward. Chief Kennedy hollered for them not to touch the body. "Let me get a good look before you go messing with anything." He and Officer Sutton approached Bessie. I neared as well. I shuddered as I watched a trail of tiny black ants crawling up the dead woman's right arm. "Stay back!" Jerry waved me away.

I backed up gladly, falling into the arms of the younger of the two EMTs. "You okay, lady?"

"Yeah." I held my breath, then released it slowly. Was it my imagination or did the forest seem darker now . . . and colder?

Jerry ordered Sutton to call for the coroner. In the Town of Ruby Lake, that means Andrew Greeley, a sweet old fellow who looks about ninety but is only seventy-one, according to his birth records. Mr. Greeley owns the local mortuary and doubles as Ruby Lake's coroner.

Then Jerry had Officer Sutton escort me back to the McKutcheon house. "And see that she stays there!" he commanded his subordinate.

Two hours later, I gave my official statement, in the home's musty living room. I squirmed on a sofa that felt and looked about a hundred years old—and not in a vintage or antique good way.

There wasn't much to tell really. I explained that I'd gone for a hike and had been lucky, or unlucky, enough to have stumbled on the body.

"And you didn't see anybody? Hear anybody?"

I shook my head again. I'd been shaking it so much in response to his repetitive questions that I was getting a crick in my neck. "No, Jerry. Just the bird."

He rolled his eyes.

I rubbed the back of my neck. "Can I go now?" I'd tossed my binocs in my pack.

Chief Kennedy rested his arm on the mantel of the huge stone fireplace that took up the middle of the far wall. "Yeah." He bounced his fingers on the wood mantel. "So the last time you saw Bessie Hammond alive was . . . ?"

"I told you. Yesterday morning on our bird walk."

"Right."

"What about the others?" I asked, meaning the young men and women staying at the house. "Did they see or hear anyone around the property?"

Jerry grinned. "Only you. Tell me something, Simms. Did you and Bessie get along okay?"

My heart skipped a beat. "As well as any two people," I answered diplomatically.

"Right," Jerry repeated way more slowly than the first time.

This seemed like a good point to take my leave. Before Jerry started jumping to conclusions and those conclusions led him to me. Jerry's never had a particularly good opinion of me, so it wouldn't take much to push him over to the negative side. I said goodbye, grabbed my day pack and stood. I shook the pack. "You sure you don't want to search this before I leave?"

"Already did," Jerry said smugly. "While you were in the bathroom."

I huffed. "Don't you need a warrant for that?" I'd only been gone for a minute to freshen up and he'd searched my things?

Jerry folded his arms over his chest and wiggled his jaw. "I called to you to ask your permission while you were"—he paused—"in the facilities. Guess I misunderstood your reply."

I called him every name in the book. Well, in my head, I did. I wasn't fool enough to do it to his face. I threw my day pack over my shoulder and headed for the door.

"You need a ride?" Jerry asked.

"I'd rather walk!" I threw the door open and slammed it behind me. "That arrogant, snooping, son-of-a—"

9

A devilishly handsome man unfolded himself from the dusty rocker to the right of the front door. "Care to finish that thought?"

My words caught in my throat. "H-hello, Mr. McKutcheon."

He smiled and laid his hand on my upper arm. "Call me Gus, remember?" A shadow passed across his hazel eyes. "Police giving you a hard time?"

I nodded and stepped away. Gus's fingers skittered down my arm. "What are you doing here?"

"I live here. I'd ask what you're doing here but the police—and my boarders—have already filled me in."

"You heard about the murder."

His brow shot up. "I heard about the body. Was it a murder?"

I started to speak, then caught myself. Was it a murder? "Well, I-I think so." Softly, I added, "I believe Mrs. Hammond's neck was broken."

He pursed his lips. "Perhaps she fell out of the tree." He followed me as I started down the porch.

"I suppose . . ."

The two police cars, the ambulance, and Mr. Greeley's hearse stood in a semicircle at the side of the house. Could it have been as unfortunate and innocent as that? Could Bessie have simply fallen out of the sycamore to her death?

No, she didn't look like a woman who'd fallen to her death. Her body had looked so . . . composed, not messy like she'd just fallen twenty feet. And where were the bruises and scrapes? Wouldn't she be covered in bruises and scrapes if she'd fallen from a height?

"It is a possibility, isn't it?"

"Bessie had to be sixty if she was a day," I said. "Assuming she could climb a tree, what would she have been doing climbing one? I don't think she was the tree-house type."

"No," Gus said, matching me step for step. "You're right, of course." He turned his eyes on me. "This was murder." He wore a short-sleeved white polo shirt and black trousers with perfect pleats.

Ice formed in my toes.

"I was heading back to the diner. I was working when I got the call about all this." He waved his hand at the official vehicles cluttering his yard. "I should be getting back," Gus said. "Let me give you a ride." He gestured to an old white pickup with mud-spattered sides and tires. The vehicle had Maine plates.

Though it was something I could not put my finger on, this man gave me the creeps. What did Moire see in this guy? Sure, he was tall, dark, and handsome. But he seemed too good to be true. He also seemed like he was trying a little too hard to be affable.

Why was it, too, that I felt an undercurrent of danger in every other word he spoke?

The passenger side door squeaked as Gus opened it.

He looked at me expectantly. "I don't bite," he said, revealing two rows of perfect white teeth with the merest gap between the two top incisors, which seemed designed to give him character.

"That remains to be seen," I replied, climbing in. Despite my reservations, I was beat. My legs quivered like jelly in an earthquake and my arms felt like lead. I put it down to lack of food and overstimulation. Seeing a murder victim was something I'd never get used to.

"So how long have you been working at Ruby's Diner?" I asked as we rumbled and bounced down the unpaved road, through the woods that led back to town.

"About a week. I'm thinking of settling down here permanently. If I can make ends meet." That would explain running a hostel and working in the diner.

"I hear you're the cook." Though he didn't dress like one. Where were the grease and ketchup stains?

Gus chuckled. "Manager, chief cook, and head bottle washer."

That seemed like a lot of responsibility for a guy who'd only been working on the job for a week. "How long have you known Moire?" I asked, thinking maybe they had been friends before he'd come to town.

I gripped the armrest as he shot through several bumps in the road in succession.

"Since I got to town," he said, giving me a quick look. He flexed his fingers around the steering wheel. That wasn't telling me much. Gus wasn't much of a sharer.

I didn't get much more out of him after that. He dropped me off in front of Birds & Bees, then did a U-turn and pulled into a space across the street at Ruby's Diner.

"Should I be jealous?" I heard a voice bellow genially.

I turned to the left. Derek Harlan, my boyfriend of sorts, and Paul Anderson, the owner of Brewer's Biergarten, the business next door, sat outside at a table along the sidewalk. A chilled pitcher of beer and two weeping mugs sat between them. I smiled and waved. "Feel free!"

Brewer's had once been a retail garden center. The owners had gone out of business at that location and relocated to a spot outside town. After sitting empty for a spell, Paul and his partner, my ex-boyfriend Craig Bigelow, had remodeled the old shop and turned it into a bustling little *biergarten*. An outdoor space accommodating twenty or so tables and an outside bar were the only buffer between Birds & Bees and the interior of Brewer's Biergarten.

Unfortunately, there was no buffer between Paul and me. My friend Kim, without consulting me first, had offered Paul the use of an empty apartment in my house while his house was undergoing renovations. I hadn't even gotten used to Esther living under my roof and didn't think I'd ever get used to Paul living there.

Esther and Paul lived on the second floor in small side-by-side apartments. I smiled at the thought of them driving each other crazy.

Even more unfortunate than Paul and my ex's business being next-door was Derek's bonding with him. Derek and Paul were new BDBs, best drinking buddies or BBFs, best beer friends. Whatever you called it, it was DMC, driving me crazy. Derek thought Paul was great. I wasn't so keen on the guy myself but, like they say, we don't pick our friends, they pick us. In my case, I hadn't even picked my renters. I'd inherited one and had the other foisted on me.

Such is life.

Derek and Paul invited me over. I went around to the opening in the low brick wall enclosing the outdoor seating area. Derek pulled over a chair for me to join them. "You don't look so good," he remarked, leaning back in his seat. "Everything okay?"

"Yeah." I fiddled with my hair, discovering a small twig and half a dead leaf in the process. I could only imagine how awful I must look. Then again, not nearly as awful as poor Bessie Hammond had looked. "Can we talk about this later? Right now, I could really use a bite to eat. And some of that." I pointed to Derek's icy beer stein.

Paul rose quickly. "I'll bring another glass." He scurried over to the bar that backed up to the side of my store. A lone redheaded waitress was putting together place settings. Several tables were occupied with hungry and thirsty customers.

Paul returned with a fresh mug and poured me a glassful of beer.

I drank half down before stopping myself.

Derek chuckled.

"Sorry." I blushed. "I guess I was thirsty."

"I'll say!" He sniggered again.

"What would you like to eat?" Paul inquired. "I've got the new wood-burning pizza oven going." He cocked his brow in a questioning manner.

Hot, gooey cheese and fresh-baked dough. There was no saying no to that. "Absolutely," I said. "Mushroom, onion, and olive?"

Paul beamed. "You got it."

"No, wait!" I called as Paul turned to go. I glanced at Derek. Onion breath and kisses don't go well together. "Hold the onions."

Paul nodded and went off to the kitchen to put my

order in. He returned fifteen minutes later with hot lunch and a fresh, cold pitcher.

We all dug in.

"It's fortuitous that you're here," Derek said, draping his arm comfortably over the back of my seat. "When you pulled up, Paul and I were just talking about a proposition that he has for you." Derek blinked and looked at Gus's pickup parked across the street at the diner. "Who was that guy, anyway?"

"His name is Guster McKutcheon. He works at the diner."

"I see," Derek said, thoughtfully.

I wondered if he really was jealous and found that the idea didn't make me feel bad at all. "He's dating Moire Leora." I slammed back the dregs of my beer. "And that's all I'd care to say about that for now."

I gave Paul and Derek the eye, then wriggled my fingers at Derek. "So what's this proposition that Paul has? And whatever it is," I added, before giving either man a chance to reply, "the answer is no."

Derek chuckled while Paul sat back with a snort and laid his hands on the table. "Well, how do you like that?!" He pulled free a slice of pizza, leaving a trail of cheesy goo, and bit down hard. He turned to Derek. "This is what I get for trying to do a girl a favor?"

"That's *woman*," I said, folding my arms across my chest.

"Okay, woman," Paul said. "Boy, it's no wonder Craig—"

I cut him off quickly. "Do not go there."

Paul held up his hands. "Sorry, Amy."

Derek interrupted our bickering. "Give Paul a chance, Amy." He laid his hand on mine. "I think you're going to like his idea."

I tipped my glass to my lips and sipped. "Okay," I said, "spill."

Paul dropped his half-eaten pizza on his plate. "Birds and brews," he said proudly.

I frowned. "Huh?"

"Birds and brews," Derek said enthusiastically.

I gaped at them. "How much did you two have to drink before I arrived?"

Derek grabbed my hand. "Paul's come up with an idea to hold a monthly—"

"Maybe weekly if it really takes off," interjected the pub owner.

"Sure," said Derek. "The idea is to hold the event here at Brewer's Biergarten. He's going to call it Birds and Brews."

"And," I said slowly, not understanding what they could possibly be thinking, "you're going to do what—hold a happy hour for birds? See how many beers it takes to get our feathered friends blotto?"

Paul laughed. "Those are all excellent ideas," he chided. "But that's not what I was thinking."

"What exactly are you thinking?" I asked Paul, before turning to Derek and saying, "And what does it have to do with me?"

"You're the birds part," Paul replied.

"The birds part?"

"Yep." Paul rose, stretching an invisible banner in his hands. "Birds and Brews. We'll meet once a month initially. I was thinking on Tuesday evenings. I've noticed Tuesdays are a bit slow around here. It'll be good for business." He turned his seat around and sat back down. "For both our businesses."

"So what do you think, Amy?" Derek asked, anticipation in his eyes.

I stood. "I think I'm leaving. Thanks for lunch."

Derek jumped to his feet. "You don't like the idea?"

"I haven't heard one yet!"

Derek took a deep breath. "Birds and Brews. A gathering of bird lovers and beer lovers. You supply the bird knowledge. I don't know, I'm just spitballing here, but maybe you have a specific bird that you lecture on each time, or some aspect of bird-watching."

He turned to Paul for support and Paul nodded his encouragement. "And Paul here supplies the beer."

Paul nodded some more. "That's right. Maybe we can coordinate. I'll come up with a pairing of one of our in-house craft beers or some other artisanal brew to match up with whatever bird you care to spotlight for each gathering."

"What, like a pilsner and a plover?"

"Sure, or a good kölsch with a kestrel," Paul shot back.

"Birds and brews," I said, understanding finally dawning on me. I wanted to tell Mr. Paul Anderson that that was the dumbest idea I'd ever heard.

Unfortunately, it wasn't. It was a great idea.

Not to overly encourage the man or fuel his already overinflated ego, I chose my words carefully. "I'll think about it."

Derek squeezed my hand.

"Great." Paul stood. "I'm thinking we start this Tuesday. Seven o'clock okay with you?"

"Tuesday? This Tuesday?" That was only a couple of days away.

"Sure, why wait?"

"Because these things take time to organize. We have to send out emails, put up flyers. Gauge the public's interest."

"Nah." Paul waved away my concerns. "We'll start small. It'll be a dry run, so to speak. What do you say?"

I turned to Derek. "Do you have any plans for Tuesday?"

"Me?" Derek pointed to his chest. "A couple of client meetings in the morning. And I'm picking up Maeve from school at three." Maeve was Derek's young daughter.

"Tuesday night?"

"I don't think so, why?"

"Because I expect you to be here."

Our lunch concluded and my alliance with the devil-next-door completed, I begged my leave. Derek offered to walk me home and we exited to the sidewalk together.

"By the way," Paul called from the table on the other side of the pony wall, "you're the bird lady."

Derek and I stopped. "So?" I asked.

"So can't you do something about that darn woodpecker that keeps waking me up in the middle of the night?"

I laughed. "Number one, as much as I am the bird lady, as you say, I'm not Dr. Dolittle. I don't talk to the animals and they don't talk to me. Number two, I'd hardly call six thirty in the morning the middle of the night." I urged Derek to move on.

"It is for me," replied Paul. "I run a *biergarten*, remember? Nighttime is prime time. While you're home snuggled in your little kitty jammies, I'm on my feet serving customers."

I blushed, my shoulders tensing, but I forced myself to say nothing, move on. How did this guy know I wore pajamas with kittens on them? Who squealed?

10

We paused outside the door to Birds & Bees. "Do you want to tell me what's really going on?" Derek began softly.

I sighed and collapsed into his arms. "Bessie Hammond is dead."

"So that was what all those sirens were about." Derek explained how he had been driving across town when the police and ambulance had screamed past him.

"I'm afraid so. And I'm the one who found her."

Derek wrapped his arms around me and squeezed gently. "Do you want to talk about it?" He ran a gentle hand over my scalp.

"No," I said, looking him in the eye. "But I need to."

Derek smiled. "Let's sit." He pulled me over to a small wrought-iron bench in the shade of the front porch. The bluebird house sat empty—nesting season was over—but several wrens pecked away at the feeder hanging over the porch rail.

I let the whole story out. How I thought I'd seen a dead body being tossed from the window of the old

McKutcheon house. About the bird-watching hike I'd organized, then hiked out to the McKutcheon property so I could snoop. How I'd gone back again that morning to snoop some more. I'd even told him about the widow in the lake, for what it was worth.

Derek nodded. "I've heard of this widow-in-the-lake thing."

My brow rose. "You have?"

Derek rubbed his forehead. "Yeah. Amy told me about it." Derek's ex-wife's name is also Amy. Lucky me. "She and her girlfriends think it would be fun to take part in the annual vigil this Saturday."

"No offense, but your ex is a nut."

Derek chuckled. "I dare you to tell her that."

Amy Harlan was a temperamental fashion- and looks-obsessed fiend, if you asked me. But no, I wasn't telling her that to her face. "There's an annual vigil?"

"So Amy says. It's not a big deal. Apparently, a small but dedicated—"

"Crazy," I interrupted.

Derek smiled and continued. "—gathering meets on the anniversary of the widow's death at the magic hour. Hoping for the widow's appearance."

"Oh, brother." Was it material to Bessie's murder that the anniversary of Mary McKutcheon's suicide was this week? Did it have anything to do with everything weird that had been going on? I shook my head. No, it couldn't.

"Hey, you don't have to tell me it's crazy. I'm only repeating what I heard."

"When is this *magic hour*?" I wrapped finger quotes around the two words.

"Sunrise."

"Did you know that the widow in the lake was a McKutcheon?"

Derek stiffened. "No, Amy didn't tell me that. Or, if she did, I wasn't paying attention."

"Yep. Mary McKutcheon." I glanced back inside the shop. "Esther says the McKutcheon house is cursed. I don't want to believe her." I paused before continuing. "But the next thing I know, I lead a bird-watching hike there and Bessie Hammond winds up dead."

"And you're certain it was murder?"

"Yeah, I don't know what else it could be."

"Maybe this Bessie woman fell out of the tree? She might have climbed up to get a better look at some bird," Derek proposed. "You did say she was an avid birder."

"That's what Gus McKutcheon suggested," I replied. "I don't buy it."

"Was she the athletic type?"

"I rather doubt it. Not to mention, she was in her sixties."

"You can't picture Bessie Hammond climbing a tree?"

"Not without laughing." We smiled at each other.

"Were you and Bessie close friends?" Derek, relatively new to town, said he hadn't known her.

"No. I barely knew her. But still . . ."

"I understand," said Derek, patting my leg. "Are you going to be okay?" I nodded. "I'd better go. I promised Dad I'd help him with some yard work this afternoon."

"What about Bessie?" My eyes darted out across the lake. I could just make out the peak of the McKutcheon house. Bessie Hammond had met a violent death out there . . .

"What about her? I'm sure Chief Kennedy and the Ruby Lake PD will find out what happened." He kissed me quickly on the lips. "You will let the police do their job, won't you?"

"Of course!" I said, maybe a smidgen too quickly.

"Good," answered Derek. "Because butting into a murder investigation could land you in a heap of trouble."

I grinned. "That's what lawyers are for, right?" And that had proven to be the case more than once. A little case of murder had been the reason for our initial meeting.

As Derek headed to his car, his words replayed in my mind. "Heap!" I blurted out.

Derek paused beside his car. "What?"

"You said heap."

His brow went up. "And I meant it."

"No," I said, shaking my head. "There was a heap, a mound really, out at the cemetery on the McKutcheon property. We all saw it, our entire bird-watching group, yesterday on our hike."

"So?" Derek unlocked his door. "It's a cemetery. It's supposed to have mounds."

"But this one looked fresh."

"Fresh?" Derek bent his head, entered the vehicle, and pulled the door shut behind him. He rolled down the window and beckoned me closer. "Tell the police," he said. "Let them check it out, Amy." He turned the key in the ignition and the little engine sparked to life. "That's my advice." Derek waved his finger as he said, "As your lawyer."

Derek's car disappeared toward downtown, modest though the city center is. My eyes were drawn to Ruby's Diner. More specifically, to its new manager, chief cook, and head bottle washer, Guster McKutcheon. I'd seen a body mysteriously tossed out an upstairs window of his house early the other morning, heard tales of his ancestor, the widow in the lake, and discovered Bessie Hammond's body at the base of a tree on his property.

It didn't take a genius or a big leap of imagination to know that something strange was going on out there. The question was, what?

Come to think of it, when Abby first spotted the cemetery, Bessie had made some flip comment about how graves couldn't hurt you and we'd all end up in one someday. Who could have predicted that not twenty-four hours would go by before those words proved prophetic for Bessie herself?

My thoughts were interrupted by a grip on my shoulder that made me jump as if the widow in the lake had laid her wet, icy clutches on me. "Ahh!"

"What are you hanging around out here for?" snapped Esther, dusting her hands on her store apron. "It's time for my break." She pulled off her apron and foisted it on me. "Get to work."

I did. It kept my mind of things. Off scary, troubling, and sad things like murder.

By Monday morning, the news of Bessie's Hammond death had spread through Ruby Lake. Lance Jennings, several years my senior, came by fishing for a quote. "Get lost," I said, barely glancing up from my sales ledger, open on the front counter. "And you can quote me on that."

Lance is a reporter for the *Ruby Lake Weekender*. He's about forty years old and forty pounds overweight. He lets his wavy black hair run a little too long, in my opinion, but that was probably to lessen the sight of his receding hairline. Sometimes I thought the only thing thicker than his nose was his head.

"Come on, Amy. I can't go back to the office without a scoop."

I frowned. Lance's father owns the paper and runs a tight ship. I'd been in the paper's headquarters a couple of times to place store ads. Lance's *office* was nothing more than a tiny, cluttered cubicle next to the janitor's closet. "I don't know what I can tell you that you probably haven't already heard from the police."

Lance groaned and shoved his pen back in his shirt pocket. He wore a cheap ecru linen suit that looked like it had come off the assembly line pre-rumpled. "All Jerry will tell me is that Bessie Hammond got her neck broke." Lance kicked his shoe against the counter and only stopped when I gave him the stink eye. "He's not giving me anything else. No motives, no suspects."

I'd perked up when Lance said that bit about the broken neck. "So it was murder!"

"Yeah, I suppose so." Lance looked surprised at my reaction. "What else could it be? They're certainly treating it like a murder. Being all tight-lipped and tight—"

I slammed shut the sales ledger. "Did he say what Mrs. Hammond was doing out there? Or how long she might have been dead?"

Lance waved his notebook, pages fluttering like doves' wings. "No. I'm going to see Greeley when I get done here." He leaned over the counter toward me. "Can't you give me anything?" he wheedled. "You might have been one of the last persons to see Bessie Hammond alive."

"There was an entire group of us, Lance. Not just me. Besides," I said, rising and leading Lance to the front door, "that was the day *before* she was killed. All sorts of people probably saw her after that." I held open the door. "Why don't you go find them? Talk to them."

Lance stumbled out to the porch. "But—"

A thought suddenly occurred to me. Several, actually. I grabbed Lance's sleeve. "I'll make you a deal. You see what you can find out about who else might have seen Bessie in the hours leading up to her death and I'll do the same. I'll talk to my bird-watching group. They'll talk to me."

Lance wiped a line of sweat from his brow. "You've got a deal." Lance held out his clammy right hand and we shook.

"Great." I motioned for Lance to scoot over. I threw up the CLOSED sign and locked the store behind me. "Let's stay in touch." I hurried down the walk toward the street. "Don't forget to let me know the minute you find out anything!" I hollered as I stepped off the curb.

"Same here!" Lance called back.

I waved goodbye over my shoulder and waited impatiently for a string of cars to pass. A public bus was sitting idle at the bus stop outside the diner and I wanted a word with its driver.

One of those last people to see Bessie Hammond alive might very well have been a bus driver. After all, Bessie had made a point of saying she didn't drive. She stated she'd ridden the bus to Birds & Bees the morning of our hike.

This bus.

I trotted to the door and pushed it open. The bus was quiet and empty. "Hello?" My voice came echoing back.

"If you're looking for the driver, he's inside the diner."

I bristled. I knew that voice. "Hello, Gertie."

"Simms." Gertie Hammer stood on the sidewalk. She raked her brilliant blue eyes over me like a pair of death-capable lasers. "You're like a modern-day Medusa."

"What's that supposed to mean?" I pulled the door

shut and stepped away from the bus. Gertie was the town curmudgeon; at least she acted like one around me. It was Gertie's house that I had bought and was living in, though she'd later tried to con me into selling it back to her for her own self-enriching purposes. I'd refused, which added to the list of things she disliked about me. I'd inherited Esther because of Gertie. It seems we all have our own crosses to bear.

"It means you're like some deity of death." Gertie pulled herself up to her full height, which was all of four foot nothing. She wore a baggy blue dress that drooped to her knees and low-heeled black shoes that might have been in fashion in the forties—the 1840s. A purse the size of a small suitcase hung off her shoulder. I couldn't imagine what all she carried around in there. Instruments of torture, perhaps?

I frowned at her. "Medusa had snakes for hair and turned people to stone."

"I heard about poor, poor Bessie Hammond," Gertie said with a smile. "You turn people into skin and bones. Seems to me, that's pretty much the same thing."

"Yes," I said. "What happened to Mrs. Hammond was a terrible thing." I fingered my hair. Maybe it was time for a trim or a new style. I mean, snakes? Really? "Did you know her?" I decided to take the high road and avoid a verbal confrontation. There was little to be gained in such sport and lots of time to lose.

"Sure, I knew her." Gertie stepped aside and snarled at a young boy as he pedaled by on his bicycle. "I know everybody."

That was quite likely true. "What about her husband?"

"He's been dead for years."

"I didn't know that."

"Died in a boating accident." Gertie turned her eyes to the lake.

"Oh," I said again. A sudden breeze off Ruby Lake set the little hairs of my arms on end.

"His body was never found." Her eyes gleamed devilishly.

"You mean, he—" I pointed toward the lake, now filled with recreational boaters and swimmers. Were Bessie's husband's bones rattling around out there at the bottom of Ruby Lake with Mary McKutcheon's bones?

It was too gruesome to dwell on.

"I remember it like it was yesterday." Gertie pulled a rumpled pale blue handkerchief from the front pocket of her dress. She blew her nose, rubbed it fiercely, and then returned the hankie to its home.

"Was the accident recent?"

Gertie sniffed. "Ten years ago yesterday, as I recall."

"You mean . . ."

"That's right." Gertie shifted her purse to her opposite shoulder. The bag must've weighed a ton. "The same day that ole Bessie got herself killed." With that, Gertie Hammer turned on her heel and hobbled up the street. I watched as she disappeared inside the town post office.

I stared at my reflection in the window of Ruby's Diner, wondering where and when I, and the whole Town of Ruby Lake for that matter, had entered the twilight zone.

11

I pulled open the door to Ruby's Diner. Lana Potter stood behind the hostess stand. "Hi, Lana. Is Moire here?" Looking around the diner, I didn't see her out front. I did see the back of Gus McKutcheon's head through the pass-through window to the kitchen.

Lana shook her head, her raven hair flouncing. "She's taking a break upstairs. Can I get you a table?"

Peering over Lana's shoulder, I noticed a man in a blue-gray bus driver's uniform sitting alone at the counter. There was an empty stool beside him. "I think I'll sit at the counter today."

"Help yourself. I'll be with you in a minute."

I told Lana to take her time and approached the counter. "Is this seat taken?" I asked the uniformed man, more to break the ice and get him talking than anything else.

"Nope, help yourself, young lady."

I jumped on the stool. Gus turned, set two hot plates on the stainless steel counter. He looked at me and blinked. "Hey, Lana!"

"Yes?" Lana moved languidly toward the pickup counter. She walked like a model and had the looks to match. Lana Potter must certainly be giving Tiffany a run for her money in terms of attracting the attention of the males that frequent the diner.

"Order's up. Table three."

Lana reached for the plates. Gus said something in a low voice. Lana laughed huskily, then shook her hips all the way to table three.

"So what's good today?" I asked, picking up my menu and turning to the bus driver. His paper place mat held a plate with a bacon sandwich with a big bite out of it, French fries, and a shallow bowl of coleslaw.

"Can't go wrong with the special."

"Is that it?" My mouth watered. Bacon has that effect on me.

"Yep." He lifted his sandwich, as if to prove his point, and took a giant bite. His jaw worked back and forth. He swallowed, grinned, and patted his paunch. "Hits the spot."

I looked at the million-calorie meal on my neighbor's plate, half of them fat. "Sure looks good." I told Lana I'd have the same. There's nothing like ordering what a man's having for lunch to get on his good side.

Lana looked at me uncertainly. "Are you sure?"

I nodded. "Coffee, too. Cream and sugar."

Lana shrugged, wrote up a ticket and placed it on the pass-through counter.

"I'm Amy." I lifted my silverware, took my napkin, and draped it across my lap.

"Neal." He had pale brown eyes and a complexion to match. He removed his cap and placed it on the counter, revealing a head of thick, curly black hair.

My coffee arrived and I dumped in some cream and sugar. "I've seen you around town. It must be tough driving a big bus like that around town all day. Especially during the height of the tourist season."

Neal fisted several fries and shook salt over them. "I don't mind. Keeps food on the table." He brought the fries to his mouth and downed them as one.

That it did. "Well, I don't think I could handle it. I have a difficult enough time maneuvering my minivan."

Neal chuckled appreciatively. "What exactly do you do?"

I explained that I ran Birds & Bees. "That's it there." He turned his neck as I pointed out the window.

"Yeah," he said, returning to his meal. He took a loud sip of coffee before saying, "I've seen it but never been in. Birds don't do anything for me." He paused and smiled. "Unless they're breaded and deep-fried."

Lana slid my bacon sandwich special down before me. "Can I get you anything else?"

I said no. Lana refilled a couple of customers' drinks, then pushed through the swinging doors to the kitchen. She sidled up to Gus and began whispering in his ear. His hand fell on the small of her back.

"I had a lady on the bus yesterday," said Neal, catching my ear. "She was really into that whole bird-watching thing."

"You did?" Bingo.

He nodded, took another loud sip, and then said, "The only reason I remember is because she got herself killed."

I took a bite of coleslaw, figuring that, of all the food items on my plate, it was the least damaging to my health. "I heard about that." I took my time. I didn't want to spook him. Sometimes talking to a person and trying to get any useful information out of them was like reeling in a difficult fish. "You gave her a ride?"

"Yep, picked her up at the stop outside the high school. Her house must be near there. I don't usually get many folks coming out this way on a Sunday morning. Those I do get are on their way to church."

"But Mrs. Hammond wasn't going to church?"

Neal's brow went up. "Bessie Hammond. That was her name, all right." He wiped his full lips with his napkin. "You knew her?"

I explained how she'd been a member of my inaugural bird-watching group.

"That makes sense," Neal replied. "She said she was going bird-watching." He paused, chuckling. "And maybe a little ghost hunting as well."

"Ghost hunting? What did she mean by that?"

"I have no idea. A joke, I guess. She had a big pair of binoculars around her neck. Said nobody could read a clue like her."

"What time was this? Do you remember?"

"Of course, I remember. Like I told the police, Saturday and Sunday mornings I hit that stop three times."

"What time did you pick up Bessie Hammond?"

"Six fifty in the a.m. On schedule." Neal tipped his coffee mug. "I stick to my schedule. Not that I get many folks at that stop Sunday mornings. I keep telling my boss at the transportation department they ought to cut that run, but what do I know?"

"Was Mrs. Hammond alone? Did anyone board with her?"

"Not a soul. Who'd want to?" Neal chuckled and shook his head. "I don't know what makes a person

want to get up early on a Sunday morning and go looking at a bunch of silly birds." He tapped the side of his
skull with a fat finger. "Bird brains, if you ask me."

The driver looked suddenly stricken and added quickly,
"I mean, no offense to you or the lady." He hung his
head, staring into his coffee mug, though I wasn't sure if
it was sudden-found remorse or unhappiness that his
coffee was gone and no more was forthcoming.

"You said you gave her a ride," I started. "Where did
you take her?"

"The marina."

"And you never gave her a ride back?" I pretty much
knew the answer to that question, but I wanted corrobo-
ration. The more I could learn about Bessie's movements
Sunday morning, the closer I might come to learning
what had led to her death.

"Nope." Neal had polished off his sandwich and now
attacked the remaining fries after slathering them with
ketchup. "Saw her picture this morning in the *Weekender*."

"Today?" The town paper only comes out on week-
ends, hence its name.

"Yep. They put out a special edition."

Leave it to Lance's dad, William Jennings, to run a
special edition of his newspaper to try to capitalize on
the murder.

"Nice obit. The lady would have been pleased. Well"—
Neal slid off his stool, extracting a ten-dollar bill from a
thick black wallet and laying it next to his ticket—"back to
work."

I nodded thoughtfully as I bit into my bacon sandwich. I promised myself I'd only eat half and save the
rest for later. Unfortunately, the bacon on white toast
had other ideas and I left behind an empty plate.

Self-control was not one of my strong suits. Leaving the diner, I walked around back to the private stairs leading to Moire's apartment. I wanted to get Moire alone and, with Gus McKutcheon tied up in the kitchen, this was the perfect opportunity.

Or so I thought.

I knocked on the door. Gus answered, his lower half wrapped in a fluffy white bath towel. "Oh." I stepped back in surprise and stumbled off the tiny landing.

Gus reached out, caught my hand, and pulled me toward him. "Hey, there! Be careful, kitten!"

I smelled musk as he pressed me close to his bare chest. I felt the blood rush to my cheeks and forehead. And what was with that kitten crack? Did everyone in town know what kind of pj's I wore?

"Who's there?" I heard Moire call.

"Your friend Amy!" Gus shouted. One hand tugged at the towel hanging precariously on his hip bone.

"Oh?" Moire's surprised voice was followed a moment later by the woman herself. "Hello, Amy." She ran a hand through her damp hair.

I gaped, struggling for words. "I—that is, I—"

"Yes?" Moire belted her green fleece robe and wrapped her arm around Gus's waist.

Wow. Not only was Guster McKutcheon the diner's manager, chief cook, and head bottle washer, as he liked to proclaim, he was also sleeping with the boss!

After merely a week, no less.

"I wanted to let you know that Paul Anderson and I are starting a new birds-and-brews event. We'll be meeting one Tuesday a month at Brewer's Biergarten, starting this Tuesday. I hope you can make it. Both of you." I managed a weak smile.

Gus and Moire looked at each other in poorly hidden amusement.

"Uh, sure, Amy. Thanks." Moire's hand was on the doorknob. "Was there something else?"

I shook my head no. There was so, so much more. But where to begin? I'm pretty sure I muttered some sort of goodbye before fleeing down the stairs.

The next thing I knew, I was at the marina, staring at boats.

I was drenched in embarrassment-induced sweat and part of me felt like jumping in the lake to cool off. The other part of me thought about Mary McKutcheon's and Mr. Hammond's bones swishing around the dark bottom of the lake somewhere.

That part of me won. I remained on dry land. A man and a woman were clearly visible in the glass-sided control center atop the marina's main building. Several gulls basked in the sun near the rooster weather vane at the peak of the shingled rooftop. I was about to climb the steps leading to the center when I noticed a police car roll up and park nearby.

I ducked my head and turned left quickly. I rounded the corner and took a peek. Chief Kennedy exited the squad car. He was in uniform and making straight for the marina manager's office on the ground floor, directly below the control center.

Now was not the time for amateur sleuthing. At least, not directly under Jerry's nose. Harsh sunlight beat down from the sky, bounced off the flat lake, and hit me in the eyes. Using my hand for a visor, I surveyed the rows of docks.

I was in luck. Two men were moving about on the small orange-topped motorboat I'd seen out alone on the lake the morning of the storm. A sign that hung over the side of the boat advertised fishing expeditions and scenic tours. A phone number and web address were prominently displayed.

My feet thumped loudly as I walked along the long, narrow dock. Gulls lifted off as I approached. Their squawks had the opposite effect of what the birds might have intended because I found the noise oddly soothing, natural.

Normal. There wasn't a lot of normal going around lately.

A heavyset man with a thick black beard was folding a net on deck. He stopped when he saw me. The blue-and-white horizontal-striped shirt and baggy cargo pants made him look doubly wide. The second man had disappeared, probably gone belowdecks.

"Good morning!" I waved. "Catch anything?"

The bearded man spat over his shoulder but his aim was poor and his spittle landed in the boat not the lake. He didn't seem to mind. "See for yourself," he said in a friendly manner. The burly man gestured toward a water-filled fiberglass holding tank built into the motor-boat's side.

"Permission to come aboard?" I quipped. He nodded and I gingerly stepped across from the dock to the boat. The boat rocked unexpectedly toward me. I felt myself falling for the second time in the space of an hour. This time, instead of a half-naked man in a towel, it was a fleshy, calloused hand that reached out, saving me from cracking my skull against the gunwale. I pushed my hair out of my face and straightened my blouse. "Thanks. That was close." Thank goodness I'd worn shorts and not a skirt.

The fisherman chuckled. "My license doesn't allow me to catch women," he said. "Only fish." A big-brimmed camo hat covered his head and shaded his piercing eyes.

I'd have found those words disconcerting from most anybody else, but from him they seemed harmless. I peered into the tank. Half a dozen fish, varying in size from six inches to over a foot, swam in circles within. "Perch?" I'm not a fish person. Birds I can identify, but not fish. They all look the same to me. I imagined bus driver Neal felt that way about birds. Neal. Something he'd said—and something I'd seen before or hadn't seen—nagged at me from a hidden corner of my mind. What was it? I squeezed my eyes shut, deep in thought, but was interrupted by the fisherman.

He chuckled and joined me at the tank. "See the ones over here with the black spots?"

"Yes?"

"Those are bluegills. Them two stripey ones are crappies. The big olive-green one is a large-mouth bass."

"Yes, I see now." Though how black spots led to a fish being christened a bluegill was clear as the mud surrounding the lake's edge. I guess it was no different than a lot of birds whose names make no sense to me, like the red-bellied woodpecker that had been driving me from my sleep on recent mornings. "Did you catch anything Friday morning, Mister . . . ?"

"Captain Ethan Harrow. Call me Ethan."

"Amy Simms." I shook his hand. My hand now smelled fishie and some sort of slime seemed to have taken up residence on my palm. I wiped my hand against my shorts. "So, did you catch anything Friday?"

Ethan cocked his head. "Friday?" He rubbed his chin between his thumb and forefinger. "I don't recall. Why?" I sensed a growing suspicion.

I explained that I lived across the street and had been bird-watching at the time. "I'd been surprised to see anyone out on the lake during the storm."

"Friday." He nodded, thoughtfully. "Yeah, I was out. How did you know it was me?"

I explained that I had recognized his boat. "It was the orange roof," I explained.

Ethan seemed to take my interest at face value. "I didn't haul much, as I recall. What I can't eat, I sell to the Lakeside Market. I was alone that morning. No crew. No customers."

"Customers?"

"Tourists. They pay me to take them fishing. Not Friday. Bad weather. I didn't stay out long, myself."

I watched the little fish swimming in hopeless circles as I framed my next question, the question that mattered most. "Did you notice anything odd that morning?"

Ethan sat back against the captain's chair and motioned for me to sit beside him. "How do you mean, odd?"

I scratched at my leg. I sometimes scratch when I'm nervous or restless. "I don't know. Anything that seemed out of the ordinary?"

Ethan shrugged and pulled a chubby cigar from a small pouch hanging beside the wheel. "Nothing."

"Nothing?"

"Lady"—the fishing captain poked his cigar at me— "I was only looking for fish. Not to mention, there was a squall going on. It was too loud out here to hear anything less than a cannon shot." He lit up with a gold lighter. "You mind?"

I said I didn't. It was his boat, after all. I already smelled of fish, so smelling like a cigar too couldn't be much worse. "Have you ever been to the McKutcheon house?" Maybe I could work around to my subject by coming up on it from another angle.

"That old place? I know folks are living there again. But I've never been up. Why?" Ethan looked over his shoulder at the house, barely visible through the trees. "What's so special about that house?"

"I like old houses," I answered. "In fact, I live in one. I'm sort of a history buff. I have an interest in historic houses and their stories."

"Oh," Ethan said slowly. He slid off his seat. "In that case, you ought to talk to my young assistant. He can probably tell you all about it. More than me, that's for certain."

My heart quickened. Finally, I might be getting somewhere.

The captain crossed to the hatch and yelled down. "Hey, Jean! Come on up, will you?"

Jean?

Jean Rabin's head popped up from the hatch. He looked at me and smiled. "*Bonjour.*" He crossed to where I sat and kissed me on both cheeks. "Welcome aboard."

I tried to voice a reply, but my mouth had turned dry as soot. Ethan picked up a jug and poured me some water in a plastic cup, which he handed to me. I drank it down.

"You okay?" Ethan asked. He and Jean looked at me with concern.

"I'm fine." I forced a smile. "I guess I don't have my sea legs yet."

Ethan's brow went up in amusement. "We're tied up and barely moving."

"I don't do so good on boats. Remind me to tell you about the time I went whale watching in Bar Harbor. I didn't see a single whale, but I did get a good look at my shoes every time I bent over to puke!"

Both men laughed.

"Amy was asking me about the McKutcheon house, Jean. She's one of them history buffs."

Jean flashed his teeth. "Is that so?" I detected a bit of disbelief in his speech and it wasn't just the French accent. "You must come and visit us again, mademoiselle."

"Again?" asked Ethan, between puffs of his cigar that sent clouds of smoke over the bow.

"I did see the house briefly . . ."

Jean planted his bare feet and grabbed a coil of thick rope from the stern. He placed it in a small locker, then flipped the lid closed. "Amy is the one I was telling you about, the one who discovered the unfortunate dead woman in the forest."

"Is that so?" Ethan tossed his cigar over the side. Ecofriendly didn't seem to be in his vocabulary. "Not a pretty sight, I'll bet. Not a pretty sight at all."

Jean plopped himself down on an orange foam cushion on the deck and crossed his legs. Bare skin showed through where the knees had worn away or been cut to appear so at the knees. "What exactly would you like to know about the house?" He wiped his hands across his T-shirt. "I have not been long here. But I'll tell you what I can."

"I hear Guster McKutcheon is using the house as a hostel. How many guests are there?"

Jean scrunched up his lips and counted with his fingers. "*Un, deux* . . . I should say *sept*—seven. Counting me," he said, pointing to himself. I tried to do some quick math in my head. How many people had I seen at the house? Did his number add up? And what about the body I'd seen ejected from the window? Though I was more and more beginning to think that everybody else was right and I was wrong. Maybe I could get Kim's boyfriend, Randy, to take me to the dump. I wanted to get a look at this dressmaking dummy and see if that dummy had made a dummy out of me.

"As for the house history," Jean was saying, "you must ask Mr. McKutcheon himself. Perhaps you should come for a supper?"

"Umm, well . . ."

"Tonight?" Jean turned to Ethan. "You must come, too, sir. My way of repaying you for the job, monsieur."

"Yeah, why not?" Ethan said quickly. "You got any whiskey up there, or should I bring a bottle?"

"I am certain we can accommodate you, Mr. Harrow, sir."

Much as I loathed the idea, I had no choice but to agree. Notwithstanding whether I'd seen or only imagined a man being tossed in cold blood out a second-floor window, I had seen Bessie Hammond with her neck broken out there. I did not want to be next.

With the fisherman at the house, too, I knew I'd be safe.

12

"Are you kidding me?" shrieked Kim. "Half-naked?"

I shook my head. "Half-naked and wearing only a bath towel."

Kim hooted. "Why do I miss all the fun?"

I threw a sofa pillow at her. It missed and tumbled helplessly end over end across the floor until it came to a stop in the fireplace. Great, now I had a soot-covered pillow. How was I going to explain that to Mom? I dug my spine into the back of the sofa. "I was shocked. I mean, Gus had been in the diner not long before that. I saw him with my own two eyes. Canoodling with one of the waitresses, no less!"

"It was probably nothing. I worked in a restaurant one summer. There's a lot of harmless flirtation that goes on. Trust me."

"I suppose so."

Kim helped herself to a glass of wine from the bottle over the fridge. "I guess Moire's in love. Good for her."

I pulled a face. "She thinks she's in love, but she's in flames."

Kim settled down beside me. "What do you mean?"

"I mean there's something wrong about this guy. There's been at least one murder out at his property."

"That doesn't make it his fault."

"It doesn't make it *not* his fault," I argued back. "Besides, he's a player."

"He can play me anytime."

"Would you cut that out? I'm trying to be serious here."

"Okay." Kim tilted back her glass and took a swallow. "Let's be serious for a moment. Whatever, and I mean *whatever* is going on between Gus McKutcheon and Moire is none"—Kim tapped my hand—"none of our business."

I bit down on my lower lip. "But you didn't see the way Lana and Gus were carrying on at the diner—"

Kim cut me off. "But nothing. Like I said, that could have been simply a harmless flirtation. Gus is a good-looking guy. Maybe Lana is coming on to him a little bit. So what? I think it's already clear from what you told me that Gus wants Moire. And boy, does she sure want him!"

"But—"

Kim pressed a finger to my lips. "Butt. Out."

I grabbed her wineglass and tossed back the rest of the red. "I suppose. I'm not happy about it though."

I made Kim promise to wheedle me a ride out to the dump the next day, or as soon as possible, with Randy, so I could get a look at whatever it was that those young men had been throwing out the window. I'd never been out to the county dump and he had some experience going there, what with his need to occasionally rehab his properties and dispose of the ensuing debris.

"Now get out of here," I said with love. "I've got a dinner date with the devil."

"Not before you shower first," Kim retorted. She sniffed my side and pinched her nose. "You smell like Popeye the Sailor Man. You show up reeking like that, not even the devil will want to sit next to you."

I showered and dressed, then drove the minivan out to the McKutcheon house. We'd agreed on eight o'clock—a little late for an early riser like me. Maybe Drummy would let me sleep in tomorrow.

Chills ran up my spine as I followed the unpaved track past the park and out toward the old farm. It was getting dark. I'd left the lights of town far behind. Only my headlights provided illumination and that wasn't much. The lenses were cloudy with age and only a dim, yellow light spilled forth.

A row of dark clouds hung in the distance. A squall was coming up—like the one the other morning. I turned on the CD player. I needed some Broadway tunes to clear my head. After several minutes, I shut it off again. *Guys and Dolls* was sounding too much like *Guys and Ghouls*.

I bounced along the narrow, uneven dirt road. A dense canopy of trees kept the stars from my sight. Finally, after what seemed like hours but was only minutes, and a final blind curve, the track opened onto the wide, ill-kept and weed-infested yard. I pulled up to the house several feet from Gus's pickup. No other vehicles were present. Where was Ethan Harrow's car?

My first thought, and I knew it was crazy, was that they'd murdered him. But that really was crazy, plain

and simple. His car would still be here . . . unless . . .
unless they moved it from sight afterward.

Besides, Mr. Harrow might have boated over to this
side of the lake and walked up to the house.

I shook the farfetched thoughts from my brain. If I
didn't stop speculating, I'd never go inside. And I really
wanted to learn more about Guster McKutcheon and his
boarders.

I knocked, and a moment later, Dominik Lueger
answered the door. He wore jeans and a short-sleeved
black turtleneck shirt. His goatee appeared freshly
trimmed. *"Guten Abend."* He bowed ever so slightly.
"Good evening."

Dominik invited me inside. Despite it being summer-
time, the wood fire in the massive fireplace in the living
room blazed brilliantly. I followed him to the dining room.
Gus McKutcheon and young Jean Rabin sat on opposite
sides of an aged cherrywood dining table. Open bottles of
beer and wine sat beside a silver platter holding an assortment of cheeses and crackers.

Gus rose and greeted me. "Welcome, Amy. Come sit
next to me. We're so glad you could join us."

"Thanks for having me. I hope Jean didn't overstep
his bounds in inviting me." Yellow wallpaper peeled off
the walls. The same mustiness I'd noticed the first time
I was in the McKutcheon house was still present. It
would probably never disappear completely.

"Not at all. I'm thrilled." Gus pulled out my chair and
I sat, nodding my hellos to the others.

"Where's Mr. Harrow?" I caught a whiff of musky
cologne. Gus wore a rumpled white sweater and dark
slacks.

"I'm afraid he couldn't make it this evening," answered my host. The small flames of the two tall ivory candles on the table flickered.

Jean, seated across from me, added, "A couple of tourists on their honeymoon paid for an evening cruise."

"Tonight?" I said. "It looks like rain."

Jean merely flapped open his napkin and settled it on his lap.

"May I?" Gus's hand reached across my place and scooped up my long-stemmed wineglass. He filled it with a California white wine and returned it to me. "Cheers," he said, lifting his own glass. "To a pleasant evening and a profitable future." The others joined in and I followed suit.

Dominik excused himself to see to the meal. Moments later, the girl Channing, whom I'd met earlier, entered with Dominik and two others—a young blond woman with vermillion nails and a redheaded young man, both casually attired. I was glad I hadn't dressed up for the occasion, having settled on a simple blue skirt and silver-gray crew-neck sweater.

Gus rose. He took the shallow casserole dish that Channing had carried in on a silver platter. "Thank you, Channing. Everything smells delicious." I agreed. He set the stew on the sideboard and turned to me. "Amy Simms, meet Channing Chalmers."

"We've met," I said.

Channing leaned the empty platter against the wall. "The day that—"

"Of course," said Gus.

"Channing is such a lovely name," I said. "Did your parents name you after Carol?"

Channing gave me a blank look.

"Carol Channing. She won a Tony award for best actress in a musical for her portrayal of Dolly in *Hello, Dolly!*"

"Sorry, no." Channing moved over to the sideboard and slid open a drawer containing serving utensils.

Gus rested his fingers on my elbow. "Do you know Annika and Ross also?"

I said I didn't and we exchanged introductions. Annika's accent was much like Dominik's, if not identical. Ross said he was from Ireland.

Gus clapped his hands softly. "Now that the food has arrived and everyone is here—"

"Everyone except—" Annika started, as she walked languidly toward the table.

My host shot the girl a nasty look that no one missed and she froze momentarily. Uneasy looks passed among the lodgers.

"Let's eat then, shall we?" Gus motioned for everyone to be seated. Channing sat across from me, with Jean to her right.

Annika plopped into the empty chair beside me. She dropped her face to her plate and picked up her fork, jamming it into the mashed potatoes.

The meal was simple farm fare, beef stew, mashed potatoes, homemade biscuits, and spiced applesauce. The dinnerware was old but serviceable.

"Did you prepare the food, Gus?" I asked, between bites of mouthwatering braised beef.

"The kids took care of everything," he answered expansively.

"Lucky you," I said. "This meal is wonderful. I wish I could get my boarders to cook for me." Of course, Paul Anderson probably survived on frozen dinners and Esther would probably feed me canned cat food. "This is the most savory beef I've ever tasted."

"That's goat." Channing pointed her fork at the meat on my plate. "We raise them."

I froze. Goat? I had a half-masticated mouthful of goat in my mouth? I forced a smile, then forced myself to swallow. I held out my water glass and Jean poured from a porcelain pitcher. "Thanks," I gasped.

"The gang has been indispensable. I give them room and board in exchange for helping get the house in shape. I'm afraid I don't have the money to do it all myself. Nor to pay them."

Gus picked up his wineglass and toyed with it. The candle flames, reflected in the glass, danced like spirits. "They work on the side for spending money. Many have jobs around town."

"Yes, and we get a free home for the summer," added Dominik.

"As Gus said, some of us work part-time in town on the side," added Ross, who sat at the other end of the table. "For instance, I've been helping at the market, bagging the groceries." He was a good-looking, affable young man with ginger hair and a body he didn't look like he'd quite grown into yet. I imagined he was the youngest of the group. Through his open shirt collar, I saw he wore a thin gold chain around his neck, bearing a charm.

I nodded. "Like you, Jean, working on Mr. Harrow's boat." It was a nice setup for everyone, it seemed. "How did you all find each other?" I asked. "Ruby Lake, North Carolina, isn't exactly New York City."

Gus answered. "I placed a small ad on several internet sites looking for lodgers in exchange for room and board."

The others nodded. I still didn't understand what had

made these young people choose our sleepy little town, but it wasn't my place to pry. And what did it matter?

"Are you from Ruby Lake, Amy?" inquired Annika. "What do you do?"

I explained that I was born and raised here, left for college, then came home. "I wanted to be closer to my family."

"Amy owns Birds and Bees across the street from the diner," added Gus.

"Oh," Channing exclaimed. "I adore birds." She knotted her hands at her chest. "They speak to me."

"Maybe you could do me a favor and speak to the woodpecker who's been waking me up at the crack of dawn every day."

Channing laughed. "You don't mean that. Woodpeckers are adorable. We had many back home in Melbourne."

"Australia?"

She nodded.

"I thought from your accent that you were English."

Channing wiped her lips with the linen napkin from her lap. "I was born in London but my family moved to Melbourne when I was a baby, for my father's work."

"And now you're here," I said. "A long way from home."

"I wanted to see America."

"We all did," said Jean. "This was the only way we could afford it."

"Lucky for me," Gus said.

"What made you decide to come back?" I asked Gus.

He smiled. "I got tired of the cold."

"Ruby Lake gets cold, too. But not as cold as I hear Maine can get."

Gus looked at me quizzically.

"I noticed the Maine license plate on your truck."

Something unreadable passed across my host's eyes. "You notice a lot."

I looked away for a moment. The others had gotten eerily quiet. "What did you do in Maine, Gus? Were you in the restaurant business?"

"No. A little of this, a little of that."

"A jack-of-all trades, eh?"

"I prefer to think of myself as an entrepreneur. I see an opportunity and I take it."

"You think you can find some opportunities here?"

"I hope so."

He seemed to be making a good go of things so far: a house full of energetic and unpaid young men and women to help him get the farm up and running, managing the Ruby Diner, and dating its owner.

"Did you grow up here?"

"Never been here before in my life. But I knew the house had been sitting empty and decided to try to make it a McKutcheon home once more."

"Are you familiar with the story of the widow in the lake?"

Annika dropped her spoon on her plate. "Sorry," she mumbled.

"Please," Gus said, rolling his eyes. "That old story? Sure, I've heard it. When you've got a family that's been around a region as long as mine, there are going to be a few stories." He smiled. "Some good, some bad. What was her name? Mary? My great-great-something-or-other.

"I mean, may she rest in peace and all that, but I prefer to concern myself with what's real." He banged his hand on the table. "The nuts and bolts of life. Not the goblins and ghosts. I'll leave the otherworld to others." He reached for the wine. "I prefer my spirits in a bottle."

"Have you seen such a thing as a spirit rising from your lake?" asked Jean, leaning forward on his elbows.

I admitted I hadn't.

"Do you still believe you saw something here in this house?" Dominik asked. "Such as you informed the police?"

Color rose to my cheeks. "I don't know what I was thinking—"

"Now, now, Dom," Gus said. "Let's not put Amy on the spot. She is our guest. Amy was only doing what she thought was right."

"Thank you," I sputtered. "It was early and it was raining," I began in my own defense. "And my house is so far away—"

"Hel-looo!" A woman's voice called from the kitchen, interrupting my rambling explanation.

Gus stiffened. "You'll excuse me." He threw down his napkin, rose quickly, and disappeared.

Gus's lodgers and I eyed each other uncomfortably for several minutes. He returned carrying a sheet cake. "Vanilla cake with orange buttercream."

Our host cut generous slices and passed them around the table on ornate dessert plates. I was full but I was also dying for something to cover the taste of that goat on my tongue, so I didn't refuse my fair share. A good buttercream can cover the taste of just about anything. Even if it doesn't, who cares? It's still a mouthful of buttercream.

No mention was made of the woman who'd shown up at the kitchen door. Who was she? Who shows up out of the blue, at night, in the middle of nowhere?

Too bad I couldn't ask Gus those questions. Her voice had seemed vaguely familiar too . . .

I told myself to relax. Maybe she was the cake delivery person. Something about this house and Gus McKutcheon was getting under my skin and I needed to exorcise it, whatever it was. If I could figure out what had happened to Bessie Hammond and what had happened at this house the other morning—and get rid of Drummy the woodpecker—maybe I could get my life back to normal . . . or, at least, somewhere in that general vicinity.

And despite how I downplayed things with Mom and Kim, I was anxious and excited to see where my nascent relationship with Derek might lead.

Gus pushed back his chair and the others took this as their cue to do the same. Like a well-orchestrated troupe, they began lifting items from the dining table and removing everything to the kitchen.

"Want the tour?"

"Of course." I was dying to see the rest of the house. Who knew what secrets it held?

We started downstairs, but I'd already seen most of the ground floor, so it was the upstairs that interested me most. Once we climbed the steps, my senses came alert. A couple of the bedrooms held two twin beds each, separated by a night table. Another contained a couple of cardboard boxes and a mattress on the bare floor. Gus's bedroom was nothing special. A high bed with a dark blue comforter, a small television on a chair in the corner, and an open suitcase balanced atop a small chest with a padded top.

The only item of any interest at all was an antique-looking brass telescope on a mahogany tripod standing in the far corner near the window. It had probably sat there a hundred years.

"I haven't had time to really get settled in," Gus said, as if reading my mind.

Gus explained that there was one upstairs bathroom that they all shared. Finally, we came to the room I wanted to see the most. I couldn't help wondering if he'd saved it for last for some purpose of his own. He must have known that this was the room that I had reported seeing the struggle and ensuing murder occur in.

Gus turned the glass knob and pushed the door open. He bent and flicked on a small lamp next to the door. "Voilà. The scene of the crime."

My eyes widened.

"Sorry," Gus said. "A lousy joke. Come on in." I followed him into the bedroom. Sounds of laughter spilled up the stairwell from the kitchen. "I'm thinking of adding several bunks."

I nodded. The bedroom was dark, the lamp cast formless shadows. Through the open curtains, I could make out Ruby Lake, glimmering in partially obscured moonlight. I thought of the story of the widow in the lake and wondered what her life must have been like, to have her husband taken away from her at the height of his life, brutally and senselessly murdered.

The room was barren. The hardwood floors bowed ever so slightly as I put my weight on them. Many of the planks appeared water stained. I crossed to the window, resting my hands on the window ledge. The dark form of my house was barely visible in the distance.

I looked down and shivered. Memories raced toward me. I moved my gaze to the black forest, drawn by the lonely sound of an owl. Bessie Hammond's life had ended under one of those trees. Who had killed her and why? Her killer might be someone in this house. I bristled. He might be the man standing behind me now.

A hand gripped my shoulder and I let out a small scream.

"Are you okay?" Gus eyed me anxiously in the dim light given off by the lamp on the floor.

I turned and started for the door. "It's late," I said. "I'd better be going."

Gus led me back downstairs. I called out a goodbye to the others. Jean poked his face around the kitchen door and waved. Channing sat cross-legged in a tall wingback chair in the living room. She lowered her book and smiled. "Good night, Amy." The fire was nothing more than embers.

"Thanks for having me."

"Before you go." Channing stood and twisted her foot against the rug. "I was wondering . . ."

"Yes?"

"If perhaps you might have some work for me at your store. As you heard the others speak, we are all trying to earn some spending money."

"Now, now, Channing," interjected Gus. "We don't want to put our guest on the spot."

"That's okay. I don't mind." I smiled. "Let me think about it and see what I can come up with. The business is still in its infancy. I couldn't give you many hours and I couldn't pay you much." Not to mention I now had Esther on the payroll and even Cousin Riley, all thanks to Mom.

Channing gave me a quick hug. "That's not important. We have everything we need here. I only want a little cash for extras."

"I get that. Let me get back to you. Why don't you stop in the store in a day or two and we can talk some more?"

Channing agreed and Gus McKutcheon walked me out to my car.

I watched him return to the front porch and reenter the house. Even after having dinner with the guy, I failed to see what Moire saw in him. I guess that's what makes love so mystical and mysterious.

A drop of rain hit the windshield as I twisted the key in the ignition. Looking up, I noticed a flash of movement from the small attic window centered under the peak of the roof. The curtain was pulled back to one side. A woman's face peered down at me.

A moment later, a man appeared. A moment after that and their silhouettes melted together.

13

"Have a good time last night?"

"Yes," I answered. "How did things go here? Smoothly?"

"Of course," replied Esther, waving her feather duster around like she was d'Artagnan fighting off Cardinal Richelieu's troops. I'd asked her a hundred times not to use a duster made out of feathers in a store catering to bird lovers, but she didn't seem to grasp the concept.

"That's good." I flipped through yesterday's receipts, smothering a yawn. I'd slept poorly and this time I couldn't blame it on a woodpecker. Too many thoughts were pecking away at my brain. I'd tossed and turned like a dinghy in the ocean during a Cat 5 hurricane.

"Your boyfriend came by." Esther kicked up some more dust as she ran the feather duster along a row of shallow butterfly-feeder dishes. I ordered mine from an artist based in Asheville, North Carolina. Overripe fruit, or a sponge soaked in sugar solution, both worked great to attract butterflies.

"Derek?" My hand went automatically to my hair. I'd skipped breakfast and raced through my usual morning routine. I had the feeling my canary-yellow Birds & Bees blouse matched my sallow complexion.

"That's your boyfriend, isn't it?"

"What did he want?"

Esther stared at me like I was a birdbrain. "He wanted you."

A feeling of dread started to creep up my toes. "What did you tell him?"

"I told him you were having dinner with Gus Mc-Kutcheon at his house."

I shot up from my stool, and receipts went flying and fluttering to the floor. "What did you tell him that for?" I chased after the paper slips as they skittered across the hardwood.

"Because that's what you were doing." Esther pulled a face, shook her head, and strutted off. "If you need me, I'll be taking my break."

I stared after her, a wad of receipts clutched in my hand. "Great, just great," I mumbled. What would Derek be thinking?

I tossed the receipts into the bowels of a damaged wooden birdhouse I kept under the counter for the purpose. The birdhouse had dropped from the sales shelf, splitting the roof. I couldn't sell it, but that didn't mean I couldn't find a good use for it—and I had. I'd finish sorting through the receipts later.

I grabbed my purse and headed for the back door and my van. "Kim's due in any minute, Esther. Please don't take off before she gets here!"

"Where are you going?" Esther sounded petulant.

"I've got an errand to run!" I slammed the door behind me before Esther could catch me.

I parked in the public lot off the town square. The offices of Harlan and Harlan were on Main Street near the Chinese restaurant. If Derek hadn't moved to Ruby Lake to practice law with his father and be closer to his daughter, we'd have never met. Whether that was fate or mere chance didn't matter. I was happy.

Two floor-to-ceiling windows ran the length of the office front. The entrance was on the right with a small seating area and a desk for their part-time receptionist-slash-secretary. Ben Harlan's office was on the left with his desk facing the street. Derek's office was in the rear with a small window that looked out on the alleyway. Derek was living in the apartment above the offices.

Peeking in the front window, I saw Ben Harlan bent over his desk, quietly poring over some papers. I rapped a knuckle on the glass. Ben smiled and waved me in.

The secretary was nowhere in sight. Ben came out to greet me and he invited me to sit in his office.

"Actually, I was hoping I might have a quick word with Derek." I looked down the quiet hall. "Is he in?" Derek had said he was going to have a couple of client meetings today. "I only need a minute." To explain myself and set things right. Thank you very much, Esther Pester.

"Sorry, Amy. Derek's not here at the moment. He and Amy had a thing."

My jaw twitched. Amy the Ex? I wanted to ask what sort of thing Derek might be having in the middle of the workday with Amy the Ex but was too polite and much too uncomfortable to ask. "Oh, I see . . ."

Ben's brow went up as he laid a hand on my upper arm. "Is there something I can help you with?"

"No." I struggled to keep my disappointment from showing. I smiled. "I guess I'll catch him another time."

"Are you sure you won't join me for a cup of coffee?" Ben hefted the glass carafe at the coffee bar between a pair of comfy guest chairs.

"Thanks, but I'd better get back to the store. Besides, I don't want to keep you from your work." I pushed open the front door. A cool breeze wafted over me. The temp was only supposed to reach into the low seventies today, according to the weather folk.

He splashed some coffee into a mug and replaced the carafe. "Please say hello to Barbara for me. Tell her not to be such a stranger." Ben fiddled with his navy-blue tie. "I kind of look forward to our time together, I don't mind telling you."

I cocked my head. "Didn't you and Mom go out last night?"

"No." Ben shook a sugar packet back and forth. "I haven't seen her for a few days now."

"That's funny, I thought—" I stopped myself. Hadn't Mom said she was going out with Ben last night?

"Yes?"

"Nothing," I said, recovering from my near-fatal faux pas. I didn't want to get Mom in trouble with Ben. "I'll be sure to say hi for you. Do the same for me with that son of yours?"

Ben promised he would.

Out on the street, I decided a strong cup of coffee was actually just what I needed. And not the stuff I made at Birds & Bees. Though I had a decent coffeepot and bought only grown-in-the-shade, bird-friendly-certified beans, it tasted more like the coffee you get out of a vending machine in a hospital waiting room, and I wasn't sure why.

What I needed was something better, more full-bodied,

that went down like hot liquid gold and filled the recesses of the soul. Only one place I knew fit the bill.

I headed across the town square to the Coffee and Tea House. The owner, Susan Terwilliger, stood at the counter. "Hi, Amy. What can I get you?" Fluffy brown hair hung in loose waves along her cheekbones and matched the color of her eyes.

"Coffee," I replied. "The biggest size you've got."

Susan swung into action. "Coming right up." Besides running her own business, Susan's got four school-aged children, three boys and a girl, plus a husband who's a dentist. Somehow, she still managed to have more pep than me at my best.

"Something to go with that? I've got a couple of new items I'm trying, fresh walnut bars and mini breakfast tarts."

I looked in the glass case, drooling over the choices. "What's in the tart?"

"Pancetta and onions. They're made in-house."

"Too savory." I needed caffeine and sweets. "I'll take a walnut bar." What was Derek doing with his ex-wife, and why had he told me had meetings with clients all day?

Now I would have to wait until tonight, at the inaugural Birds and Brews event, to get the scoop. And to explain my dinner with Gus McKutcheon. Not that Derek was necessarily going to ask for an explanation or that I even owed him one. But I wanted everything to be on the up-and-up between us.

I'd been in a long-term relationship with one lying louse already. I wasn't going to let history repeat itself.

I started for an empty table and noticed the skipper of the boat *Sunset Sally* seated alone in the corner. "Good morning, Captain Harrow," I said, balancing my cup and plate. "Mind if I join you?"

He nodded to the vacant chair beside him, moving his big-brimmed camo hat to the other end of the table. The fisherman was drinking black coffee and had devoured three of the mini tarts as evidenced by the three empty tins.

I sat and adjusted my mug and plate in front of me. "We missed you last night at dinner. How did the cruise go?"

Ethan Harrow laid his mug on the table, cradling it in his tanned, rough hands. "Cruise?"

"Uh-huh." I broke off a corner of walnut bar and nibbled. "I was afraid it might rain, but then we had nothing but a sprinkle." The boat captain seemed out of sorts this morning. Dark circles rimmed his watery, red eyes and he'd only managed to utter a single word so far.

He wiped his nose with the back of his arm. "Got cancelled."

I ignored the fishy odor emanating from my tablemate. "Too bad." I doused my coffee with cream and sugar. "Who knows? Maybe one day I'll take one of your cruises myself."

Ethan Harrow cleared his throat. "You might want to stick to dry land." He clamped his fingers over his hat and stuck it on his head.

"Excuse me?"

Harrow rose slowly, his hands braced on the table. His belly bumped the table and coffee leapt over the side of my cup and spread in a shallow puddle across the tabletop. "Not everybody is meant to be on the water." He tossed some money on the table. "Or in it."

I sat there, mouth agape, as the surly captain plodded out the door.

"Chasing away my customers?" Susan smiled and tossed a clean rag over my spilt coffee.

"Sorry about that." I lifted my mug and plate so she could wipe away my mess.

"No problem. What did you say to him?"

"I have no idea." And I didn't.

I spent the afternoon working in the store alongside Kim. Mom came in around six and Esther agreed to work the evening shift with her so that I could participate in the Birds and Brews event coming up at Brewer's Biergarten next door.

"Birds and brews," snorted Kim, arms folded behind her back as she stared out the front window. "What a kooky idea."

"Kooky or not, it could be a boon to business." There had been a dismal lull in traffic that afternoon, which always depressed me. "We did give out several flyers for it."

"True," said Kim, "but maybe the people who accepted them were looking for something to line their birdcages with—or needed paper-airplane building material."

"Very funny." I removed my apron and hung it on the hook behind the counter. "I'm going to freshen up, then head next door." I paused at the stairs. "Are you sure you don't want to come?"

"To Birds and Brews?" Kim looked amused. "Not a chance. You're the bird lady, not me. Besides, I've got a date with Randy." She slid up in front of me and dropped an arm over my shoulders. "And speaking of dates, is Derek going to be there?"

"I hope so," I said. "He did tell Paul he'd come. But

now . . ." I'd explained to Kim how Esther had spilled the beans about my dinner at the McKutcheon house.

"Just tell him the truth. Derek's a big boy. He'll understand." Kim gave me a friendly shove up the steps. "It's not like you actually had a date with the sleaze; you were merely a guest at a dinner held in his house, one of many guests."

"True," I said from the second floor, looking down. "I still don't get why Ethan Harrow didn't show. Or why he acted so brusque with me earlier today."

"You think too much, Amy Simms," Kim replied. "Maybe the guy had a headache or got out of the wrong side of bed this morning. Or maybe he got a letter in the mail that he was being audited and his boat was being repossessed!"

I couldn't help smiling as I returned to my third-floor apartment and got ready. Kim was right. I was overthinking things. I took a quick shower and put on a clean pair of slacks and a green Birds & Bees polo shirt. I wanted to look good but be sure to advertise my store, too. This wasn't a social event, I reminded myself, this was business.

If Derek showed up, maybe there would be a little pleasure, too.

14

Thirty minutes later I was at the *biergarten* with several bird reference books in hand. Mom and I had barely had a chance to talk, but she promised she'd still be awake when I returned.

"Where's Derek?" Paul asked. He was standing beside the hostess station a couple of steps inside the main door of Brewer's Biergarten, in jeans and a black T-shirt.

A long-haired young blond woman with way too many curves gave me a smile. Bambi rocked a hip-hugging black skirt that really should have been several inches longer, and a white blouse that pulled taut across her chest. No doubt Paul Anderson personally did the hiring for the business.

"Isn't Derek here?" I asked, a little disappointed. I looked at my watch. We weren't due to start for twenty minutes yet. There was plenty of time for Derek to arrive.

"I haven't seen him." Paul jerked a thumb over his shoulder. "I've got a bunch of bird lovers in the banquet room though. I stuck everybody there for now, but we can move outside, if you prefer?"

"Outside might be better." The weather was crisp and cool. I always preferred fresh air to indoor air. It was so much more invigorating. "Maybe we'll even spot a bird or two." The fresh air might also help to keep everyone awake during my lecture.

"Okay." Paul made a notation on a ledger atop the podium and rubbed his hands together vigorously. "I've got to check on the beers. Candy here will get you set up."

Okay, so her name was Candy, not Bambi. I'd been close.

"Follow me?" Candy said. Without waiting for a reply, she turned with a sashay of the hips that drew Paul's eyes. I tailed her to the banquet room.

"Hello, everybody!" I called cheerfully. "We're going to meet outside, if that's okay with you all?" I saw that Floyd Withers, Karl Vogel, Ed and Abby Quince, and the others from our bird walk had come—all but John Moytoy and Lana Potter. I wasn't surprised not to see Ms. Potter put in an appearance. She didn't strike me as the bird-watching type, so I'd been surprised she'd joined our nature walk in the first place. If anything, I pegged her for the man-eating type.

I was especially heartened to see several new faces as well, and said so.

Murmurs of approval followed my suggestion that we move the party to the courtyard, and Candy led our small group outdoors, where a couple of servers had already pushed several tables together for us. I took a seat at one end of the long table and invited everyone to find seats.

Our first order of business was introductions. I started with myself and we worked around the table.

Paul, Candy, and a second server showed up with several trays. One held three tall pitchers of light-colored beer. The others held various snacks, mostly typical bar fare like pretzels and peanuts, but there were also some tiny sirloin sliders that looked and smelled delicious— and a glass bowl filled with peeled hard-boiled eggs that made me question Paul Anderson's palate.

Candy went around filling beer steins while Paul explained what we'd be drinking.

"I chose an American-style pilsner for our first meeting. Something light and refreshing. Best served chilled." He lifted his mug and sipped. "Umm. The pilsner has its origins in the city of Pilsen, located in Bohemia, now part of the Czech Republic," the bar owner explained. Anderson outlined the story of the beer's origins. He was more knowledgeable than I'd expected. "But we brew this lager right here at Brewer's Biergarten once a week. I hope you like it. I call it Happy Pil." He smiled. "Get it?"

"To Birds and Brews!" Floyd said, raising his glass.

We all joined in.

"Maybe you should knock down this brick wall and combine your two businesses," Karl suggested.

Paul beamed. "That's not a bad idea."

I made a face. "It's not a good one either," I quipped, which provoked loud laughter.

Paul clinked his glass against mine. "Hey," I said, taking a tentative sip. "This is good."

"Love it," said Karl. "What do you think, Floyd?" The ex-chief-of-police helped himself to two of the sirloin sliders.

"Very good, Mr. Anderson," agreed Floyd, pulling his mug from his face. Karl and Floyd sat nearest me on my left.

Karl snorted. "You got foam on your mustache!"

Floyd reddened and dabbed at his face with a napkin.

"Thank you for hosting us," Walter Kimmel said softly.

"Yes," added Clara Kimmel. "You have a lovely establishment." Her eyes rose to the strands of white lights strung from tree to tree across the courtyard. It really was quite pretty.

"What birds are we going to talk about?" inquired Otelia Newsome, who was seated between Walter Kimmel and Ed Quince.

"I'm glad you asked, Otelia." I pushed back my chair and stood. I had decided on a discussion of the northern cardinal. What better bird to begin our new social group on than North Carolina's state bird? I had prepared a short lecture on the widely recognized red bird. Afterward, I hoped the others would contribute with their own thoughts and stories.

I anticipated Paul would have more to say on the beer, too. But I'd wasted my time. Our maiden Birds and Brews event quickly turned into a somber wake for Bessie Hammond.

"I don't get it," moaned Ed, before I'd even said the first word of my prepared talk. He held his head in his hands. "Who'd want to kill poor Bessie?" The guy was really shaken. Why? Of course, the two had worked together at Lakeside Market. Bessie and Ed had been more than bird-watching buddies. They had been ex-colleagues and maybe friends.

I sat back down. "I don't know," I answered softly. "But I'm sure the police will find out soon enough."

"Her husband!" Floyd said rather loudly.

"Floyd!" I was shocked. Floyd Withers was normally so quiet, so polite.

Floyd gave me a sad puppy-dog look. "Sorry, Amy."

He turned on his seatmate. "Karl said it first. I was only repeating."

The ex-cop merely shrugged. "Bessie was a pain in the patooty. We all know that. At least, those of us who knew her know that."

"Didn't Bessie's husband die some time ago?" I asked. "That's what Gertie Hammer told me."

"Yes," hissed Ed.

Karl looked like he wanted to say more but I gave him a look of warning.

Ed shot Karl an angry look but it was Ed's wife, Abby, who spoke next. "Bessie Hammond is dead. I'm not saying I'm sorry or that I'm going to miss her, but shouldn't we be talking about birds and beer? That is what we've come for." She snatched her mug and drained it before giving her husband an ugly look.

Ed ignored her. "What was Bessie doing out in those woods anyway? All by herself. I mean, that doesn't seem right."

I didn't know what to say. It didn't seem right to me either. "Did she often go for bird walks alone?"

Ed shook his head no.

"What do you know?" Abby said acidly.

"Maybe she saw something interesting on our walk Saturday and wanted to go back for a second look," suggested Floyd.

"True," said Otelia. "She might have wanted to return to get more pictures."

Pictures!

"Her and that fancy camera of hers," scoffed Abby Quince. She snapped her napkin and folded it on her lap. "What good does it do her now?"

My heart was racing. That's what had been gnawing at me. That was what was wrong with the scene I had stumbled on, Bessie slumped against the tree. She'd had her binoculars, but not her camera. Why wasn't it around her neck, too? Would she have left it home? It didn't seem likely, not if she was bird-watching. So what had happened to her camera?

Floyd rested his elbows on the table and his chin on his fists. "You remember what Bessie said in Amy's van the other day, on the way to the lake?"

"What do you mean?" Karl replied.

"We were talking about murder. You remember, Amy. About how good you were at solving them."

I picked up the thread from there. "And Bessie claimed that if there ever was another murder, she'd be the one to solve it."

Floyd nodded soberly. "Now, instead of solving a murder, she's the victim of one."

"And it's going to be up to somebody else to solve her murder." Karl snapped a pretzel in two. "I've half a mind to do it myself. But I am retired." He slid both halves of the pretzel across his tongue.

The table fell silent a moment.

"Bessie Hammond was a hussy," Clara Kimmel said quite unexpectedly, breaking the silence. "Hammond the hussy." She hiccuped, then popped a handful of salted peanuts in her mouth and chewed, her pointed jaw moving sharply side to side.

I goggled at her.

"Excuse me." Walter rose unsteadily. "Men's room?" He looked expectantly at Paul Anderson, who was seated at the opposite end of the long table. Paul, who'd had a bewildered expression on his face for the past several minutes, gave directions to the facilities.

"Sorry I'm late." A man's lips brushed my cheek.

I shot around. "Gus! What are you doing here?" My

cheek burned where he'd kissed me. What had the man been thinking?

"You invited me, remember?" Gus replied. "I just came from the diner. We had quite a rush for a while there." His charcoal trousers were unwrinkled and his white button-down shirt spotless. How did he manage to always look so clean and unsoiled working in a kitchen?

Gus grabbed a chair from a nearby empty table and pushed it close to mine.

I'd invited him? I wanted to say why on earth would I do that, but then I remembered. I had invited him. Him and Moire when I'd burst in on their afternoon love-making session the other day. I stifled a groan of regret.

"Hey, I know you. You're from the diner," Floyd said.

Gus smiled. "That's right, Gramps."

Floyd fumed and Karl patted him on the shoulder. That was when I saw Derek standing on the sidewalk, looking into the courtyard with an unreadable expression on his face.

Oh, dear. Gus McKutcheon was sitting right beside me, his knees practically touching mine. Touching! My fingers flew to my cheek. Had Derek seen Gus kiss me?

I smiled wanly, pulled my fingers away from my burning cheek and waved to him. Every head at the table turned to see who I was waving to.

"Hey, buddy!" Paul called. "Join us."

Derek leaned his hands on the brick pony wall. "If I say yes, do I get free beer?"

Paul agreed and Derek came through the courtyard side entrance. He was wearing his blue pinstriped suit, one of my favorites—it brought out the blue in his eyes. His slate-gray tie hung loosely knotted around his neck. Paul handed him a full mug of pilsner and he shambled over to me. He looked tired. "Evening, Amy." He glanced at Gus. "Who's your friend?" Of course, he knew darn well who he was.

I cleared my throat. "This is Gus McKutcheon. I told you about him, remember? He recently moved into his family's old property across the lake."

Derek, to his credit, smiled and shook Gus's hand. "My pleasure."

"Have a seat," I said, pulling another chair close to me on the opposite side.

"Did I miss much?" Derek stuck his hand in a bowl of pretzel twists.

"We were remembering Bessie Hammond," I explained.

"More like discussing Bessie Hammond's death," Paul replied.

"Who'd want to kill poor Bessie?" wailed Ed once again, rubbing his chin against his chest.

"Floyd here thinks Bessie's husband did it!" shouted Karl.

"That was you," Floyd hollered back. "I was only repeating what you told me, Karl!"

"Bessie's husband has been dead for a decade," I explained to Derek.

"I'm sorry to hear that."

"He drowned in Ruby Lake," I continued. "On the anniversary of the day that Bessie herself was murdered."

Derek's brow shot up. "That is weird." He looked across me to Gus. "I'll bet you didn't know what you were getting yourself into when you decided to move to Ruby Lake, eh, Gus?"

"So far," Gus responded, "I'm finding it quirky but delightful. Are you a local?"

"No, a recent transplant." Derek explained how he'd moved up to be nearer his daughter and work in the family business.

"What business would that be?"

"I'm a lawyer," said Derek.

"Ah, any particular specialty?"

"General practice. In a small town like this, it's best not to over specialize. Speaking of which, Amy tells me you're running the Ruby Diner and operating a youth hostel as well."

Walter returned to the table just then, looking wobbly and pale. "I believe we will call it an evening." A bead of sweat ran the length of his hairline. "Clara?"

Clara eyed him silently, then stood and grabbed her black purse. "Thank you for a lovely evening," she said rather mechanically, nodding to one and all.

The Kimmels left shoulder to shoulder, climbed into their dark Buick, and sped away.

Ed hiccuped. "Maybe we should be going, too?" He looked hopefully at his wife. "Sorry, Amy. I'm afraid this is all my fault. I never should have mentioned Bessie."

"That's okay, Ed. I'm sort of glad you did. Can anybody here think of anyone who might have wanted her dead?" I cut off any stupid remarks from Karl by saying, "Besides her dead husband?"

Ed shook his head glumly. "Not me."

Abby merely chewed her lower lip.

"I didn't know her that well," Otelia said, playing with her half-empty mug.

"Was there anyone in particular that she had been fighting with?" Bessie wasn't the most pleasant woman I'd ever met, but had she been vile enough to provoke someone to murder?

"I have no idea," Gus said quickly. A little too quickly, I thought.

"Me either," said Floyd. "I've known her for years from shopping at the grocery. And I knew her husband, Arthur, from the bank." Floyd was a retired banker. "They seemed like quiet, ordinary people."

"The police still can't figure out what she was doing on my property." That was Gus again. He seemed to be doing his best to distance himself from Bessie's murder. I realized I couldn't fault the man for that. I'd probably be doing the same thing.

"The two of them never got in trouble with the law, I can tell you that," Karl added. As Ruby Lake's former chief of police, he'd be aware of any brushes with the law the Hammonds might have had or any encounters with unsavory elements.

"What about you, Ed?" I called down the table. "You probably knew Bessie better than anyone here. Can you think of anyone who might have wished her any harm?"

"Just what are you implying?" Abby glared at me.

"Sorry," I apologized quickly, though I had no idea what for. "I only meant that you, Ed, worked with Bessie at the Lakeside Market for so many years. In fact, didn't you, too, Abby? Maybe if you think about it—"

"Funny thing is," began Ed, "Bessie wasn't in church Sunday. We always see her in church, don't we, dear?" He continued when his wife didn't respond. "Remember, you remarked how she wasn't there?"

Ed looked at his wife as she said, "I think it's time we left." Abby stood and Ed followed suit.

"This is a disaster," I muttered. I crumpled my meeting notes and tossed the wadded-up paper on the table.

"Say, Candy!" Karl waved to the young lady as she frolicked toward the table. "Got anything sweet?"

She shook her head and smiled. "I'll bring you the dessert menu."

Karl gave Floyd a wink. "I think she likes me."

"Are all bird-watchers this flighty?" Paul joked.

I rolled my eyes at him. "This is your fault."

"My fault?"

"Birds and Brews was your bone-headed idea."

Paul slammed back his beer. "Don't worry, next month's meeting's bound to be better."

"I'm not so sure there's going to be a next meeting."

"Bah," Paul said. "Lighten up. Don't let this whole murder thing spoil the evening, Amy."

"Besides," said Derek, "it's not like there's going to be a murder before each meeting of Birds and Brews."

I looked at him skeptically.

"Paul's right," added Gus. "Mrs. Hammond's death is unfortunate, but we have to go on with our lives. We can't bring back the dead. Yep." He banged his fists against the table. "Go on with your life. That's what you do."

"You're one to talk, Gus," I said. "Your great-what-ever killed herself after her husband got murdered by a bunch of marauders."

"Mary McKutcheon?" Gus appeared amused.

"What's your take on this whole widow-in-the-lake story?" Derek asked. "My ex tells me quite a tale."

"That old rumor?" scoffed Gus. "If you ask me, it's nothing but bull. After her husband was killed, Mary probably moved to Florida to live with relatives," he said with a laugh.

Derek leaned across me toward Gus McKutcheon. "You don't believe it?"

"As much as I believe in Santa Claus and the tooth fairy." Gus stood. "Nice meeting you all." He leaned toward me and I cut off what looked like another move to kiss my cheek by standing and extending my hand.

Derek pushed back his chair. "I'll walk out with you."

"Can't you stay a while?" I asked. "I've got some wine upstairs. Or I could make a pot of coffee, if you prefer?" Derek really did look tired.

Derek shook his head. "Sorry, it's been a long day." His fingers lightly brushed my arm. "Goodnight, Amy."

Floyd, Karl, and Otelia quickly followed.

I looked down at Paul, who had remained seated after waving goodbye to everyone. "Next time you get a good idea to boost business, leave me out of it." I gathered my purse and keys from the table.

"Cheer up, Amy," Paul replied, diligently smoothing my crumpled notes and riffling through the pages. "You've already got next month's talk written."

15

"Anita stopped by," Mom explained. "We're doing a little baking."

"Of what?" I gasped in an odd, alien, duck-sounding voice. It's really hard to talk, pinch your nose, and hold your breath all at once. "The undead?" I'd come home from Brewer's Biergarten hoping to drown my sorrows. Instead, I found myself drowning in stench and gray smoke.

I pushed open the kitchen window and flapped my hands like mad.

Mom pouted and wiped her hands down her apron. "We were trying something new." She turned to Anita. "Too much brewer's yeast, you think?"

Anita nodded and dropped a big, smoking pot in the sink. "Yep. Too much brewer's yeast, Barb." She turned on the tap and squirted liquid soap into the aluminum pot. The accompanying sound of sizzling and tortured metal had me preparing to duck for cover.

I crossed to the sink and looked at the blackened stock-pot. A large metal baking tray containing lumps of . . . something brown with black and gold singe marks, sat at the edge of the counter. "What exactly were you baking?" Half the ingredients from the pantry were spread haphazardly along the kitchen counter. Some had spread to the kitchen table.

"Don't worry," said my mother, seeing my critical eyes wander over the mess. "I'll clean it up."

"I'll help," promised Anita.

I held the twisted baking tray under Mom's nose. "We're trying to create our own breakfast bar," she said, sounding rather defensive.

I eyed her archly. "Breakfast barf is more like it."

"Breakfast cookies and bars are all the rage," Anita explained. "We thought we'd give it a shot. Maybe get an investment from one of those venture capitalists."

"It's going to take a capitalist with a sense of adventure, that's for sure."

"Very funny." My mother snatched the pan away from me and began attacking it furiously with a butter knife and steel wool. "Where's Derek?"

"Home, I guess."

"You two getting serious?" Anita said, fighting to keep her hair out of her eyes as she scrubbed the pan in the sink.

"About as serious as Mom and Ben," I shot back.

Mom ignored the remark. "How was your event?"

"Noneventful." I grabbed the wine from the fridge along with bread and cheese and made myself a simple sandwich. "The group spent most of its time eulogizing and theorizing."

"We may have overdone it on this last batch, but the previous batch isn't so bad. They're right over there beside the blender," Anita said. "You should try one."

"What do you mean *eulogizing and theorizing*?" inquired Mom.

"Maybe later," I replied, noncommittally. "We spent the whole time talking about Bessie Hammond."

"More wake than wingding?" Anita said with a wink.

"It's important to express your grief when a loved one dies." Mom dried her hands on the kitchen towel. Mom should know. Dad's passing had been hard on her. And me.

"I know." I bit into my sandwich and chewed, deep in thought. "I tell you, there's a whole lot going on in Ruby Lake that I don't think most of us ever see more than the tip of."

"What do you mean?" Anita plopped into the chair beside me, a glass of water in hand.

I thought about Ed and Abby, Walter and Clara, Gus McKutcheon, and even Bessie. "I mean, I get the idea there are a lot of people holding in a whole lot of secrets." I cleared a lump of bread in my throat with a drink of red wine. "And I'm not sure I want to know what some of those secrets are."

"Amen to that." Anita nodded sagely.

"They're on the house." I handed the chief of police a brown paper sack filled with what must have been a quarter pound's worth of roasted, unsalted peanuts. He would have pilfered that much from the store bins himself anyway.

We stock a variety of wild bird food in bins up near the front, across from the sales counter. Kennedy treats it like his own personal snack center.

Jerry Kennedy eyed the bag in his fingers. "You know bribing an officer of the court is illegal."

"So is murder," I said, folding my arms over my chest. "Are you going to answer my question or not?"

"What's to answer?" Jerry stuffed the bag of peanuts into the pocket of his light brown Windbreaker. "All you're doing is speculating and throwing crazy ideas around."

Jerry and I were alone in the store. Esther and Mom had the morning off. Kim was supposed to be at work but hadn't shown up and hadn't called in. I'd like to think that wasn't like her, but it was.

"What's crazy about Bessie Hammond being murdered on the anniversary of her husband's drowning in Ruby Lake? Weird, I grant you. But crazy? No."

"Like you said, Simms." Jerry had helped himself to my store coffee, filling to the brim the stainless steel mug he'd had the audacity to bring into Birds & Bees. I wanted to tell him I wasn't running a convenience store, but his being here was all my fault. I'd invited him to the shop in the hopes of sharing what little I knew and learning what the police might have uncovered about Bessie Hammond's murder.

"Bessie Hammond got her neck snapped. Her husband, James, drowned. The only thing the two things have in common is that they both involve dead people!"

Outside, I noticed Cousin Riley look up from the flower beds, his attention drawn to the chief's strident voice. Mom had him pulling weeds.

I felt like pulling my hair out. "I still say there's more to this case. Something deeper."

Chief Kennedy slanted his eyes at me. "There is no case, Simms. At least, not for you." He thrust his thermos in his other pocket. "Mind your birds and bees. James Hammond drowning ten years ago and Bessie getting herself killed on the same date are no more than coincidences."

"Come on, Jerry. Even you can't believe that." The phone rang. I let it go to voicemail. Whoever it was could wait.

"It happens all the time," Jerry argued. "I knew a man who died on his own birthday."

"But, Jerry—"

"No buts about it." Jerry held open the door and gestured that it was time to leave. "And no, I repeat, no butting in!"

"What happened to Bessie's camera, Jerry?"

"What camera?" Jerry leaned against the open door. A hesitant customer in the doorway looked from him to me, caught in the crossfire.

"Come on in," I said with an encouraging wave. "I'll be right with you."

The woman hesitated on the porch, then entered. I repeated that I'd be right with her, then stepped outside with the chief. "Bessie had a camera with her when we went on our bird walk the other day," I said, lowering my voice. "A very expensive camera."

"So?"

"So, I remember"—and could unfortunately picture clearly—"that Bessie did not have her camera with her when I found her. Her binoculars were around her neck, but not her camera."

"So?" Jerry repeated. "What's your point?"

"Where's Bessie's camera?"

Chief Kennedy shoved me ever-so-gently aside. "How the heck should I know? Maybe she left it at home. Didn't want to carry it around. Was out of film or just not in the mood to be taking pictures!" Jerry bounded off the porch and into the sunlight.

"It was a digital camera. She didn't need film. Are you saying you didn't find any sign of her camera at the crime scene?" I called desperately as Jerry headed down the walk. He'd parked his squad car at the curb.

Riley stood, dusting his dirt-black hands on his denim jeans and enjoying the show.

"No!" barked Jerry. He yanked open the door and plopped behind the wheel. "And if I find any sign of you at any of my crime scenes, you'll be spending the night in jail!"

The door creaked behind me. "Excuse me," began the woman who'd come in, "can you tell me the price of those twenty-pound bags of safflower seeds?"

"Of course," I said. I held up a finger. "I'll be with you in a second. I promise." There was one more thing I wanted to quiz Jerry about. If he could tell me the exact time of Bessie Hammond's death, give or take, I'd be able to figure who might have had the opportunity to murder her. All I had to do was find out where everyone had been at the time in question.

But when I turned around, it was to the sound and sight of the police cruiser peeling away and heading up-town on Lake Shore Drive.

"What was that all about?"

"Oh!" I turned and smiled. "Good morning, Channing. I didn't see you there."

The young woman pointed next door. "I stopped at the pub." She looked embarrassed and twisted her sandal into the porch. "I put in an application. I hope you don't mind? I know you said you might have something, but I wasn't sure and I really could use a job."

I grinned. "No, of course I don't mind. I understand completely. You have to consider all your options." I caught Riley, on his knees in the topsoil, ogling Channing. She had on a pair of skinny jeans and a white blouse with a frilly collar open at the neckline. If I'd had her cleavage, I might have forgotten a button or three myself.

My cousin considers himself something of a ladies' man. The ladies consider him more the town clown. Not that they meant that in a mean-spirited way, only that Riley can't be taken too seriously. "How about sweeping the sidewalk when you're finished, Riley?"

"I'll get right on it!" Riley promised.

I pulled Channing inside. "Come on in. Let's talk where we've got some AC." And no prying ears or ogling eyes. Then I spotted my near-forgotten customer. I told Channing where to find the refreshments and promised I'd be with her shortly.

After disposing of my customer—and happy to make my first sale of the day—I checked the answering machine. The sole message was from Kim. I couldn't make out half of what she was saying because she sounded like she was either blubbering, drunk, or both. Either way, the gist of her garbled message was that she wouldn't be coming into the store to work today.

Great. I caught up with Channing, who had made herself a cup of hot chamomile tea. She sat in one of the pair of rockers, legs crossed. "Thank you for seeing me, Ms. Simms."

"It's Amy, remember?" I said. "How did it go at the *biergarten*?"

"Mr. Anderson said he was very sorry but that he didn't have any openings at the moment. Still, he had me fill out an application. He told me to leave my number in case something should open up."

"I'll bet," I muttered.

"Pardon?"

"Have you ever worked retail before?" I sat beside her, resting my feet.

Channing shook her head in the negative. "Only briefly in a friend's boutique."

"Not to worry." I clamped my hands on my knees. "We run a simple operation around here."

Channing's face lit up. "You mean you'll hire me?"

I nodded. "Only part-time, mind you. And, like I said, I can't pay much."

Channing reached over and squeezed my hand. "I don't need much, Amy. A few hours a week. I do have my chores at the house. And it's only for the summer," she gushed. "Then I'm going home."

"Ten hours a week okay to start with?" We agreed on a rate and schedule. I figured I could afford to help out a needy young adult. I'd been one myself not so long ago. It might mean tightening my own belt, but my jeans had been a little too snug for comfort of late.

Besides, if anything, having Channing around would give Esther someone to boss around besides me.

I spent the rest of the morning and afternoon cooling my heels, assisting customers, and straightening up the store in the dead times in between.

I left a message at Derek's office and on his cell phone. Both calls had so far gone unreturned. That was nothing unusual, normally, what with him being a busy attorney, but today it got under my skin.

I called Kim, too. The only phone she's got is a cell. My call went straight to voicemail. "Whatever you're doing, call me back," I pleaded. "And ask Randy if he'll give me a ride to the dump."

I heard a beep and then, "The dump!" sobbed Kim. "Did you have to say the *dump*?"

I pulled the phone away from my ear and stared at it. All the while I could hear Kim sniveling mournfully.

"What's wrong?" I asked, returning the phone to my ear.

"What's wrong is that-that-that—"

"Yes?" I was getting worried now.

"Randy dumped me!" Kim shouted thickly. "He dumped me and said he was going back to his wife!"

16

"No! You mean he's getting back together with Lynda?"

"He's already back with that—that—" I heard my friend gulp air and sigh loudly. Something metallic rattled in the background. "That Lynda!"

"Kim, I am so sorry!" But I was only a little bit surprised. A customer walked in and Riley followed behind. I motioned for him to assist her.

Riley raced over to my side at the counter. "I don't know nothing about birds, Amy!"

"I'm on the phone here, Riley. Handle it," I insisted. Riley slithered off after the squat woman in a magenta summer dress as she examined the birdhouses, pinching her chin between her fingers.

I stepped out the back for some privacy and spent the next twenty minutes listening to Kim spill her guts.

"I sold one!" Cousin Riley squealed enthusiastically as I walked back inside the now empty store.

"Aunt Betty will be so proud," I deadpanned.

Riley bobbed his head. "Yeah. Mom only thinks of me

being good with my hands." He extended said hands, his fingernails loaded with garden dirt. "Wait'll she hears I'm good with selling stuff, too."

"That's terrific, Riley." I draped my arm over his left shoulder. "Now, listen to me. I have to go out."

"But—"

I cut him off. "It's an emergency." Of sorts. Kim needed me.

"But who's going to mind the store?"

I looked him dead in the eyes. "You are." Heaven help us all.

Riley took a step back, bumping into the cash register. "Oh, no!"

"Oh, yes." I planted my hands on his shoulders. "You can do it." My cousin had gone pale. I threw him a lifeline. "Listen, call my mom or your mom or even Esther, if you want. I'm sure one of them can come down and lend you a hand."

Like his twin sister, Rhonda, Cousin Riley has thick brown hair, hazel eyes, and a generous nose. Those eyes now glistened with fear. "When will you be back?"

"I'm not sure," I said, grabbing my car keys and purse. "A couple of hours tops." Who knew how long it would actually take to bring Kim down to earth, back to the living?

It took me about fifteen minutes to get across town due to the summer tourist traffic clogging the main road. The tourists come for the boating, the hiking, and the fresh air as much as they come for the quaint taffy-, trinket-, and fine-art shops in town.

Though it was the middle of the day, the curtains at

Kim's Craftsman-style bungalow were pulled tight. I parked in the drive behind Kim's car and raced up the porch steps.

The front door was unlocked, so I let myself in. Kim was parked on the black leather sofa watching a soap opera. A big bowl of popcorn sat between her legs and the clothes she was wearing looked like they'd been slept in. The popcorn was half gone. So was Kim, by the looks of her.

Kim looked at me through a pair of swollen, red eyes that the sorriest, saddest puppy dog in the world could not have matched.

"You want to talk about it?" I helped myself to a handful of popcorn. "Scoot over."

Kim obliged, pulling a throw pillow along with her. We watched the soap for a little while. I had no idea who all these people were and why they were all conniving against one another, but when one regal woman accused a second, younger woman, with a nose that looked like it had been chiseled by some modern-day Michelangelo, of stealing her husband, I figured it was time we quit. I grabbed the remote and cut the power.

"Hey!" complained Kim, shooting me a dirty look. "What did you do that for? It was just getting interesting!"

I grabbed the popcorn bowl from between her thighs. "I think you've had enough TV and enough of this. I, on the other hand . . ." I shoveled another mouthful of buttered popcorn into my mouth and chewed with exaggerated side-to-side movements of my jaw. "Mm-mm, good."

Kim smiled. "You're an idiot. No, correction," she said, punching her white satin throw pillow. "I'm an idiot."

"So how did you find out?" I asked softly.

Kim turned up her lip. "I went to his house this morning and Lynda answered the door." She twisted the pillow in her hands so violently I thought it might rip in two. "Wearing Randy's pajamas."

"Ouch." At least this time Kim wouldn't be blaming me for the breakup. She'd broken up with Randy briefly some months ago over something I had innocently said, and she'd taken it the wrong way. This time, the blame was all on Randy.

"Yeah," she sniffed. "Ouch."

I grabbed her hand. "I'm sorry. You know he didn't deserve you, right?"

Kim smiled. "I guess so. I thought we really had something, too." She tossed her hand. "All this time, he kept saying the divorce was going to be final any day. Instead . . ."

"Yeah." Instead the creep had dumped my best friend and gone back to his wife. "Men are jerks," I said, fully prepared to toe the line in support of the woman who was like a sister to me.

"Don't worry, Amy, I'm sure Derek is different."

I thought about it, but only for a second. "Yeah, I think so. I'm pretty certain he'd never go back to Amy the Ex." The woman was a piece of work and then some. I told Kim what had happened at the Birds and Brews gathering, especially the parts about Gus and Derek.

"I wouldn't dwell on it." Kim managed a small smile, though her cheeks still looked rather puffy and her forehead was mottled pink and white. "Talk to Derek. He'll understand."

"Talk to him? Wouldn't that be nice? I haven't managed to be alone in a room with him for what seems like days." The wheels in my head spun like hamsters in a rodent spin class.

Kim caught the look in my eyes. "What?"

"All this man stuff. And what I told you about Gus McKutcheon coming on to me."

"*Maybe* coming on to you," countered Kim.

"Maybe coming on to me," I aped with a roll of the eyes. "Anyway, I know you said I shouldn't, but I really think I ought to say something to Moire Leora about the guy."

Kim sighed. "Not that again."

"Yes, that again. What's wrong with giving a woman a heads-up that her lover may not be so . . . devoted, shall we say?" I thumped her in the chest with the pillow. "You of all people right now should appreciate the thought."

"Even in my sorry state, I know better than to stick my nose into somebody else's love life."

"Ha!"

Kim scrunched up her face. "What's that mean?"

"It means you're always sticking your nose in mine."

"That's different," she said with a dismissive toss of the hand.

"Different?" I crossed my arms. "Different how?"

"You're like family. Family's always sticking their noses in each other's lives."

I had to agree and said so.

Kim drew her legs up. "Do you want a drink?"

"No," I said. "Neither do you." One glass of wine or two and Kim's ebullient. More than that and she's on a bus to morose-ville. In fact, she was three-quarters of the way there now. I needed to get her headed back in the opposite direction. "Besides, alcohol and breakups don't mix."

Kim pulled a face. "That makes no sense at all."

She was right, of course, but all my hair could fall out and my teeth turn green before I'd admit it—especially since I'd already just agreed with her on something. I didn't want her to think we were going to start making a habit of that. Our relationship would be forever changed if I let Kim think she was always right. "Let's get out of here," I suggested.

Kim's brow went up. "And go where?"

I smiled. "How about a little bird-watching?"

"Bird-watching?" Kim's nose, already red from crying her heart out, wrinkled up. "Amy, I've told you a million times that I'm really not much into this whole bird-watching thing. Let's watch another soap."

"What if I told you what we're really doing is looking for clues?"

"Clues?" Kim quipped. "Can't we go looking for booze instead?"

"Another time," I answered. "We're going searching for evidence that will lead us to Bessie Hammond's killer. What do you say?"

Kim curled her lip. "So, no booze, huh?"

I shook my head no as I said, "Definitely not."

"Fine." Kim caved. "Then I'd say, lead on, Sherlock." She stood, dusting bits of popcorn kernels and granules of salt from her dark clothing. "Anything is better than sitting around here feeling sorry for myself." Kim picked her purse up from the floor. "Besides, I can always feel sorry for myself while I'm helping you look for clues."

"That's the spirit!" I said. I headed for the door. I took the popcorn with me.

* * *

I parked the van at the marina and we followed the same hiking trail I'd led my little birding group down the other morning. The sun was heading to the west now, but I knew we still had several hours of daylight before we had to worry. I did not want to be in the woods after dark. Only killers and their sexy but witless and doomed victims dared do that.

Through a break in the trees, I spotted Ethan Harrow's boat, the *Sunset Sally*, bobbing in Ruby Lake along with dozens of other vessels, large and small. I could make out the captain by his size. There were three others aboard, probably his mate, Jean, and a couple of charters. Fishing poles dangled off the stern.

"I'm thirsty," complained Kim, stumbling along behind me. She stopped and leaned a hand against a pine. She pulled off a shoe and watched two small pebbles drop out. "You didn't tell me we'd be roughing it," she groused as she slid her moccasin back on her foot. "I would have worn better shoes."

I ignored the bellyaching remarks and urged her on after taking a look around to recalculate my bearings. Our bird-watching group had come this way, I was sure of it. I pulled my teeth across my lower lip and swatted a horsefly that had it in for me. I pointed. "The little cemetery I was telling you about is that way." I turned. "So, that means Bessie was found over there." I pointed about twenty degrees to my left.

"Can't we turn around and go home?" Kim moaned. "I'm starting to think this isn't such a good idea." Her shirt was drenched in sweat and she was pink in the face—this time from exertion and sun exposure rather than crying and psychological distress. I took that as a good sign. "We've been walking for hours."

"Don't exaggerate. It hasn't been that long. Come on,

Kim. It can't be more than a couple hundred yards further. And keep your eyes open for—"

"I know, I know. You've told me a hundred times: We're looking for clues," she said, her voice rising in pitch. "Whatever *they* might be." She threw her hands in the air to show her growing displeasure.

"*And* Bessie's camera," I reminded her, ignoring her attitude.

"Yeah, yeah. A camera."

She hobbled along after me, and before long we came to the sycamore where I'd discovered Bessie Hammond's corpse.

"That's it," I whispered, pausing at the clearing. The ground all around had been trampled by the feet of the police and rescue personnel.

Otherwise, there was not a single trace of death. Except that it somehow hung in the air, like a specter that I couldn't shake. A chill ran up my arms and I rubbed them.

Kim had edged closer. "So this is the spot, huh?"

I nodded in silence.

"It looks to me like the police have been all over this place." She squatted and ran a hand over the trampled undergrowth. "I doubt if even our pal Jerry could have missed a digital camera lying around."

"I suppose you're right," I admitted. My voice came out a whisper. I felt like I was standing in a funeral parlor rather than a forest.

We kept our eyes on the ground and circled the clearing, round and round for ten minutes or more, then stopped. "Nothing," I said glumly. "No camera, no scraps of clothing, blood stains—"

"Yep, none of the things they find on TV." She kicked the ground. "Plenty of footprints."

"Too many," I agreed. Me, the police, the EMS crew, and who knew who else had tramped around the old sycamore. If the killer had left any footprints, there'd be no way to discern them in this mess. Besides, I was sure that the police would have followed any prints that might have been worth following.

I was frustrated. Where was Bessie's camera and what images might it contain? If I could find her camera would I find a photo of her killer?

"You know, Amy, Bessie's camera might never have been here at all. She might have left it home the day she was killed."

"Why would she do that?"

"Why not?"

Kim was right. Why not? "We'll search her house next."

"No we won't!" Kim said, pushing out her chest.

"Fine, I'll do it myself." I stuck my tongue out at her.

Kim ignored my antics and rubbed her hands together. "Okay, so we're done here. I can't wait to get home and take a long, hot shower. Let's boogie."

"No."

"No?"

"Not yet." I blew out a breath. "Come on," I said. "There's a small cemetery over there. I want to get a look at it."

"What for?" Kim asked.

"We saw it the other day and, well, you might think it sounds silly, but I thought I saw a fresh grave."

Kim appeared amused. "The day of your hike?" I nodded. "You do realize that Bessie Hammond was with you that morning?" I nodded again. "Then, you do realize that she can't possibly be buried in that grave you say you saw?"

"Yes," I answered slowly, "but what if someone else is?"

The blood drained from Kim's face. "You mean—" She brought her right hand to her shoulder, then threw it forward.

"Yep." The body I thought I saw being tossed from the Mc-Kutcheon house upstairs window.

Kim wiped her forehead. "Did you ever tell Jerry about it?"

"About the cemetery? No. To tell the truth, it never crossed my mind to. Besides, he'd probably laugh at me."

Kim grinned. "That's true." She turned and waved over her shoulder. "Well, have fun with that. I'll meet you back at the van."

"Wait!" I shouted. "Where are you going?"

Kim spun on her heels. "I told you, back to the van. You can lead me out into the forest of death to look for clues but I am not—not, I repeat—going to a cemetery in the middle of a deserted forest."

She shook her head in a scolding fashion. "You know things like that creep me out. No," Kim said firmly. "I appreciate you helping me get out of my funk, but I'm not so far out of it as to step foot in a cemetery!"

I gaped at her retreating figure. As she reached the edge of the clearing, she froze in her tracks and shouted. "Hey!"

I stood there with my arms crossed over my chest. I was a little ticked off that she'd abandon me now. When we'd come this far. "What?"

I watched as Kim bent down. As she did, she waved urgently. She had me curious now. I had no choice but to jog to her. "What is it?" I huffed, shocked that such a short jog had left me gasping for breath.

Kim pointed to a thick patch of wild grasses. "That."

Her eyes scanned the ground and her fingers fell over a foot-long stick that she picked up. She used it to spread the slender leaves. "See? That shiny silver and red thing. Do you think that could be Bessie's camera?"

I bent beside Kim, rubbing shoulders with her. I pushed my hands through the grass for a better look. "No," I said, unable to hide my disappointment. "It's only a knife."

Kim reached in and plucked it from its hiding place. "Too bad." She sounded as frustrated as me. She bounced the knife in the palm of her hand.

"Hold on," I said. I snatched the knife from her and turned it over and over in my hand. "Oh, dear . . ."

"What's wrong?" asked Kim, rising and dusting off her knees.

I grabbed on to her leg and pulled myself up, my knees burning. "The centipede."

"What?" Kim scratched her head.

"It's the centipede." I held it between us. "At least that's what Ed Quince calls it."

Kim lowered her face closer to the knife. "Do you mean to say you recognize this particular knife?"

I nodded slowly. "I'd recognize it anywhere. It belongs to Ed Quince."

"One of your bird-watchers?"

I nodded once again.

"Why does he call it the centipede?"

"Because he claims it's got over a hundred uses," I replied. But that wasn't the question. The question was: What was it doing there?

17

Bessie Hammond hadn't been stabbed to death, but that didn't mean one of those hundred uses hadn't been to threaten her with the knife's sharp-looking, four-inch blade before brutally snapping the woman's neck.

I didn't see any visible signs of blood on the blade, but I knew that didn't mean much. I slipped the knife into my pocket.

"Are you sure it's his?"

I patted my pocket, feeling the hard steel against my thigh. "I'm sure. Ed used it when we were out walking the other morning. Did you notice the Red Deer Dairy Farm name and logo on the handle?"

Kim said she had. "So?"

"Ed's knife had that same logo. How many knives like those do you suppose are in Ruby Lake?" Let alone out lying around in the woods near the sight of a recent murder. Everyone in town knew that Red Deer was a small, locally owned dairy located in the next valley. A knife bearing its name and logo wouldn't be widespread.

"What are you going to do?" A gray and white stratus cloud edged across the sky, threatening the sun.

"I'm going to ask Ed Quince about it. Come on, you win. We're getting out of here." Talking to Ed Quince had taken precedence over poking around an old family cemetery, no matter how curious I was to get a closer look.

Besides, I could always come back later on my own.

"Amy, are you crazy?" Kim struggled to keep pace as I hurried back to the parking lot. "You've got to turn that knife over to Jerry. That knife could be evidence."

I shook my head. "Maybe. But we don't know that for sure. We're not even positive that it belongs to Ed. I mean, I'm pretty sure, but you never know."

"Let the police figure that out."

I stopped and laid a hand on my friend's arm. "What if we take this knife to the police," I conjectured, patting my pocket, "and then we find out that Ed's still got his knife? Can you imagine how that's going to make us look?"

Kim pulled a face. "Kennedy will have a field day."

"We'll never live it down. Is that what you want?"

"Fine. You go talk to Mr. Quince," Kim decided. "Personally, I'm going to go soak in a tub till I transform into a raisin." She grinned. "Then I'll help myself to a little of the old grape."

"Deal." Kim seemed to be doing better. At the very least, helping me look into Bessie Hammond's murder had gotten her mind off the breakup, at least temporarily. That was the best that could be hoped for. Broken hearts take time to mend. "I'll drop you off at home and then try to go talk to Ed."

As we reached the parking lot and climbed in the

van, Kim asked, "Can we stop at the five-and-ten before taking me home?"

"What for?"

"I've got a picture of Randy next to my bed, but not for long. I thought I'd buy a dartboard for the kitchen so I can put it up there and throw darts at his stupid face."

I laughed but sped past the five-and-ten and went straight to Kim's bungalow. The last thing she needed was to be drinking and hurling needle-sharp objects at the walls. I'd only be helping her patch said walls the next day.

I stopped at Birds & Bees. Cousin Riley sat on the porch bench beneath the front window, sipping a light beer. "Aren't you supposed to be minding the store, Riley?"

"Aunt Barbara's inside assisting a customer." He waved his near-empty bottle toward the store. "I'm on break."

"I'm not so sure this is a good idea." Riley appeared flummoxed. "Drinking beer in front of the store." If he wanted to drink outdoors, he could go next door to Brewer's Biergarten and buy himself a beer. The bottle in my cousin's hand looked like one from my fridge.

"Fine." Riley started to rise. "I'll go up to your place."

"Never mind," I said quickly, one hand on the door. "You're good where you are."

Riley shrugged and slumped back against the bench while I went inside.

"Excuse me." I tapped my mother on the shoulder as she hovered near a man and woman discussing birdbaths. "Any chance you know where the Quinces live, Mom?"

Mom told her customers she'd be back with them in a moment. "Ed and Abby?" Mom asked, stepping away and stuffing her hands in the pocket of her apron.

"Yeah. That's them. They're part of my bird-watching group."

"They live at 1212 Windmere. Why?"

My jaw dropped. "How did you know that?" I'd have settled for a general idea, like the name of their neighborhood, but my mother knew their exact address?

"Your father and I used to socialize with the Quinces when you were little. Don't you remember?"

I said I didn't. "Thanks, Mom. You've got things under control here, right? Great." No way was I going to wait for an answer counter to what I needed to hear. I gave her a peck on the cheek. "Bye, Mom."

"You're leaving?" She left the *again* unsaid.

I jiggled the van keys. "Places to go, things to do."

"Wait, why are you off to see the Quinces?"

"Bird stuff," I said, vaguely. I stepped back out. Riley had stretched out on the bench and his eyes were shut. I gave his feet a gentle kick. "Back to work, Riley."

He struggled up. "But you're back. I thought I was done."

"Well, I'm gone again. Go help your aunt Barbara."

Muttering words his mother would wash his mouth out with lye soap for using, Riley headed indoors. The store was in good hands with Mom, and Mom was in relatively good hands with Riley.

I jumped behind the wheel and headed for Ed and Abby's house. The two-story brick colonial wasn't hard to find. Their subdivision on the south side of Ruby

Lake was a small enclave with one road, Windmere, snaking in one edge of Lake Shore Drive and coming out another.

Ed, dressed in baggy blue overalls and a white T-shirt, stood in the front yard hacking ineffectually at a waist-high firethorn hedge that separated his lawn from his neighbors'.

I watched from the curb for a minute, waiting for the overture to *Kiss Me, Kate* to wind down, then climbed out. It was curtain time.

"I think those shears of yours need sharpening!" I veered across the lawn toward Ed.

Ed Quince lowered his clippers and stared at me a moment without recognition. He ought to have been wearing leather gloves. They didn't call that bush *fire* and *thorn* for nothing.

"Ms. Simms?" He ran the back of his arm over his damp forehead. "What are you doing here?"

"Hi, Ed." I reached into my shorts pocket. There was no sense beating around the bush, so to speak. "I wanted to ask you about this." I held my hand out, palm up, the knife in plain sight.

Ed looked at it a moment, then jerked his head nervously toward the house. His eyes quivered. "Where did you get that?"

"It is your knife, isn't it?"

Ed gulped. His eyes bulged as the color began rising up his doughy, stubbled face. I was afraid he might be having a heart attack. "Where did you find it?" he managed to spit out.

"The question is, where did you lose it?" Ed reached out for the knife but I closed my fist around it and pulled back.

Ed glanced once more at the house. Whatever he was

looking for, I didn't see. "Come on," he gestured. "I don't want to talk out here."

I hesitated for a moment as I slid Ed's knife back in my pocket. Where was he taking me? What would he do with me when we got there? Hack me to pieces with those blunt hedge clippers of his? That sounded rather unpleasant. And painful.

Ed was silent as he led me around the side of the house and back to the detached garage. Outside the garage, he paused and took a long drink from the green garden hose curled up in a mulched flower bed beside the screen door. Thirst quenched, or maybe he'd been stalling for time while he thought about what he wanted to say, Ed pushed open the screen door. I stepped inside. The garage smelled of must, mildew, and gasoline. The overhead door was closed.

The dark garage, with its wood-paneled walls, was silent as a tomb.

"You didn't answer my question," Ed said, his voice low and thick.

"You didn't answer mine." I inspected the garage. There were a million weapons here that I could defend myself with, like that three-tined hoe hanging on a peg or that steel shovel.

Ed scratched behind his ear with his free hand. He hadn't let go of those shears yet. Had that been intentional? How much danger might I be in?

"I guess I lost it Saturday."

"On our bird walk."

"Yeah, I guess so."

"Are you sure?"

Ed drew himself up. "That's right. On our bird walk."

"Are you sure it wasn't the day after?"

Ed's eyes drew closer to his nose. "You mean the day Bessie died?"

"I mean the day Bessie was murdered."

Ed crossed to the door and looked through the screen toward his house. Was he worried about his wife? "Now, look here, Amy, I've had that knife for years. It was a present from our distributor. You give it back to me." He held out his lumpy palm and took a step in my direction.

I took a step back. "You didn't return to the lake the next day?" He shook his head no. "You didn't go there with Bessie, or to meet up with her?"

"No! Of course not!" Ed's face reddened. "Now give it to me."

"Why would Bessie go back to the lake the day after we went there, Ed?"

Ed coughed. "I don't know. Maybe she wanted to do some more bird-watching. You'd have to ask her that question and you can't very well do that." Ed paced the small one-car garage.

"No. But I can ask everybody else that knew her."

Ed glowered. "Why would you want to do that?"

"Because I want to know who killed her," I retorted. "Don't you?" He had seemed terribly shaken by her death.

Ed waved the shears around. "Of course, I do. But that's what the police are for." To my surprise, Ed suddenly bent over and began sobbing violently.

I softened my tone. "You miss her, don't you?" I stepped closer and draped a hand across his back.

Ed nodded and sniffled. "I don't know why anybody would kill her, Amy." He looked up at me. "Really I don't. You've got to believe me."

I reached into my pocket and handed Ed his knife. "I found it out by the lake. On McKutcheon's property. Not far from where Bessie was found."

For a moment, Ed stopped breathing as he stared at the knife in his hand. I had no idea what he was thinking and only hoped those thoughts didn't involve contemplating another murder—mine. If the gasoline fumes didn't kill me, the retired grocer might.

"Are you going to tell Chief Kennedy?" He tapped the trimming shears against the side of the workbench.

"I don't know," I said. I honestly didn't. I didn't want to aid and abet a killer, but I didn't want to humiliate Ed for no good reason. He was a married man and Ruby Lake was a small town.

"Fine," he answered, glumly.

He seemed resigned to the fates, but I could sense his eyes pleading with me not to tell the police about finding his knife in the woods, and I shifted my feet.

"You and Bessie had been colleagues. But you were more than that, you were close friends," I declared, softly. "Were you"—I hesitated, but what I was thinking needed to be asked—"more than close friends?"

Ed turned his back to me. "We had a fling. Just once." His voice dropped even lower. "It was after the company picnic out at the lake. Her husband had died by then and Abby hadn't wanted to attend."

Ed spun back around. "We never talked about it again and we never"—he rolled the tip of his tongue over his lips—"did it again."

"Might Bessie have threatened you in any way?"

Ed rubbed the point of the shears against the back of his knee, then set them on the worktable. "How do you mean?"

"I mean, was Bessie blackmailing you?"

Ed laughed. "Of course not!"

"And what about Abby?" I turned my eyes toward the house. "Did she know?"

"No."

"Are you sure?" Women had a way of sensing these things.

"I'm sure," Ed replied, but he suddenly didn't appear so sure.

I wasn't so sure myself.

"Besides," he said, "Walter's the one you ought to be talking to. Leave me out of this. Bessie was a mistake I made a long time ago."

"Walter? You mean Walter Kimmel?"

But I got no answer. Ed had said all he was going to say. He snatched up his shears and jammed them onto a rusty hook on the garage wall. A minute later, he disappeared inside his house, leaving me standing in the garage alone.

I glanced at my watch: six o'clock. By now, Esther should be at work. Mom wouldn't be all alone at Birds & Bees, assuming Riley had left long ago.

That meant I was free to check out Bessie Hammond's house. Kill two birds with one stone, so to speak. I knew Bessie lived somewhere on this side of town from what the bus driver, whatshisname, told me. I just didn't know exactly where.

The bus driver. I needed to call him, too. He remembered giving Bessie a ride to the marina the day she was murdered. Maybe he had noticed whether or not Bessie had her camera with her that day.

I sat in the van outside Ed's house, pondering my current dilemma: how to find out the address of Bessie Hammond's house. Then I remembered that I'd had all my participants fill out a form listing their name, address, and telephone contact info. I dug my phone out of my purse and called Mom.

"Birds and Bees, where everything is on sale all the time!" snapped a familiar voice. But it wasn't my mother's voice.

"Esther?" I said. "Is that you?"

"Of course it is. Is that you, Simms? What are calling your own store for?"

I took a calming breath. I decided not to ask what all that sales talk was about. Some things were better left unknown. Esther's antics definitely fell into that category. "Would you put my mother on, please?"

"I can't. She's busy with Ben."

"That's good." I tapped my finger against the dash. "Listen, I don't want to disturb her. Do me a favor."

"What kind of favor?"

"I need you to go in the file cabinet in back and get me Ms. Hammond's address."

"What do you need that for? The woman's dead."

"That's just it," I said. "I-I was thinking of sending flowers."

"To a dead woman's house?" Esther was practically shouting. "The woman lived alone. What do you want to send flowers to a dead woman's deserted house for?"

I gnawed the inside of my cheek. "Please, Esther, would you just get me the address? I'll hold."

Without another word, Esther banged the phone against the counter. I then heard low voices in the background. That must have been Mom and Ben Harlan. I was glad they were spending a little time together, even if it was in a retail store.

After an eternity, Esther came back on the line. She spat out the address like she was spitting out a mouthful of bees.

"Wait, slow down!" I pleaded. "And let me get something to write with!" I fished around in my purse for a pen and paper, settling on a mascara pen and a one-dollar-off coupon for codfish. "Go ahead."

Esther repeated the address and I read it back to her. "Okay, bye."

"Wait!"

"What is it now?"

"How's everything at the store?" I felt a little guilty about the way I'd been neglecting the business.

"Busy. Lots of customers. Plenty to do. And your cousin Riley says the fire damage is nothing to worry about. Nothing a good coat of paint won't fix. Bye."

"Wait . . . what? Esther? Esther?"

I closed my eyes and counted to ten.

I shouldn't have bothered. The world still looked the same when I opened them again. Except this time both Ed and Abby were glaring at me from their living room window.

I waved weakly and sped off.

18

My cell phone was ringing as I pulled up to the Hammond house, a two-story redbrick colonial with black shutters. An elderly couple sat on the front porch of the house next-door, while a sheepdog pranced about their front lawn. A curled-up copy of the *Ruby Lake Weekender* lay on the path leading to Bessie's house. They ought to have known better than to deliver a newspaper to a dead woman. The *Weekender* had reported her death, after all. It had been front-page news.

I slowed but kept moving. How was I going to get into Bessie's house? How was I going to get into Bessie's house without being seen?

I'd never broken into a house before and felt a little uncomfortable with the idea now. What if I was spotted by one of the neighbors and they called the cops? I'd be humiliated and thrown in the slammer. That wouldn't be good for me or my business.

Worse still, what if relatives of Bessie's had come to town for her funeral and were staying at the house? I knew she'd had no relatives in town and that their one grown son lived in Michigan—Mom had told me that—but was he in Michigan now?

I turned the corner to the next block. Gray clouds had moved in from the south, casting an early twilight. This residential street was far quieter. In fact, I'd parked at the curb in front of a house that appeared empty. The front lawn was overgrown with weeds and the shrubbery needed trimming. All the curtains on the windows facing the street were shut. A weather-worn FOR SALE sign on a wood post had been hammered into the grass at the edge of the porch. I recognized the Realtor as the one Kim worked with part-time.

The phone chirruped in my purse, reminding me of the recent call. I looked at the screen: one missed call and one voicemail. I hit the voicemail button as the phone started ringing once more. It was Derek.

"Derek, hi!"

"Hi, Amy. I'm glad I caught you. I was afraid I was going to have to leave another voicemail."

"I'm sorry I missed your call. I was driving." I killed the engine, leaving the keys dangling in the ignition.

"Am I interrupting something? I can call back."

"No! Not at all." I took a deep breath. The last thing I wanted to do was let him go, now that we were talking. "How are you? I miss you."

There was a beat of silence. "I miss you, too. It's been a hectic couple of days."

He did sound tired. "I'm sorry to hear that. Is there anything I can do?" I thought fast. It wasn't too late, and breaking into Bessie Hammond's house shouldn't take all that long. "How about if I cook us some dinner?"

"Sounds good. I'd like that. Then we can talk."

Talk? It felt like someone had hit my heart with a

sledgehammer. When a man says he needs to talk, it usually meant one thing: The Breakup.

I had a growing sense of impending doom as we made plans to meet at my apartment in two hours. We said some other stuff, too, but, to tell the truth, I was barely paying attention. Dread had taken over my soul.

We rang off. A few large drops of rain fell, splatting like little wet bombs against the glass—not enough to cause trouble, just enough to smear the bug goo baked on my windshield.

I checked for prying eyes once more. Reasonably sure that the coast was clear, I grabbed my purse and exited the van. My plan was to act like I was interested in purchasing the house that was for sale. That way, if any neighbors did happen to see me walking around the abandoned house, they'd take me for a potential buyer and not call the cops on me as a potential burglar.

I strolled up to the house, swinging my purse from my shoulder, pausing occasionally to shake my head or place a finger along the side of my chin as if admiring the house's charms and inspecting it for potential flaws— of which there were many. The sweet smell of gardenia filled the air. The tall, leggy bushes bursting with white flowers flanked the steps leading to the house.

After what seemed like a suitable amount of time, I angled around to the back and smiled. The setup was perfect. The sodded backyard was bound on three sides by tall holly hedges in dire need of Ed's shears. The view of the houses on either side was blocked. That meant the people living in those homes couldn't see me either.

Wishing I'd worn a long-sleeve shirt and denim jeans instead of shorts, I pushed through the thinnest spot in the holly that I could find, into Bessie's yard. A pair of cardinals chirped their indignation at my invasion of their space and flew up to the top of Bessie's chimney. The birds bobbed their heads and stared down at me as I wiped myself off. A neglected, algae-lined birdbath sat askew on the back lawn, surrounded by a ring of gravel. A lone birdfeeder hung off the rear wall of a screened-in patio.

I looked left and right. On this side, too, the neighbors' houses were barely visible due to the tall hedges. I approached the patio and tried the door. Bingo. It was unlocked. The screened patio enclosure contained little more than a cheap white PVC patio set and a few houseplants in need of watering. A pair of sliding doors led into the house. The curtains were pulled wide. I could see into the living room with its flowery upholstered furniture in shades of dark reds and purples. Several dreary paintings in gaudy frames, the mass-produced sort you'd find in any big, cheap department store hung from the walls. I tried the nearest slider. It jiggled but held. So did slider number two.

Now what?

I could break the glass, but that didn't feel right. Jerry Kennedy would probably even claim it was illegal. I returned outside and looked around the house more carefully. A window on the second floor was slightly ajar. It was practically an invitation. Maybe Bessie's ghost had left it open for me because she wanted me to find her killer.

At least that was what I was going to tell the cops if I got caught. I found an aluminum extension ladder behind the shed and leaned it up against the screened porch. The porch's roof appeared solid enough. I could only hope that it held me.

Although I climbed slowly, the ladder rattled so loudly

that I feared I'd attract the ears and eyes of Bessie's neighbors. I heaved myself up onto the gravel- and tarpaper-covered patio roof and surveyed the area. Several lights were on in the surrounding houses but I saw no one in the windows.

I wiped my hands together to rid them of the tiny pebbles that had become embedded in my flesh and stood, taking stock of my surroundings. I looked down. Mistake number one. I'm not a big fan of heights, especially heights with no railing. I turned quickly and faced Bessie's house. The sooner I got inside the less likely I'd be spotted or fall to my death. The window stuck to the sides of the rails for a moment but gave in when I put my shoulder into it.

I stuck my head inside. It was a bathroom. Pink tile, pink sink, pink tub, pink toilet, and fluffy pink bath rugs. On the plus side, I heard no threatening voices—or barking dogs, pink or otherwise, with teeth the size of daggers looking for their next meal. I slid over the sill and onto the toilet seat.

The house was silent. I gaped at myself in the bathroom mirror. I was a wet wreck. I'd deal with that later. I stepped out into the hall. I expected that Bessie either kept her camera in her bedroom or in an office of some sort, if she had one. There were doors at each end of the hall, separated by the stairs.

I started on the left and found myself in a sewing and craft room. Bessie had a very nice, if older looking, Kenmore sewing machine on a long table under the back window. Another long table held several bolts of cloth and various odds and ends, including a tape measure and a pincushion. I opened the accordion doors to the closet. Bessie was, had been, a well-organized person. The closet held systematically organized and labelled translucent bins of fabric, yarns, and ribbon. I dug through them randomly.

No camera.

At the other end of the hall, I found the master bedroom. The whole room smelled like rosewater. The heavy brocade curtains were pulled and refused to let in even a modicum of light.

My hand fumbled against the wall and flicked the light switch, and the bedside lamps on either side of the bed sprang to life; not much life, because the bulbs couldn't have been more than fifty watts, but there was enough of a yellowish glow to see by. An ornate, dark wood four-poster bed sat atop a sea of beige wall-to-wall carpet.

I was a little worried about the neighbors noticing the lights, but closer inspection of the hanging drapes told me they were blackout curtains. I was safe from discovery.

Pulling open the nearest nightstand drawer, I found books—fiction, nonfiction, and crossword puzzles—and a tube of hand cream. Bessie had said she was a whiz at crosswords. But there was no camera here either.

I opened the second drawer and discovered a pair of knitting needles holding a work in progress whose ultimate shape and use I couldn't discern, and half a skein of the thick lavender yarn she was knitting it from. A handful of plain white envelopes lay beneath the twist of yarn. There were five envelopes, all the same, no postmarks and no addresses.

I opened the first and withdrew a sloppily folded sheet of yellow legal-pad paper. It was a note to Bessie:

Bessie,

For the last time, please stop calling me. I don't care if you do tell Clara. I can't live this way any longer. I want it to stop.

Walt

Walt? That had to be Walter Kimmel! He had been behaving oddly at the Birds and Brews get-together. And this had to be why. He'd been having an affair with Bessie Hammond.

Had Bessie told Clara about the affair? Had Walter killed Bessie to prevent her from doing so?

I quickly scanned the other letters. More of the same. The first had been more pleasant, then Walter had clearly grown increasingly upset that Bessie refused to let him go and forget their affair.

There had been more to Bessie Hammond than I ever could have imagined. The police must not have noticed the letters. I might have missed them, too. They could easily have been mistaken for empty envelopes waiting to be used. Plus, Bessie had been murdered out in the middle of the woods. The police might not have performed more than a perfunctory search of her house.

I'd have to let Jerry know about their existence, if I could think of a way to do it without getting myself arrested.

My heart pounded. I'd found a bombshell, but no camera, so I kept looking. There was no camera in the dresser nor in the—no surprise, well-organized—hall closet. I planted my hands on my hips while I did a slow turn around the room, trying to imagine where Bessie might have kept her camera. Assuming it was here in the house at all.

"Time to try the downstairs," I said under my breath. I didn't know if it was the spookiness of being in a dead woman's home or the fear of getting caught in that home, but I found myself tiptoeing around, as noiseless in my search as possible.

I had not seen a computer of any sort in the house yet either. That could be on the first floor as well, assuming she had a computer at all. Even my own mother seemed quite uninterested in the things. It was less than two years ago that she had agreed to a cell phone. Maybe Bessie had felt the same way. Besides, she seemed to have had another hobby: dating the town's married men. That must have kept her quite busy.

I turned off the bedroom light and was exiting into the upstairs hall when I heard the distinct, and not a little unsettling, sound of a car door slamming.

I hurried to the edge of the stairs, hoping to get a glimpse of the car, but my view of the living room window was blocked from that vantage point. I raced back to the master bedroom on tiptoes and eased back the heavy drape. Officer Sutton was starting up the walkway.

A small cry escaped my lips as I dropped the curtain. I clamped a hand over my mouth. My whole body quaked and I thought I'd faint. "Ohmygod, ohmygod, ohmygod," I heard myself muttering.

My mind raced. Did he know I was here? Had someone called the police to report a break-in? Had he seen the curtain move just now?

Bending low, I ran from the bedroom, determined to escape. I made it to the bathroom right when I heard the sound of the key turn in the front door lock.

Without thinking, I stepped into the tub and shower combo and gently pulled the pink shower curtain closed.

I was dead meat.

I could see the *Weekender* headlines already: "Amy Simms Found Hiding in Dead Woman's Bath."

I should have been nicer to Lance.

I held my breath as I listened to the sound of Officer Sutton moving around downstairs, his leather shoes squeaking as if to announce his coming.

Please, please, please don't let him come upstairs, I prayed.

But he did. I could hear his heavy steps, *clomp, clomp, clomp*, up the carpeted steps. He moved from one end of the hall to the other. I imagined what it was going to be like when he pulled the shower curtain open and discovered me. Would he shoot first and ask questions afterward?

Should I say something now before he did pull his gun? Or would it be better to surprise him?

I didn't get a chance to make a decision. Whistling, Officer Sutton entered the tiled bath. I squeezed my eyes shut, my body tense as if a million volts of electricity were running through me. I prayed to every god I knew and then some.

Officer Sutton's feet squeaked across the tile. He paused. I heard the sound of a window slamming shut. I'd forgotten to close the window behind me! Dumbdumbdumb.

I swallowed a groan.

A second later, Sutton's steps came toward me in the tub enclosure. He paused. I could see his dark outline through the opaque vinyl curtain. The outline moved and I pressed myself against the back tile, hoping to disappear into the wall.

Sutton began whistling once more as he left the bathroom. I strained my ears, listening to each step as he moved back downstairs. A moment later, I heard the door slam behind him.

I sank to the bottom of the tub and opened my eyes.

That had been close. Too close.

19

I ran my hands over my face, surprised to discover that I'd been crying. I pulled back the curtain, climbed out of the tub, and wiped my face on a fluffy bath towel hanging from a hook across from the sink.

One look in the mirror told me I was even more of a wet wreck now than I had been ten minutes before. I ran to Bessie's bedroom and inched back a corner of the drape. Sutton was gone. I watched his tail lights receding in the distance.

"Time to go," I whispered. After the close call, I decided it was best not to press my luck and search the downstairs. Figuring it was best to leave the way I'd come, I went back to the bathroom, slid open the window, and bellied over the ledge to the screen porch roof. The top of the ladder poked up.

OMG! What if Officer Sutton had noticed the ladder?!

The sight of a ladder leaning up against the house would surely have set off alarms in his head. I'd dodged a bullet. Just maybe, literally.

I scolded myself for my stupidity and told myself that

I needed to be smarter, a whole lot smarter, about how I went about things from now on.

Back on the ground, I returned the ladder to where I'd found it. I then hitched my purse over my shoulder and forced my way back through the hedge. As I popped out on the other side, a fat drop of rain landed on my nose, reminding me that some things were beyond my control.

I trotted out to the front. The sooner I got out of there, the better. As I jogged, I thrust my hand in my purse. I wanted to have my car key ready to go the minute I hit the street.

I skidded to a stop in the middle of the damp lawn. My open purse went flying. Cosmetics, coins, and expired coupons spilled across the overgrown grass.

That was the least of my problems.

The van was gone.

Tripping over my purse, I raced to the curb, looking up and down the street. "I parked it right here!" I said aloud, stamping my foot. "What on earth?"

I was stuck there. And I had a date with Derek in less than two hours.

A few sparse, icy raindrops fell—not enough to cause any trouble. I picked up my purse and shoved everything helter-skelter back in. I had to call somebody. But not the police. At least, not yet.

Mom doesn't drive, so I called Aunt Betty. Unfortunately, the call went straight to voicemail. I considered calling one of my cousins, Rhonda or Riley, but didn't want to explain myself to them.

Should I call Kim? She'd had a tough enough day herself. Besides, by now she'd probably downed an entire bottle of chardonnay. I needed somebody sober.

As much as I hated to, I phoned Derek. "Hi, Derek."

"What's up? You're not cancelling on me, are you?"

"No, not at all. In fact . . ." How was I going to phrase this? "I was wondering if you could come pick me up."

There was a beat of silence before he answered. "Pick you up? Aren't you at your place?"

I cleared my throat. "Actually, no."

"Well, okay. You want me to pick you up. Can do. Tell me when and where."

"How about now? I read the address off the empty house and gave Derek directions as best I could how to get there. Not being from Ruby Lake, he was unfamiliar yet with much of the town.

Derek promised to get there as soon as he could.

The sky opened up and I ran for the vacant home's porch. I was soaked to the bone before I'd made it halfway.

Derek pulled up fifteen minutes later. His headlights were on and his wipers were working full tilt. He honked and I made a dash for it. He leaned over and threw open the passenger door. I jumped in.

"You're soaked!" he said. "And shivering!"

"Y-yes," I said. "Th-thanks for coming."

Derek pushed some buttons and turned some knobs in the cockpit and warm air began blowing from the vents. "Sorry, I don't have a towel," he said, starting down the road. "Let's get you home as soon as possible."

Derek parked next to the rear entrance of Birds & Bees. I unlocked the door and led us inside.

"Mind if I take a hot shower before fixing dinner?" I asked, once we were inside the apartment.

"I'd mind if you didn't," he said with a laugh.

I told him to help himself to drinks and whatever was in the fridge while I went to get cleaned up. I showered, blow-dried and combed out my hair, threw on the merest hint of lipstick, and slid into a comfy but, hopefully, sexy green pantsuit.

By the time I got back to the kitchen, Mom was seated at the kitchen table with Derek. A bottle of wine sat between them.

Mom rose and gave me a squeeze. "Amy, Derek told me all about what happened." I had explained the circumstances of my standing in the freezing rain outside an empty house and my missing van to Derek on the drive back to my place. "You have to call Jerry!"

"I know," I said, reaching for a hunk of cheese from the platter on the table. "I don't suppose you want to do it for me?"

Mom rolled her eyes. "You're a big girl, Amy Simms. This is serious. Somebody stole your van." She pointed to my phone on the counter. "Now pick up that phone and call him. You agree with me, don't you, Derek?"

Derek nodded. He was grinning.

I picked up my phone. "I'll get even with you later," I vowed. I called the police station. To my relief, Chief Kennedy was out. Anita, the dispatcher, took the call. I explained the situation.

"There's been a big wreck out by the highway," Anita explained. "Everyone's all tied up. Are you okay?"

I said I was, and Anita promised to take down the report and said someone would get back to me. I left out the part about the exact location of my van when it was stolen.

"Don't worry," Anita said encouragingly. "I'm sure we'll find your Kia."

Sure, I thought, unless it's part of that wreck out near the highway.

"See, that wasn't so hard." Mom held a plate of her homemade cookies under Derek's nose. "Care to try one of my breakfast cookies, Derek?"

Behind my mother's back, I waved my hands and shook my head no, but he didn't seem to be getting the hint as his hand went out to select one. I cut between them. "Now, now, Derek. You don't want to spoil your dinner now, do you?" I pushed the tray toward my mother.

"Oh." Mom looked from me to Derek and back. "I didn't realize. Don't let me spoil your evening." Or kill my boyfriend, I thought. At least, he was my boyfriend for a little while longer, I supposed.

"Don't worry," I replied as I filled the carafe and started a fresh pot of coffee. "You won't." Whatever Derek wanted to talk about might, however. I needed a hot beverage. The rain had seeped into my bones. "I was thinking spaghetti." I reached into the cupboard for a box of noodles. "Is that okay with you?" Derek nodded his approval. I filled a six-quart pan with water and placed it on the stove to bring it to a boil.

"I can't believe that Walter Kimmel and Bessie Hammond were lovers," Mom said, fetching three mugs.

"And don't forget," I said, "Ed Quince was having, or had, an affair with Bessie, too."

"Ed Quince?" One of the mugs slipped from my mother's hand. Derek extended his hand and caught it. "Sorry."

I filled them both in on what Ed had told me about his relationship with Bessie. I also explained how Kim and I had found his pocketknife at the scene of the crime. "Well, not exactly at the scene of the crime, but near enough," I said. "And Ed didn't exactly have a plausible explanation for what his knife was doing there."

Derek nodded thoughtfully. "You turned the knife over to the police. I'm sure they'll examine it thoroughly."

"Actually . . ."

"Yes?" Derek's eyebrows rose.

"I gave the knife back to Ed."

"What?" Derek and my mom said in unison.

"Why on earth did you do that?" Mom asked.

"That knife could be evidence in a murder investigation, Amy," Derek complained. "You should have turned it over to the police the minute you found it."

I poured the coffee and reached for the sugar. "I felt sorry for Ed." I found a jar of tomato sauce in the pantry and brought it out.

Derek frowned. "Feel sorry for yourself." I cocked my head at him and he elaborated. "Because when Chief Kennedy finds out about this you are really going to be in hot water. And I'm not talking hot shower this time."

I sighed. No doubt Derek was right. "In the beginning," I said, searching the utensil drawer for the jar opener I knew was in there somewhere, "I could never imagine that anybody would want to harm, let alone murder, Bessie Hammond."

Unable to find the jar opener, I handed the jar to Derek. The top deftly came off in his hand. "Now, I'm seeing that plenty of men might have preferred shutting her up for good."

"Not only the men," Derek conjectured, "but their wives."

"What do you mean?" asked Mom.

"I saw Ed and Walter's spouses at Brewer's Biergarten the night of the Birds and Brews thing. No pun intended, but something was brewing under the surface with those two. I could feel it. Heck, I could see it." He turned to me. "You must have seen it too, Amy, right?"

I agreed. It would have been impossible to miss the tension in the room that night.

Derek continued. "They might not have wanted Bessie spreading stories about their straying husbands to their friends and neighbors."

"So true." I lifted the lid of the pot. Bubbles were forming nicely on the bottom. "Did I tell you that Kim broke up with Randy?" It was time for a change of direction in this conversation—take the heat off me, so to speak—so throwing Kim to the dogs seemed appropriate.

Both exclaimed their surprise.

"What happened?" demanded Mom, pulling up a chair beside me.

I went over the gory details of Randy's cheating on Kim with his ex. As I talked, my eye snuck looks across the table at Derek, in a search for clues. Was he doing the same? Cheating? Could it even be considered cheating if he was seeing his ex-wife romantically? Was that what he wanted to talk to me about?

There was a knock on the door. I answered it. It was Kim. Her clothes were wrinkled and her shoes and hair were dripping wet despite the long black raincoat that she had either neglected or forgotten to button up.

She slouched against the doorframe. "I hate my life."

20

I stared out the window. My chin rested atop the empty cash register. It was the middle of the day. There wasn't a customer in the shop and I couldn't stop yawning. Not only because of the lack of stimulation but Drummy, my wood-pecking nemesis, had started banging away at the tree outside my window at five thirty in the morning. Didn't he have anything better to do at five thirty in the morning? I knew I did.

I had stared and stared out across the lake toward the McKutcheon house. It had appeared as a dark silhouette against the predawn sky. I knew in my bones that the house held secrets.

And maybe a killer . . .

I'd spent the night tossing and turning. The evening before hadn't turned out as planned. Soon after Kim arrived, Derek had made his excuses and bailed. He said he didn't want to intrude on *girl talk*. The big coward. I still didn't know what he'd wanted to talk to me about.

Kim, Mom, and I had gabbed and commiserated into the wee hours of the morning and devoured a not very ladylike quantity of pasta and pinot.

I yawned again and felt a stabbing pain in the frontal lobe, a not-so-pleasant reminder of my night.

Maybe Derek and I not getting the opportunity to have a private conversation was a good thing. If he couldn't talk to me in private, he couldn't break up with me. Yeah. Maybe that would be my new strategy. All I had to do to keep my relationship with Derek going was to avoid him completely.

"Wake up!" Esther banged the sales counter with the point of her plastic-handled feather duster.

A cloud of dust filled my eyes and nostrils. I sneezed loudly and waved my hand in front of my nose. "Don't you ever shake that thing out?"

"I just did." Esther Pester thrust the feather duster into her apron tie and stomped off. She stopped in aisle two and glared back at me. "I thought you might want to be awake when that girl gets here."

"What girl?"

The door chimes tinkled and in walked Channing Chalmers in a pair of tight blue jeans, a simple white cotton tee, and leather sandals.

Esther pointed. "That one!"

I perked up and went out to greet her. "Sorry," I said, leading the girl inside. "I forgot you were coming today." My mind had been on other things besides new part-time employees: little things like who killed Bessie Hammond, what did Derek want to talk to me about, how was Kim doing post-breakup, and how to save my friend Moire from that player Gus McKutcheon. Not to mention, my stolen van.

"Is there a problem?" Channing looked concerned.

"No, no," I assured her. "Things are a little slow at the moment, so this will be perfect." I rubbed my hands for warmth.

"Slow isn't the word for it," mumbled Esther.

I ignored her. "Let's see," I said, taking a turn around the store. "Where should we start?" I paused. Across the street, I spotted Gus McKutcheon. He walked out to his pickup truck, climbed inside, and drove off in the direction of his house.

Channing tapped me on the shoulder. "Is everything okay, Amy?" Her full, wine-colored lips pushed out.

"Huh?" This would be the perfect time to talk to Moire Leora, woman to woman. "Esther?" I waved my employee-slash-renter-slash-pest over. "Would you mind taking over for a few minutes? Show Channing around?"

"I suppose." Esther scrutinized the young woman up and down and Channing looked back rather uneasily. I couldn't say that I blamed her. I felt a little bad leaving her in Esther the Pester's clutches, but now was the time to strike while the striking was good. I'd already seen one good friend get dumped on by a guy. I couldn't let it happen to another. Not on my watch.

"Great. Channing, this is Esther. Esther, this is Channing." I untied my apron and handed it to Channing. "I'll be at the diner if you need me. I won't be long. Promise."

I took a deep breath before opening the door to the Ruby Diner. It was showtime. Moire Leora stood at the register in full uniform. The diner was half-empty. It was no accident that I'd chosen the middle of the afternoon to try to talk with her. This was the midday slump. There'd be fewer distractions. The biggest distraction being Gus McKutcheon. It would have been impossible to talk to my friend with him in the kitchen.

"Hi, Moire, can I talk to you for a minute?" Out of

the corner of my eye, I saw Lana watching us from a stool at the counter. Apparently, she was on break. Was it me she was interested in or Moire, her potential rival for Guster McKutcheon?

"Sure," Moire replied lightly. "There's a free table right up front. We can chat there."

I would have preferred someplace more private, away from the prying eyes and ears of staff, especially certain staff like Lana Potter, but didn't know how to say so without sounding crazy.

"Want some coffee?" she asked, as she reached behind the counter and poured a cup for herself. My friend Tiffany waved as she refilled the water glasses of a pair of customers seated at the counter. I waved back.

"No, thanks." I was so nervous about what I wanted to say, my stomach was already churning like a sea in a hurricane. I didn't need the additional acid rolling around in my gut. I sidestepped around a worker running a damp mop over the terrazzo floor and followed Moire.

"So," Moire said as we settling across from each other in the small booth near the door, "what's up, Amy?"

Suddenly, I didn't know how to begin. My gaze wandered across the street to Birds & Bees and Brewer's Biergarten. The brew pub, too, was in the midst of a midafternoon lull, with only a few tables in the courtyard occupied. "Did you know Gus came to the Birds and Brews event the other night?"

Moire smiled as she dumped a packet of artificial sweetener into her cup. "I'm trying to watch the calories." She stirred slowly. "Sure, he told me. I'm sorry I couldn't make it."

"You knew about it?"

"Sure, you invited us, remember? I wasn't able to get away." Moire sipped. She turned her head as the phone behind the register rang. "Gus said he had a good time. Is there a problem?"

Tiffany called out, "I'll get it!"

"No, no problem." I studied my fingernails. "I didn't realize he was interested in birds."

Moire shrugged lazily and rubbed her neck. "Gus is a man of many interests. And talents." She smirked lasciviously.

I felt my cheeks turn pink. I could have used a glass of ice water. I grabbed a napkin from the dispenser and twisted it in my hands. "I take it things are going well with Gus?"

"Very well." Moire clasped her hands, arms extended across the table. "Why?"

"I'm—I mean, how well do you know him, Moire? Gus Mc-Kutcheon has only been in town a short while."

"So?"

"So, I'm worried that maybe you don't know him as well as you should."

Moire leaned back, a look of amusement on her face. "You're worried about me, Amy? I'm a grown woman. A grown woman who's been alone too long."

"I know that. I understand that." Since Moire's husband died, she'd managed to make a good life for herself. But, until now, there hadn't been a steady man in her life that I was aware of.

"Then what does it matter to you how well I do or do not know Gus?" Her eyes beat into mine. "And what business of yours is it, anyway?"

My ears heated up. I tore the napkin to shreds and entwined the pieces back into a wrinkled lump. "I don't want to see you get hurt, Moire."

She folded her arms over her chest. "Gus makes me happy, Amy. Very happy."

I shifted in the booth. This was not going the way I'd planned or wanted. I decided to be blunt. "Where was he the day I saw the body get thrown out of the bedroom window of his house, Moire? Where was he when Bessie Hammond was murdered on his property?"

"He was around here somewhere—working in the diner when Bessie was killed." She pushed up from the booth.

"Around here somewhere? It doesn't sound like you're very sure where Gus was."

"Whatever, Amy." She looked at me with growing disgust. "Not that it's any of your business, but I have no idea where he was the day of your reported sighting of a body flying out of the window of his house."

She threw back her head as she laughed. "Gus is a big boy and I run a busy diner. I have more important things on my mind than keeping track of my boyfriend every minute of the day. Maybe you'd do better in your relationships yourself if you did the same and stayed out of everyone else's business."

That last barb of Moire's stung, though I didn't let it show. "I'm sorry, Moire." I held up my hands in supplication. "I only wanted—"

"And, furthermore, I don't care where he was!" Moire cut me off. Her voice filled the diner now as she leaned over me. "Because from what I hear, there was no body thrown out of a window. That was all your imagination." Moire tapped the side of her skull with her finger, then snatched her cup from the table. "Your overactive imagination."

I slid toward the end of the booth toward her. "Moire, if I could just—"

Her hand sliced the air between us. "We're done here, Amy."

"But, Moire, if I could only—"

"In fact," interjected Moire, refusing to let me finish a sentence or a thought, "I think it would be best if you didn't come back."

I felt as if every eye in the diner was on me now. I dropped the ragged paper napkin on the table, grabbed my purse from the booth bench, and scooted out past Moire. Her face livid, she shook her head at me in disgust, then stomped off to the kitchen.

Hanging my head, I made a beeline for the door like a scolded dog with its tail between its legs.

I felt a hand on my shoulder. "We need to talk," Lana told me.

Through the window between the kitchen and counter, Moire glared in my direction.

"Now is not a good time," I said, feeling defeated and humiliated. "No doubt you heard all that."

Lana smiled grimly. "I heard. How about later?"

"Sure," I said, though I couldn't imagine what the woman and I had to talk about. "Where do you live? Maybe I can stop by after work." Was she living with Gus? Had she been the woman I'd seen looking out the attic window of the McKutcheon house the night I'd gone for dinner? If so, why had she stayed out of sight the entire time I was there?

Lana was shaking her head even as I spoke. "No, not my place. I get off shift in a couple of hours. I'll stop by."

Moire's burning eyes hadn't left me and I was only half listening. "Sure, whatever." I waved weakly and stumbled outside. Unsure what to do next.

The squeal of brakes startled me and I looked up. The bus had pulled up at the curbside. Passengers spilled out while others waited to climb aboard.

Glancing through the big front windshield, I recognized Neal the bus driver, his blue-gray cap atop his curly dark hair. I squeezed past the now boarding passengers. "Hi, Neal. Amy Simms, remember me?"

"Birds and Bees, across the street. Sure," he replied, his voice neutral.

A woman's elbow jostled me. "Ouch." Right in the ribs. I squeezed closer to the driver. "Do you have a minute to talk?"

"Are you kidding? I've got a schedule to keep." He motioned with his chin toward his waiting passengers. "Are you in or out?"

"In," I said, making up my mind quickly. If riding the bus was the only way I'd get to talk to him, then the fare was a small price to pay. I threw a couple of dollars into the acrylic money box beside him. Every seat was taken but that was okay by me. I wanted to stick as close to Neal as possible.

He levered the doors shut and told everyone who wasn't seated to hang on. That included me. I grabbed the chrome overhead bar and held tight as he eased into traffic.

We chugged along a bit, then came to a stop at a red light. While we idled, I said, "I was hoping I'd run into you again."

"Oh, yeah?" replied Neal, without taking his eyes off the traffic signal. "What for?"

The light changed and I about fell over as we lurched forward. I adjusted my footing. "You remember Bessie Hammond?"

"Dead lady," he replied. "What about her?"

"Do you remember, the morning she rode your bus, did she have a camera with her?" I went on to describe the camera as best I could.

"Hmm." He removed his left hand from the big steering wheel and idly rubbed his paunch. "I remember the binoculars. You don't see a whole lot of riders with binoculars. Cameras, yes. Especially in tourist season." He pulled his eyes from the road a moment and glanced my way. "Can't say as I remember any camera though."

"Are you sure?" I asked as we pulled to a stop at the edge of the town square.

"Town square!" Neal shouted. "Food, shopping, and bureaucrats!" Besides the surrounding shops, in the center of town square sits Ruby Lake's government offices and courthouse.

The front and rear doors of the bus hissed opened and many folks took off. A few others climbed on.

"Are you sure Bessie didn't have a camera?" I asked again.

"No, I'm not sure at all," the driver replied, his hand clutching the mechanism that opened and closed the bus's doors. "Are you in or are you out?"

I didn't know what to say next. I couldn't blame him for not being sure. Like Neal said, plenty of people walked around with cameras, particularly during the tourist months. Chasing Bessie's camera had come to a dead end.

"Well?" Neal demanded.

"I'm out. Thanks for the ride." I stepped down into the late afternoon heat. I was miles from Birds & Bees and light-years from figuring out who'd killed Bessie Hammond and why.

21

Walking up Main Street, I glanced in the window of the Italian Kitchen and spotted Annika and Dominik, two of Gus McKutcheon's guests, seated at a table near the front. The pair were having a heated conversation. They didn't appear to have noticed me. I wondered what they were so upset about. There was only one way to find out.

Though I had little appetite, I stepped into the restaurant and asked for a table for one. There were two small tables near the young couple and I wanted to get as close as I possibly could. At my whispered request, the hostess seated me nearby. I hoped they didn't spot me or recognize me if they did.

I took a seat at the table with my back to Annika and Dominik and perused the menu. The Italian Kitchen is a small, casual restaurant serving up mouthwatering, if carb- and calorie-filled, pasta dishes. I ordered the spaghetti marinara and a glass of ice water.

Unfortunately, Annika and Dominik seemed to be speaking in German or something similarly unfamiliar to me. It didn't look like I'd be getting anything out of this except another thousand calories that I most definitely did not need. I sipped my water, listening to the incessant babble. Whatever they were discussing, it was Annika who was doing most of the talking, and she didn't sound happy. In fact, it sounded like she was admonishing her boyfriend, beating him up pretty good, in fact.

"Amy!"

I looked up. Tiffany LaChance was beaming at me. "Hello, Tiffany." I waved to an empty seat. "Join me?"

"Sorry." Tiffany shook out her blond hair. She wore a soft pink jumper with silver stitching. "I'm here with Aaron." She suddenly appeared stricken. "I'm sorry. You don't mind, do you?"

"No," I said quickly. "Of course not. Not at all." Aaron Maddley and I had sort of dated, and only briefly. And even that had been sort of pretend, as I had been using him to help me get some information involving another murder. I had then pretty much accused him and his sister of that murder and our relationship had been icy ever since. I now noticed Aaron, seated alone at a booth in the back corner.

"Thanks. I wouldn't want to do anything that would make you uncomfortable."

"Like I said, no problem. I wish you both the very best. Speaking of which, I suppose you heard about the breakup?" Kim and Tiffany had become close friends, so I wouldn't have been surprised that Kim had filled her in on her fresh breakup with Randy.

Tiffany nodded. "I saw the dress. I'm so sorry." She clasped my hand in hers.

"Dress?"

"Uh-huh. The wedding dress. It really is beautiful." She patted my arm. "Sorry, I know I shouldn't be saying that."

I leaned back in my chair and narrowed my eyes up at her. "What exactly *are* you saying, Tiff?"

Tiffany swallowed, then said, "I was working at the diner earlier when Derek came in and had lunch with Amy, the other Amy, that is. And his daughter." Words continued spilling out of her mouth as I gaped at her. "Amy had the most amazing wedding gown. Her friend brought it right into Ruby's Diner. I was so afraid I might spill something on it. Could you imagine if I spilled coffee on a brand-new wedding gown?" I eyeballed her as she prattled on. "But Amy was so happy. She said not to worry because it was covered in one of those clear plastic dress bags."

"Huh." I felt a numbness spreading through me. A wedding dress? Amy the Ex? Happy? Those three things, certainly those last two, didn't normally go together.

"Amy, the other Amy, said Maeve was getting a dress made, too."

"How-how nice," I stammered. Maeve was Derek and Amy the Ex's young daughter.

"Well, I've got to get back to Aaron. I don't want him thinking I'm ignoring him."

"No, we wouldn't want that."

Tiffany catwalked her way back to her spot across from Aaron Maddley. I couldn't blame her for the slinky walk; the woman was built for it. She couldn't help herself.

My waiter deposited a huge bowl of spaghetti covered in tomato sauce. Enough to feed a horse. Unfortunately, I felt like I'd just been kicked in the gut by one.

The waiter grated some fresh parmesan on top of my pasta until I motioned for him to stop, then departed. I turned my attention to Annika and Dominik, hoping they'd get to speaking English for a change. I listened a moment but didn't hear a sound. I twisted slowly in my chair. They were gone.

I don't know how I did it, but I managed to polish off my meal and a tiramisu for dessert. Some say misery loves company, but I think maybe misery loves calories.

Back on the street, I turned in the direction of Harlan and Harlan. I considered going by and saying hello. But I also considered that I might be making a fool of myself, what with the whole Amy the Ex and her wedding dress thing going on.

My cell phone rang and I looked at the screen. It was my mother.

"I just got off the phone with Anita, who just got off the phone with Jerry Kennedy."

"Oh?" I replied, worried. Anything having to do with the chief of police could not be good news, at least for me. "What's up?" As I listened, I saw Amy the Ex walking out of the law offices of Harlan and Harlan, hand in hand with her daughter, Maeve. The two smiled and waved at a person unseen inside, then started my way.

I'd dodged a social bullet.

"He's found your van," continued Mom. "Isn't that wonderful?!"

I said it was. I tucked my head, turned and pressed my nose to a boutique's display window to keep from being spotted by the two of them.

"Is it all right?" I only hoped the van was in one piece and drivable. I knew "good as new" was too much to hope for. The Kia hadn't been "good as new" for as long as I'd been driving it. Nonetheless, hopefully it hadn't been trashed. Maybe whoever had stolen it had decided that the old wreck was too embarrassing to be seen in and brought it back.

"He wants you to go down to the station right away."

Maeve and Derek's ex passed by me on the sidewalk without incident.

I promised I'd go straight there after getting Mom's assurances that everything was under control at Birds & Bees. As I waited, I moved under the awning of a perfume shop to get out of the sun. The bus arrived fifteen minutes later but with an unfamiliar driver. "Does this bus go to the police station?" I asked, climbing aboard.

"This bus goes everywhere, lady," replied the hefty driver, running a hand through a curly black beard. "Are you in or are you out?"

Apparently the Town of Ruby Lake cut all their bus drivers from the same cloth. I threw a couple of bucks in the box. "I'm in." The truth was, I was probably in over my head.

Inside the police station, I found Officer Sutton seated at his desk while Officer Reynolds handed a paper cup filled with coffee to a distraught-looking woman with a short brown bob, seated by the door. She'd been biting her nails.

"Thanks," she said quietly, setting her oversized purse on the floor. She'd clearly been crying.

A redheaded man was seated in a visitor's chair across from Chief Kennedy's desk. I couldn't tell who he was because his back was to me.

"Chief will be with you in a minute, Miss Simms," Officer Reynolds said. "You want a coffee?"

I declined—I'd had their coffee and it was worse than mine—and took a chair next to the woman. "How's my van?"

Reynolds smiled enigmatically. "Talk to the chief."

Sutton's desk was directly in front of me. I avoided

looking at him for fear he'd somehow figure out that I had been in Bessie Hammond's house when he'd been there.

A couple of minutes passed in silence and I'd about dozed off when the man at Jerry's desk stood and the two came to the front of the station. The stranger was a head taller than Jerry, who was a couple inches shy of the six-foot mark.

The woman beside me, who so far hadn't uttered a word, stood also. "Well?" she asked, her voice nasally.

"We'll do all we can, Mrs. Garfinkle," Jerry said, patting her shoulder paternally.

"Thanks, Chief," the young man said. He wore cargo shorts and a black football jersey. Up close, I saw that his face was badly sunburned. Was that the explanation for the aloe odor emanating from his direction? "If you hear anything at all about JJ, we'll be staying out at the Bellewood B&B for a few more days."

"I've got your number," Jerry replied. "In the meantime, I wouldn't be worrying too much. I'm sure he'll turn up sooner or later. Some folks get impetuous when they are on holiday."

I stared at Jerry in surprise.

The woman crooked her arm in her husband's and they left.

"Impetuous?" I said with a smirk. "I didn't think you even knew the word." Jerry hadn't been the brightest student in school. "What was that all about?"

"Some fella and his wife looking for his brother. They were supposed to meet up here in town." The chief planted his hands, one on his hip, the other on his holstered pistol. "What do you want?"

"My van."

A dangerous smile appeared on Jerry's face. "Oh,

yeah." He was beaming now. "The stolen van. Have a seat." He extended his hand toward his desk in the rear. He and Officers Sutton and Reynolds exchanged looks and I followed with a growing sense of unease.

"What's that smell?" sniffed Officer Sutton as I scooted past his desk.

I craned my neck. "What smell?"

Sutton tilted up his nose and sniffed the air. "I don't know." Sniff. Sniff. "Smells familiar though. Smells like—" Sniff. Sniff. "Daisies."

"Simms!" shouted Chief Kennedy.

As I hurried to Kennedy's desk, I braved a whiff of my underarm. Good grief. That was my daisy-fresh deodorant Sutton was smelling. He must have caught the scent when I was hiding in Bessie's shower. I only hoped he didn't put two and two together and remembered where he'd last smelled that particular scent.

If he did, I just might be pushing up daisies.

I sat and crossed my legs and waited while Jerry made a show of fiddling with some papers on his desk. Probably his lame attempt at creating drama and raising the tension.

I uncrossed and crossed my legs a couple more times. His lame attempt was working.

Jerry leaned back in his seat and laced his fingers behind his head. "So, you had your van stolen. What happened, Amy? You leave the keys in the vehicle? Because that would be dumb, Simms. Dumb, dumb, dumb." He shook his head with each word, the stupid grin never leaving his face.

"Cut it out, Jerry," I snapped. I was angry and embarrassed. The anger was directed at myself for leaving the keys in the ignition and putting myself in the position I was in now—a position in which I was made to look stupid and Jerry Kennedy was getting the better of me. "You know darn well I left the keys in the van." I folded my arms over my chest and glared at him. "I was in a hurry. I simply forgot them."

"In a hurry, huh?" Jerry tilted forward. He picked up a ballpoint pen and aimed it at me. "To do what exactly?"

"What? What do you mean to do what?" I shook my head, flustered. "I don't know. I don't remember. What does it matter? You got it back. How about letting me have the keys so I can get out of here?"

Jerry rolled the blue pen around between his palms. "How about telling me what you and your van were doing on Peace Street?"

I blushed.

"Only one block over from Ivy." He looked at me like he was studying a curious specimen with six legs under a microscope. "Funny coincidence that."

I pressed my tongue into my teeth.

"Did you know Bessie Hammond lived on Ivy? In fact, she lived in the house directly behind the house where your van was stolen from."

I felt my neck stiffen. It was as if Jerry was tightening a noose around my throat. "Is that so?" I managed to say.

He nodded. "That's so. Do you want to tell me what the heck you were doing out there, Simms?"

I cleared my throat. Just my luck, some thug steals my van and I end up in trouble. "If you must know—"

Jerry glared at me. "I must."

Officer Sutton chuckled in the background. I turned and gave him the stink eye.

"Sorry," Sutton said. "Got a funny text on my phone." He held up his cell phone as evidence. I didn't believe him for a second.

"If you must know," I began again, returning my attention to Jerry. "I was looking at a house."

"Yeah," quipped Jerry. "The question is: whose house?"

"A house that was for sale. You can check it out yourself, if you don't believe me. I was parked, perfectly legally," I added, feeling my confidence rising, "on Pea Street—"

"Peace Street," corrected Jerry, clearly amused.

"That's right, Peace Street, to look at a house that is currently for sale."

"You've got a house. Or rather an apartment *in* a house," Jerry said.

"It's for a friend."

"What friend, Simms?"

I wriggled. "Kim, if you must know."

Jerry snorted. "Kim's got her own house." He leaned forward threateningly and I felt myself edge back. "Admit it, Simms. You were there because you wanted to get a look at Bessie Hammond's house. You weren't thinking of breaking in, were you?"

"No."

"You trying to play detective again?"

"No, of course not." I wiped a hand down my blouse, chasing away invisible crumbs. "Yes, of course Kim has her own house. But she's looking to move and I told her I would check the place out."

He narrowed his eyes at me. "Why would Kim be thinking of moving? She's got a perfectly good house, too."

I thought fast. Not well, but fast. Sorry, Kim, I thought

before saying, "Because she just broke up with Randy Vincent and her house holds too many bad memories."

Jerry fell back into his chair in surprise. "Well, well. Is that so?" He shot an inscrutable look at his officers.

"Yes, Randy's back with Lynda. But I'd appreciate it if you didn't spread the news around."

"No, no," Jerry said rather smoothly. "Course not, course not."

Sutton lifted his head. "Kim's broke up with Randy?"

"Hey, that's something," Reynolds said from his own desk.

Oh, Lord, what had I done? I'd thrown Kim to the dogs. Or in this case, hound dogs. Within hours the entire town would be talking about Kim's ugly breakup. I might as well have had a billboard made up with the announcement in three-foot-tall letters.

"My van," I interjected. Good grief. It was like a feeding frenzy of bull sharks that had sensed fresh blood in the water. Jerry was married, heaven help his clearly sainted wife, but the other two were single. "Can I have my van?"

"It's out back," Jerry said, returning his attention to me.

"Is it, is it okay?" I could not afford to be buying a new vehicle.

"Good as it ever was. Don't you ever wash that thing?"

I ignored the remark. "Who took it? How did you get it back?"

Jerry explained. "A couple high school–age boys spotted it."

"On Peach Street?"

"Peace Street," the chief corrected. "Saw the keys sitting in the Kia and took it as an invitation to go for a little joyride."

"Ohmygosh."

"A few hours later, they either got tired, noticed the gas tank was nearly empty, or got scared. In any event, they dropped the van off outside the police station."

"And you caught them?"

"Actually"—Jerry shifted—"Anita was looking right out the front window and saw the boys run off."

"I recognized them straightaway," said Anita, coming in from her little communications cubby. "I phoned their parents, and their parents, well, let's just say I don't think Tommy and Michael McKillip will be causing any more mischief anytime soon."

I nodded. There was a pencil stuck in the loose bun atop Anita's head.

"You want to press charges?" Jerry inquired.

I thought about it for a second. "No, I suppose not. You did say the van is okay, right?" I needed some reassurance.

"Same hunk of junk it's always been."

"Then no."

"I think you're doing the right thing, Amy," said Anita. "Believe me, those boys have learned their lesson."

I'd learned mine, too. Always remove the key from the ignition when leaving my van. I stood and extended my hand, palm up.

Jerry pulled open his desk drawer, extracted my key ring, and gave it to me.

"Thanks."

"Don't mention it," Jerry said. He came around the desk and led me to the back door leading out to the police parking lot. "And don't you go near the Hammond house again. You've got no business there."

Anita followed us outside, announcing that her shift was over and she was heading home.

"Have you even bothered checking Bessie's house, Jerry? What if there's some evidence hidden there, like her camera with a picture of her killer?" The van sat wedged between a couple of police cruisers. It did look a bit tired in comparison to the slick and shiny squad cars.

Anita took my side. "Amy may have a point, Jerry."

"You and that camera again," groused the chief of police.

"Fine. I bet Bessie's camera is not even at the house," I goaded, as I reached the van. "I'll bet the killer took it. It and him are probably a hundred miles away and you'll never find either one of them!"

"That would be a sucker's bet, Simms."

"See? You agree with me!" I pointed an accusing finger.

He pushed my arm down. "Because we found that stupid camera you were yammering about, down by the lake."

"By the lake?" I felt my resolve leaking away like the air that seemed to have leaked away from my left front tire.

"That's right." The chief grinned smugly. "Bessie must've dropped it when she was bird-watching the day she was murdered."

"Are you certain it's hers?"

"It's got her prints on it and matches the description we got from you and the others in your bird-watching group."

"And?"

"And what?"

"What's on the camera? Did you learn anything?"

Jerry planted his hands on his hips, elbows out like a couple of chicken wings. "Yeah, I learned that Bessie liked to take boring pictures of birds and flowers."

"So there was nothing—"

Kennedy knew exactly where I was going. "No," he interrupted. "No mug shots of her killer, no secret messages. Nothing."

"Can I take a look?"

"Sorry." He smirked. "Evidence. You'll have to wait for the DVD release to come out." He shot a warning look at Anita, then said, "And don't you go showing that camera to her."

Anita vowed that she wouldn't and, unfortunately, I believed her. She's a stickler for the law.

"So who killed her, Jerry? Tell me that."

"I don't know," Jerry admitted. "Yet." He tapped the side of his skull. "But I've got my theories."

"Yeah," I said, "and they probably involve UFOs and little green men."

"Or widows in the lake," Anita added.

I gave her a high five.

Jerry give us a middle finger salute and trudged off.

22

The following morning, I loaded up the van with a variety of birdseed the store had collected over the month in contributions to our Seeds for Seniors program. It was an initiative I'd started a while back to provide birdfeeders and bird food to retirement homes in the area.

So far, we were supplying feeders and food to five senior living facilities. I'd been encouraged by the results and hoped there would soon be more. Watching and feeding the wide variety of birds in this part of the Carolinas had given a psychological boost to our senior residents.

And now that I had my van back, I was good to go. I could deliver some of the bags of seed that had been accumulating and, since one of those stops was Rolling Acres, I could have a word or two with Walter and Clara Kimmel. Had Ed Quince been telling the truth, or was he attempting to misdirect me in hinting that Bessie and Walter may have been doing the two-timing tango? He must have been telling the truth, because what else could explain the notes from Walter that I'd found in

Bessie's nightstand? Unless the Walt in the letters was another person altogether.

"That lady from Ruby's Diner was in to see you," said Esther, as I shouldered a twenty-pound bag of mixed seed out to the van. She did not offer to help. But that was okay. I suspected she'd collapse under the weight.

"Get the door for me, would you?" Esther leaned against the back storeroom door and I eased past her. "What woman? Moire?" Did this mean all was forgiven? I was heartbroken over our little tiff and hoped it wouldn't mark the end of our friendship.

"No, that one that looks like a she-wolf."

I dropped the sack on the floor of the van. Only one woman I knew fit that two-word description. "Lana Potter?"

"Yep. That's the one."

"What did she want?" I asked, returning to the store. I grabbed two bags of safflower seeds. Squirrels don't like safflower seeds, but birds do.

"She said she needed to talk to you."

I paused, bags in hand. "That's right. She did mention wanting to talk." About what, I still couldn't imagine. If it had anything to do with Gus, Moire, and her, I was staying out of it. I carried the remaining supplies out to the van, tossed them in and shut the door. Turning to Esther, I said, "Are you sure you can manage alone for a little while?"

"That Channing will be in around noon. Barbara's baking upstairs but said she'd come down if things get busy."

"Great." I'd left my mother upstairs baking more of her breakfast cookies. Anita was with her. They were each in good hands. My kitchen, however, I feared for.

Too bad woodpeckers, and birds in general, have such a poorly developed sense of smell, Mom's breakfast cookies could have made a natural and harmless woodpecker repellant. "How's Channing working out?"

"She'll do."

That was high praise coming from Esther. "If Ms. Potter comes by again, tell her I'll stop by the diner when I get a chance." Then I caught myself as I remembered Moire's admonition that I stay away from Ruby's Diner. "Better yet, ask Ms. Potter to leave me her number. I'll call her when I can. I don't suppose you know where she lives, do you, Esther?"

"What am I, a phone book? When's Kim coming in?" Esther demanded.

"Kim may not be in for a couple of days." I reminded myself to call or stop in and check on her. A little alone time would do her good, but too much alone time was probably not a good thing. Perhaps I could get her involved in some other activities, something to get her mind off Randy.

"What's Kim's number?" Esther asked. "Maybe I ought to call her and tell her to stop her caterwauling and start earning a living."

"Why don't we let her have a couple of days to recover before we go the tough-love route?" I pulled open the driver's-side door.

"Humph," snorted Esther. She smoothed her oatmeal-colored cotton sweater, which clashed mightily with her bubblegum-pink slacks. I ignored what looked like two gray cat hairs on her sweater. "Your generation is too soft."

I let the jibe slide over me. "Say, Esther"—I slid my purse over to the passenger side—"would you mind watching my van for a minute? I forgot something."

Esther said she would, though she didn't sound happy about it. No big deal. She rarely sounded happy about anything. I, on the other hand, was downright ebullient because I had noticed that Esther did not have her ubiquitous feather duster in her hand or anywhere on her person.

I rushed inside the store, darting left and right. I discovered the feather duster lying on the kitchen counter. I picked it up, glanced out the window and saw Esther hovering near my van, then looked quickly around the store. Where, where, where?

Finally, I found the perfect spot. An owl nesting box stood on display attached to a ten-foot metal pole near the middle of the store. I grabbed the step stool from the storage closet under the stairs, climbed up, unhooked the latch of the owl house, and thrust the feather duster inside. Some owls use the old nests of other birds, like ravens or hawks. Other species of owls are cavity nesters. Here in the Carolinas, this included everything from the barn owl to the eastern screech owl.

Esther would never find her feather duster in the owl nesting box. Not in a million years. Assuming she lived another million years, and I wasn't putting it past her that she would.

I returned the step stool to its corner of the closet, wiped the dust off my hands and, hopefully, the look of guilt off my face, and returned outdoors.

"Thanks, Esther." I climbed in the van, smiled and waved as I watched her figure shrink in the distance.

I drove up the long, upward-sloping drive that cut through the pristine green lawn fronting ROLLING ACRES, A SENIOR LIVING FACILITY. There's a large main building with several areas with bungalows off to the right. My friend Floyd Withers lives in a condo in the main building. Karl Vogel, former Town of Ruby Lake chief of police, dwells in one of the larger bungalows.

I came to a stop beside an unmarked, late-model white van. Millicent Bryant, an elegant, forty-something brunette, had a desk in the lobby. She more or less runs the place. And she more or less hates me.

Why, I didn't know. What I did know was that she wouldn't be overly glad to see me.

Okay, maybe I did go behind her back and install that first bird feeder out on their lawn without strictly getting permission. But couldn't we get past that?

I took a bracing breath, exited the van, and grabbed the first two bags of birdseed. The bird feeder was for a small hospice that had heard about our program and requested we give them a visit. I had told their director I'd be delighted and would stop there on my rounds later.

I slammed the rear door of the van closed with my shoulder.

"Amy?"

I looked up. "John! What are you doing here?" It was my friend John Moytoy, from the Ruby Lake Public Library.

He cradled a stack of books in his arms. "Delivering these. We rotate a selection of books out here every two weeks, plus bring any requested items. How about you? Can I give you a hand?"

"That's okay. I've got it. Besides, I'd say you're the one who could use a hand."

John's eyes twinkled. "Going inside?" A black-rimmed pair of reading glasses stuck out of the chest pocket of his short-sleeve white shirt.

"As much as I'd prefer not to, yes."

John raised his brow. "Something going on that I don't know about?"

"Never mind," I said. No point bothering him with my petty feud with the haughty Millicent Bryant. And I did need to get inside. Ms. Bryant had grudgingly allowed me to stash the birdseed in a small storeroom inside the senior activity center. As much as she seemed to dislike birds, the residents had become enthralled with bird-watching and the woman, despite what I might think of her, had recognized a losing battle when she was facing one.

Walking side by side with John through the automatic doors and finding strength in numbers, we said hello to Millicent Bryant, who barely acknowledged my presence but waved heartily to John. "Good to see you, John!" she cooed.

"Good to see you, too, Millicent!"

"Good to see you," I muttered, struggling with my seed up the hall. "Good grief." I ignored the small trail of millet following me on the carpet. The tiniest of holes in the plastic bag and you were playing Hansel and Gretel, only this time instead of leaving a trail of breadcrumbs, we were John and Amy and we were leaving a trail of birdseed.

"Hear anything new about Ms. Hammond?" John asked as an attendant held the door to the activities center open for us.

"Not a thing, at least nothing useful." So far.

"The police aren't any closer to figuring out what she was doing alone in the woods and who murdered her?"

"If they are," I said, stooping and resting my bags on the floor so I could open the closet door, "they aren't telling me."

John settled his books on a nearby table. "It's almost surreal to think of her being murdered." He shook his head. "A nice older lady like that."

"Yeah," I said, "a nice older lady." Only was she?

"Say, that reminds me." John ran a hand through his wavy black hair. "Are you coming to the vigil?"

"Vigil?" I grabbed my birdseed scoop and poured some birdseed from one of the bags into a five-gallon plastic bucket I kept in the closet for the purpose. I'd carry the bucket out to the feeders and refill each with the handy scoop.

"Yes. You know, the widow in the lake? Saturday morning is the big day. The hundred and fiftieth anniversary, I think. This could be the one."

I grinned at him. "You mean the one where the widow, Mary McKutcheon, finally rises from the lake?"

John nodded. "How about joining me?"

I grabbed the bucket by its plastic handle. According to Derek, Amy the Ex and her friends were really into the whole widow-in-the-lake story. That meant Amy the Ex would be there at this vigil. Perhaps Derek, too. It also gave me another excuse for prowling around, out near the McKutcheon property. "What time?"

"Five a.m."

My brow shot up. "You're kidding, right?"

John shook his head in the negative. "So you'll be there?"

I reluctantly agreed. At the very least, Drummy the woodpecker wouldn't be waking me up Saturday morning. Because I'd be up before he could.

"Tell me," I said as John lifted his books and started for the bookshelves on the wall opposite, "do you believe in this whole 'widow in the lake rising on the anniversary of her death' story?"

John shrugged, the books pressed against his belly for support. "Let me put it this way, Amy. This is one crazy world. I don't disbelieve in anything."

We talked some more and agreed that we'd meet at Birds & Bees early Saturday morning. "I'll bring a thermos of coffee," I offered.

"Better let me," John replied, giving me a pat on the arm as if to say, *thanks, but let an expert handle this*.

I got even by suggesting I bring the snacks. John would be getting one of my mother's special breakfast cookies. I chewed my lip as my thoughts swirled around the widow in the lake and the corpse in the woods, and my eyes followed John's departing backside. He had one thing right: This is one crazy world.

I grabbed my supplies and left to complete my task. After filling the feeders, I didn't bother going back indoors. I angled across the back lawn and followed one of the concrete walkways that meandered down the hill to the bungalows. I'd made a note of Walter and Clara Kimmel's address before leaving Birds & Bees.

There were three one-story bungalows to a building. The Kimmels occupied an end unit with an enclosed patio off the front. I straightened my clothing, double-checked my hair and makeup in my compact mirror, then rang the bell. Strains of "I'm Gonna Wash That Man Right Outa My Hair" from the musical *South Pacific*, one of my favorite Rodgers and Hammerstein shows, came from within.

"Miss Simms!" a voice hissed.

I spun around. Walter Kimmel stuck his head up over the ivy-covered brick wall of the patio. "Hi, Walter."

"What are you doing here?" Walter's wavy gray hair was disheveled and his nose was red. His voice came out in stage whisper. "Are you here to see Clara in some regard?"

I shook my head no and moved closer to the wall. "Actually, I wanted a word with you."

Walter's Adam's apple bobbed up and down a couple of times. "Whatever for?"

"I wanted to talk to you about Bessie Hammond."

Walter shot a worried glance in through the sliding glass door, where a small dinette set and a brass chandelier were visible. "You'd better come in. There's a door on the other side of the patio." He waved me around and let me in.

He held a martini glass in his left hand. "Care for a drink?"

"No, thanks." I looked around. "Where is Clara?" It was going to be awfully difficult to interrogate Walter about his possible affair with Bessie Hammond if his wife was lurking nearby. Men were funny that way.

"Bridge club." He glanced at his watch. "She'll be back any time." He stood on his tiptoes and looked over the wall in the direction of the main building. "I'd rather she didn't find you here when she returns. Clara can be a bit difficult about these things."

"I'll bet. Don't worry, I won't be long."

"Wonderful." Walter offered me a seat in one of two webbed chaise lounges and took the other for himself. He crossed his legs and sipped. "Such a terrible, terrible thing about Bessie." He plucked at his trousers with his free hand.

"You know," I said, "everybody keeps saying that, yet somebody disliked her enough to murder her. Any idea who?"

Walter raised his martini to his lips and gulped. "Karl Vogel tells me the police are no closer to solving her murder now than they were at the beginning. Karl says Greeley hasn't been able to pin down the time of death to more than a three-hour window."

"Three hours. Anybody in Ruby Lake could have

gone out to the woods, snapped Bessie Hammond's neck, and gotten back to whatever they'd been doing before, in that amount of time." I leaned toward Walter. "Even you."

"Me?" Walter rested his glass between his legs and tugged at his shirt collar. "What a funny thing to say, Amy. Why would I, I mean, what reason might I have had to want to murder Bessie?" He feigned amusement, but I could see I was getting to him.

I shrugged. "You were having an affair with her. You wanted to break it off. Bessie didn't."

"That's preposterous!" Walter started to rise, spilling his drink all over his lap. "Damn!" he cursed and wiped madly at his trousers. He crossed the small space and slammed his empty glass down on the glass-top patio table. "I'm not sure I like what you are implying. What right have you to come here to my home and—"

"Walter, please," I said, "I don't mean to upset you. Sit." I patted his empty chaise lounge. "Please."

Walter frowned, hesitated, then sat heavily.

"Listen, Walter. I know that you and Bessie were"— how should I put this?—"involved. I'm sure you felt bad about it." Walter's head hung to his chest. "You wanted to break it off."

He looked at me now, forlorn and weary. "I did. I really did."

"But Bessie wasn't having it."

"No," confirmed Walter, his voice a mere whisper.

I could feel my heart pounding against my chest. This was harder than I had expected. "Did you have it out with her?"

Walter smiled grimly. "More than once." His eyes were on a housefly that had discovered his martini glass and was crawling round and round its edge.

"Did Clara know about the affair?"

"No."

"Are you sure?"

Walter shook his head fiercely and glared at me. "Yes. I'm sure. And I see no reason for you to tell her." There was a threatening undercurrent in his tone.

We sat in silence for a moment, nothing but the two of us, the housefly, and a buttery yellow swallowtail butterfly that skipped silently over the bed of Shasta daisies along the edge of the bungalow. "Where were you the morning Bessie was killed, Walter?" It was an awkward question but I had to know.

"Why are you asking *me* all these questions?" Walter said, belligerently. "Why aren't you asking Ed Quince where he was and what he knows about Bessie's murder?"

So, Walter knew about Bessie and Ed? How did that make him feel? Of course, Ed said he and Bessie had only gotten together once. Had that been the truth? "I did ask Ed." I didn't add that I'd found his pocketknife near the scene of the crime.

Walter frowned. "And what did he tell you?"

"He told me that he didn't do it."

Walter snorted.

"What about you, Walter?" I asked softly.

Walter opened his mouth to reply.

"He was with me," a hard-edged woman's voice replied.

I turned my head. Clara Kimmel stood in the open patio side door. Her hand was fisted around the strap of her black leather purse. She scowled at Walter. "Haven't you had enough to drink? And what have you done to your trousers?"

"Sorry," Walter mumbled.

"Go inside and change at once."

Walter headed for the sliding door.

"And take your glass with you."

"Yes, dear." Walter, shoulders sloping, plucked up his empty martini glass and disappeared inside, pulling the door closed behind him.

I rose. "Hi, Clara. I didn't mean to cause any trouble."

Clara said frostily, "My husband was with me. At church. As we are every Sunday morning. You should try it yourself sometime. If Bessie Hammond had been there herself, worshipping instead of doing whatever she was doing out in McKutcheon's woods, she might be alive now."

"She might," I couldn't help saying, "but would that make you any happier?"

Clara opened her mouth to reply, then clamped it shut. She marched to the sliding glass door. Turning to face me, she snapped, "You can show yourself out!"

The glass door rattled as she pulled it open and quickly closed it again behind her.

23

I hurriedly left the patio. Poor Walter. I wasn't any closer to knowing if he or his wife had been responsible for Bessie Hammond's death, but those two needed some marriage counseling before one of them killed the other.

I headed for my van before Clara came at me with a frying pan or a twelve-gauge shotgun, but I hadn't gone half a dozen paces when I heard a sound.

"Pssst! Pssst!"

I paused, frowning, and turned slowly.

Floyd Withers stood in the middle of the lawn outside the bungalow to the left of the Kimmels'. His hands were cupped around his mouth. "Amy!"

I hurried over. "Floyd." I gave him a quick embrace. "What are you doing here?"

"Man, that was some hubbub." Floyd laughed, keeping his voice low. He was dressed in baggy linen shorts, knee-high white socks, and a white VISIT RUBY LAKE T-shirt.

"You heard?"

"I think all of Rolling Acres might have heard!" Floyd's eyes twinkled with delight. He pulled at my sleeve.

"Come on, me and Karl are barbecuing on his patio."
That explained the hint of mustard on the tip of his mustache. "Join us."

Floyd led me over to Karl's bungalow. Karl, dressed
identical to Floyd, with the exception of darker shorts
and a KISS A COP apron tied behind his neck, was hovering like a mother hen over a stainless steel monster of a
barbecue grill.

Karl plucked a wet cigar from between his lips. "Hiya,
Simms. Come on in!" The ex-cop waved his greasy
spatula in the air. "What'll it be?"

Meat hissed on the grill. "What have you got?" Bits
of cigar ash fell onto the meat. I decided to consider it
seasoning.

"Burgers. If you want yours medium rare," he said,
giving the half-dozen patties on the grill a quick flip,
"there's still time."

Smoke filled the patio and billowed upward. "Let's
go with well-done," I said, waving the smoke from my
watering eyes. That would burn off at least some of the
cigar ash residue. Karl's patio was a mirror image of the
Kimmels', though his furniture was a notch better.

"Me and Karl always grill Friday afternoons when
the weather's good."

"Management doesn't mind?" I was surprised open
flames were allowed in the retirement community. I sank
into a cushioned wicker chair downwind and fanned my
hand in front of my nose again. If the flames didn't kill
anyone, the fumes might.

"Sure they mind," said Floyd, taking the seat beside
me. He offered me a can of beer and I accepted.

"We ignore them," Karl said.

"Yeah." Floyd clinked cans with me. "We ignore them."

I smiled and took a sip of cold beer. "I guess grilling

on your patio whenever you feel like it is one of the perks of being a retired chief of police."

"You betcha." Karl unwrapped a plastic-wrapped bag of white burger buns and took one. He opened it on a melamine plate and slid a hot burger onto it. "Help yourself to the fixings."

I rose and took my plate. "Thanks." Ketchup, mustard, chopped onion, and pickles sat on a leaf extended from the grill. A big bowl of potato salad covered in plastic stood on the patio table. "Nice grill," I said. Men have some weird genetic thing going on with grills. They like them big and they like them shiny. And they like them to be commented upon.

Karl grinned. "Thanks." He handed off a double burger to Floyd. "Speaking of grills," the former cop said, "that was quite a grilling you gave Walter Kimmel!"

Floyd snickered.

"You really heard that?" I blushed as I removed the plastic from the bowl, grabbed the big plastic spoon inside, and heaped some potato salad onto my plate. Had I been that loud? "I was trying to be discreet."

"Ha! You are a lot of things, Amy." Karl looked me over. "But discreet ain't one of them!"

"We only caught the tail end where Clara was hollering at you," explained Floyd, reclaiming his chair. "But we surmised the rest."

"The way the ground dips around here, it's like being in an echo chamber or something," Floyd put in. "You'd be surprised what a person can hear."

"I'll keep that in mind," I said. I sat and bit into my burger. "Wow, this is delicious, Karl."

"Thanks." Karl hovered over the grill, half-eaten burger in one hand and greasy spatula in the other.

I gave them the gist of what I'd learned from Walter

Kimmel and Ed Quince. I didn't mention that I'd broken into—or at least, slipped into—Bessie Hammond's house. Even ex-chiefs-of-police might not be willing to overlook that infraction.

"Church, you say?" That was Floyd.

"That's what Clara told me, that she and Walter were attending services at the time Bessie was murdered."

"They attend the same church as me." Floyd was shaking his head. "I don't recall either of them being in church last weekend." He absently scratched behind his ear. "I don't recall seeing Ed there either."

"What about you, Karl?" I inquired. "Do you remember if they were there?"

"Not me," Karl said with a chuckle. "I'm a bit of a heathen these days. I never did care for sitting in a pew."

"What do you know about Gus McKutcheon, Karl?"

"Not a whole lot," Karl admitted. "Old town family, everybody knows that. But I don't know a darn thing about the kid. You want me to see what I can find out?"

I told him I would very much appreciate it. "How about Lana Potter?"

"Who?"

"The sexy new waitress over at Ruby's Diner," Floyd replied quickly. "I've met her. Wow." He held out his empty plate and Karl obliged him with another burger. For a small fellow, Floyd had a big appetite. "She's a real man-killer."

"You may have hit it right on the nose, Floyd."

"What do you mean?" Floyd squirted an extravagant amount of mustard on his burger patty.

I told Floyd and Karl how I suspected that Lana Potter and Gus McKutcheon were playing house. I added how Moire seemed be involved with him, too, and the way he'd practically taken over running her business.

Karl nodded thoughtfully. "And all the while, this McKutcheon fellow is cozying up to Moire Leora, too?"

"It looks that way, Karl." I chomped down on my burger. "I don't know a thing about her. Where does she live? Where did she come from? What's going on with her and Gus?"

"Sounds like a real woman of mystery," piped in Floyd.

Karl winked at me. "Don't worry, if there's any dirt to be found on this Lana woman, I'll find it."

"Thanks. I'd appreciate it. I'm worried. I don't want to see Moire get hurt."

"She's nice," agreed Floyd.

We discussed Bessie's murder some more. I'd hoped that Karl, as a former chief of police, might have heard something that I hadn't, but it wasn't the case. "Can either of you think of anyone else who might have wanted Bessie out of the way?"

"Well . . ." replied Karl.

"What?" I leaned forward, resting my empty plate on my lap.

"Well, it's only a rumor, mind you. And I don't know that it's related . . ."

"Stop prevaricating and spit it out already," Floyd scolded.

Karl fixed us with his gaze. "Some years ago, there was a rumor going around that Arthur Hammond—"

"Bessie's husband?" I asked.

Karl nodded and continued. "Anyway, I heard tell that Arthur and Ms. Newsome had, well . . ." He wrapped his middle and index fingers together.

"Otelia Newsome and Bessie's husband had an affair?" She had to be way younger than him.

Floyd nodded. "I heard that, too. I don't know if there's any truth to it."

Karl's eyes twinkled mischievously. "Maybe there is and maybe there isn't." Karl scraped the grill with a steel brush as he spoke. "I tell you this though." He aimed the brush at me and Floyd. "Arthur sure did like his chocolate."

Otelia Newsome ran a chocolate shop. And maybe Bessie slept with Ed, Walter, and who knew who else to exact her revenge on her cheating husband? All well and good, but it didn't get me any closer to solving who had killed Bessie herself. "What about Otelia's husband?"

"Never married," answered Karl.

"That's right," parroted Floyd. "She never married."

Karl popped open a beer. Tiny bubbles spewed over his hand and he shook his wrist. "She always says she's married to her business."

"If what you say about Arthur and Otelia is true," I said, "it would have given Bessie a reason to want Otelia dead, not vice versa."

"The two women might have struggled," Karl said. "In a fight, generally, there is your winner and there is your loser."

"And Bessie might have been the loser," I finished. Otelia Newsome was definitely the younger, stronger, and healthier of the two women. But after all these years, even if it was true, would a long-ago affair have led to a murder now?

Maybe. Bessie's murder could easily have been a crime of passion; so many murders are. And passion can linger and simmer and stew for years and years.

"I hope Otelia didn't kill anybody," Floyd said. "I like her chocolate, especially the banana rum bonbons. They were my wife's favorite, too."

"Tell me," I said, between sips of the beer I'd been nursing since arrival. "What do the two of you make of this whole widow-in-the-lake story?"

"My wife thought it was hooey," Floyd said first. "I agree."

Karl leaned back in his chair, fingering his now cold cigar. "I heard that back in the forties, around the time of World War II, Mary came up out of Ruby Lake for a little look-see."

Despite myself, I felt the little hairs on my forearms rise. It must have been the cold brew. "You did?"

Karl nodded. "Probably nothing to it. It was a couple of fishermen who reported it, as I remember. One of them got so scared he fell out of their fishing boat and nearly drowned. At least, that's the story I heard." The ex-cop chuckled. "If you ask me, they were probably drunk and seeing ghosts in the fog."

I told them how I'd been roped into going down to Ruby Lake Saturday morning to await Mary McKutcheon's coming.

Karl chuckled. "If you do see Mary, tell her hello for me."

If I did see Mary, I'd be hightailing it out of town. Next, I'd be having my head examined. "The two of you could come," I suggested.

"Ha! You're not dragging me down to the lake at five in the morning." Floyd slopped a second or third helping of potato salad onto his plate. "I need my beauty rest."

"Me either," said Karl. "You can go looking for the widow in the lake on your own."

"Is it just me or is this widow-in-the-lake tale bigger this year than ever before?" Floyd scratched the tip of his nose. "I've lived in Ruby Lake all my life and I've never seen such a to-do about it in the past."

Karl agreed. "Same here. Something's got folks stirred up this year more than ever. I've seen widow-in-the-lake T-shirts and souvenirs being offered at the shops, and some other fella and his wife selling MARY MCKUTCHEON—WIDOW IN THE LAKE labelled souvenirs, like mugs and bowls, from the back of their van."

"Where was this?" I asked.

"Down by the lake. In the marina parking lot," Karl explained. "Yeah, if you ask me, this whole widow-in-the-lake thing is nonsense. But if old Mary was to come back, now would be a good time," he calculated. "She could really cash in on her star status."

Floyd chuckled. "It couldn't hurt to have a famous ghost in town. Might be good for everybody's business."

"Or scare everyone off. The specter of death has a way of spoiling vacations." I couldn't see the presence of ghost-seekers increasing my birdseed sales either. I told them how Gertie Hammer claimed that Bessie's husband had drowned in Ruby Lake on the anniversary of Bessie's own murder.

Karl toyed with his mustache. "Drowned or disappeared?"

I stiffened, my eyebrows rising. "Are you saying he didn't drown? That he disappeared?" Did the police know something the rest of us didn't?

"Maybe," Karl suggested, "this husband of hers didn't die, just left." The old man winked at me. "You said he died on his birthday. Maybe, just maybe, he instead gave himself his own birthday present."

I leaned forward. "You think?"

Karl shrugged. "All I'm saying is that his body was never found."

"Hey," said Floyd. "Maybe Arthur faked the whole thing to get away from Bessie!"

And maybe he came back to town a week ago to break her neck . . .

24

Otelia's Chocolates was a bright, shiny space with a black-and-white checked tile floor and spotless glass cases filled with chocolates of every size and description.

I inhaled deeply, reveling in the scent of fresh chocolate, knowing that breathing rather than eating wouldn't add inches to my waistline.

Otelia Newsome's shop is a mere half block from Birds & Bees on the opposite side of the street, nestled in the middle of a strip of stores catering mostly to the tourist trade.

I all but pressed my nose to the glass and drooled as I waited for Otelia to finish up with a family of tourists enjoying an afternoon treat.

"Hello, Amy," Otelia said, a big smile on her face as she peered at me from behind the counter. "See anything you like?"

"I see a lot that I like. I don't suppose any of this is low cal, low fat, by any chance?"

Otelia leaned over the display case. "I use real butter, real cream, and sacks and sacks of sugar."

"So that's a no?"

Otelia chuckled. "How about a sample of my pecan praline fudge?"

I didn't say no. "And I'll take a pound of the banana rum bonbons." They were Floyd's favorite. I'd sample a mere one or two and take him the rest.

"Sure thing." Otelia handed me a slice of fudge on a bit of wax paper and I closed my eyes in ecstasy. "If I worked here, I'd gain five pounds a week," I said when I reopened my eyes. I noticed a tray of hand-wrapped chocolate bars on the edge of the counter beside the cash register. "Don't tell me you're into the widow in the lake, too?"

Otelia noticed my eyes on her dark chocolate bars. "What can I say? The whole thing really seems to have taken off all over town." She handed me a plain white bag filled with my order of bonbons. "Did you know Ruby's Diner even has a Widow in the Lake special plate?"

I said I didn't.

"Yep. And free dessert all day if she appears tomorrow."

I fingered one of the Widow in the Lake chocolate bars. The image on the front showed Ruby Lake, the silhouette of the old McKutcheon house in the distance, and a spectral-looking Mary McKutcheon floating above the lake. "Interesting." It seemed that Otelia was already cashing in on the craze, just like Floyd had suggested.

"Isn't it? I had the wrappers made up at the print shop."

I told her to throw in a bar of chocolate. I paid in cash and Otelia gave me back a handful of change. I dumped it loose into my purse and fidgeted with its clasp.

"Is there anything else?" asked Otelia.

I looked around the empty shop. "Can I ask you a personal question?"

Otelia twisted up her brow. "Shoot." There were fine crow's feet at the corners of her eyes. I hadn't noticed them before.

"Did you get along well with Bessie?"

Otelia pulled off her white smock and came around to the front of the store. She slid the CLOSED, BACK SOON sign over the doorknob, then turned to me. "Don't tell me you've heard about my lurid affair with Bessie's husband, Arthur?" She waved her hands in the air.

"I don't mean to pry."

"Yet you're doing a good job of it." Otelia planted her fists on her hips. For a moment, I thought I was in trouble. Then Otelia laughed. "As a single woman in a small town, it seems I'm often the subject of a rumor or two."

I laughed with her but part of me wondered. I was a single woman, too. Were people making up stories about me?

The chocolatier blew out a breath. "We're talking a long time ago here. A long, long time ago." I waited. "One day Bessie came in here mad as a wet hen. She accused me of having an affair with Arthur. I tried to calm her down, convince her that it was nothing but a vicious rumor."

Otelia paused a moment and glanced out the window. Sunlight slanted through the windows, casting long shadows on the tile. "I'm not sure she believed me."

"And that was the end of it?"

"Yep. Of course, not long after that, Artie drowned in Ruby Lake."

"Karl Vogel told me Arthur's body was never found."

"No, I don't suppose it was. But several witnesses

had seen him swimming earlier. He was an avid swimmer."

"Did Bessie ever forgive you?"

"I never even saw Bessie again until we all went bird-watching." Otelia hugged herself. "It must have been awful finding her out there in the woods like that."

I said it was, and I knew an opening when I saw it, and this one was as big as the entrance to the Biltmore House, part of George Vanderbilt's incredible Biltmore Estate located in nearby Asheville. "Do you remember what you were doing that morning?"

I could see by the look in her eye that she knew where I was leading, but she answered anyway without any signs of offense. "I was right here, I suppose. Making chocolates like I do each morning. Especially during the summer busy season." She beamed. "The tourists do love their chocolates."

Otelia's Chocolates was on the lakeside of Lake Shore Drive, with the lake mere steps behind. It wouldn't have taken a woman like Otelia long to cover the distance from the chocolate shop to the sycamore where I'd discovered Bessie. "I hear Arthur Hammond was fond of chocolate himself."

"Artie did like his chocolate. Probably more than was good for him. But it was his money, who was I to say no?" She shook her head, as if chasing away memories. "Besides being one of my best customers, he was a nice man. I miss him still."

There was a rap on the door and we both turned. A hopeful couple stood peering in the glass. Otelia waved to them. "Be right there!" She grabbed her smock off the counter. "I'd better open up."

I held her back. "One more thing. What made you decide to come bird-watching with us?"

She shrugged nonchalantly. "I thought it might be fun. Get me out of my shop. Meet some people." She pinched her waist. "Work off some of this."

"That makes sense."

"Of course, if I'd known Bessie Hammond was going to be there, I might not have signed up."

"Well, you won't have to worry about her showing up on next month's walk."

"No, I guess I won't." Otelia's expression was inscrutable as she unlocked the door and removed the CLOSED, BACK SOON sign. I waited for the couple to enter, then exited. The shopping strip bustled with activity.

Ahead of me on the street, I noticed a pickup truck at the curb. Through the back window I could see a man and woman necking. The door flew open on the passenger side. The woman leaned across to the driver, gave him a peck on the cheek, and then stepped out onto the sidewalk. It was Lana Potter, in her waitress uniform.

I turned my head aside but she called my name. "Amy."

"Hello, Lana." My eyes darted to the pickup, which sat unmoving at the curb. "It seems we keep missing each other. Let's go to Birds and Bees. We can talk there." Whatever she wanted to talk about, I was dying to hear.

Lana glanced over her shoulder. "I can't now."

"How about tomorrow morning?"

Lana shook her head, her long locks flowing like silk. "Make it later. Afternoon. I'm busy in the morning."

She probably had an early shift at the diner. Ruby's Diner opens at six. I remembered I'd be busy in the morning myself. Standing outside in the cold waiting for Mary McKutcheon to show herself. "Okay, tomorrow afternoon then. Why don't you tell me where you live? I can stop by. Just say when."

Lana said no. "I'll call you. At the store." She shifted her leather purse to her opposite shoulder. "I've got to run. I'm going to be late."

Lana walked quickly toward the diner, and heads turned as she did. If I walked that fast, I'd look like a lame chicken. Kim had told me so on more than one occasion. When Lana Potter did so, she looked as sulky and seductive as Brigitte Bardot in her prime. Sometimes life wasn't fair.

The white pickup came to life, the rear brake lights blinked, and the truck eased into traffic.

That was Gus McKutcheon's pickup truck. I'd have bet my life on it.

25

"Hand me the thermos." I shivered and extended my hand. "Please."

"Here you go."

John handed me the stainless-steel flask. "Thanks." I unscrewed the cap and poured myself a first-of-the-day, bracing cup of coffee. I breathed in the fumes and took a sip. "Wow, this is good."

John Moytoy smiled. "It's a mixture of several types of beans that I grind and brew myself." He was bundled up like it was the first day of winter rather than midsummer. That included jeans, a heavy, long-sleeved green-and-black flannel shirt with a T-shirt showing underneath, mittens, and a trapper cap that made him look a bit Elmer Fudd-ish.

"Maybe you should have become a barista rather than a librarian." I was shivering in my cotton shorts. At least I'd had the sense to throw a sweater over my Birds & Bees T-shirt. The open-toed sandals had definitely been a mistake. My toes felt like ice cubes.

I could just barely make out the dark form of a small fishing boat in the distance. I brought a fist to my mouth as I yawned. If I ever took up fishing, I'd stick with going after only those fish species that had the decency to keep bankers' hours.

"I can't believe I let you talk me into this," grumbled Kim, hugging herself for warmth. She'd dressed rather appropriately in jeans, sneakers, and a cable-knit sweater, so I didn't know what she was complaining about.

I started humming the opening bars of "Together (Wherever We Go)" from *Gypsy*.

"Thank you, Stephen Sondheim," Kim yawned snarkily.

"Actually, Sondheim wrote the lyrics. It was Jule Styne who wrote the music."

Kim gave me a look that might have turned the entire surface of Ruby Lake to foot-thick ice if directed toward the water rather than me.

"I wonder if we'll spot any interesting bird species." I craned my neck toward the treetops. It was too early yet for any real sightings, but come sunrise the trees would come alive with the flutter of wings and cheerful chirping song. "I spotted an American kestrel gliding over the lake earlier in the week." It had been a male with distinctive black spots along its rusty back and bluish-gray wings. The female's wings are reddish-brown.

"If you ask me, this whole escapade is for the birds," was Kim's reply.

"Buck up," said John rather cheerily. "At the very least, we should be regaled with a lovely sunrise."

Kim's mouth opened in a cavernous yawn. "I can see that on the Weather Channel."

"But you can't taste it, you can't smell it." John inhaled deeply. "Here you get to experience things with all your senses. This is so much better than TV or even books. Besides, who knows what the morning might bring? Like they say, it's the early bird that gets the worm."

"Worms?" Kim tugged at her sleeve and wrinkled her nose. "They can have them."

It may have been too early for even the early birds and squirrels, but not so for the widow-in-the-lake watchers. There had to be a good thirty or forty people presently huddled together near the edge of Ruby Lake. Some faces looked familiar and I took them to be locals. Others were clearly tourists. Even Ava Turner, our resident movie star, and her ever present assistant, Gail something. I waved Ava's way and she returned my greeting with a regal nod.

The enterprising couple selling widow-in-the-lake souvenirs out of their van had set up a small folding table, which they now proceeded to fill with Mary McKutcheon–related tchotchkes. Gus McKutcheon was nowhere in sight. I wondered what he would make of all this brouhaha concerning his long-dead ancestor.

Kim, following my gaze, said, "Look at them, gawkers and hawkers."

Then I noticed Derek's former wife, Amy, in attendance with several of her friends. I'd completely forgotten they were going to be there.

"Isn't that Amy Harlan?" Kim poked me. She'd seen her, too.

"Derek mentioned she was coming." There was no sign of Maeve, their nine-year-old daughter. "I totally forgot." If I'd remembered, I would have stayed as far away as possible, now realizing how ill-advised it was to be in proximity to Derek's ex. The women were each dressed in fancy outfits meant more for a morning outing to some fancy coffee shop than a morning of spook-watching at a small-town lake.

"Forget about her," advised Kim.

"I wish I could," I grumbled. They'd brought folding chairs that they set up close to the water's edge.

"She's always seemed nice enough to me," John put in.

"You know her?" Kim asked.

"She comes in the library with her little girl once in a while."

"Can we talk about something or someone else?" I pleaded. "Tell us what you know about Mary McKutcheon," I urged John.

While John obliged, my eyes drifted. To my surprise, Officer Sutton had also put in an appearance. He was in civilian clothes, workaday jeans, and a gray hoodie over a black T-shirt that extended below it. The hoodie was zipped up to his chin and his hands were buried in its pouch.

At the moment, Officer Sutton was chatting with a pair of bleary-eyed campers who had pitched a small tent near the lake's edge. The boy and girl looked to be of college age and sat bundled up in folding canvas camp chairs. A sluggish campfire ringed with small stones lay at their feet, sending up wisps of oak-scented smoke. The official campground was about one hundred yards back toward the marina, but rules were lax around Ruby Lake, so the pair, and several more campers, had moved closer to the lake; presumably in hopes of getting a better view of the widow in the lake, should she appear.

I had a sneaking suspicion that the only things we'd be seeing this morning were several new cases of pneumonia.

My eyes lingered on Officer Sutton a little longer. Initially, I had thought Dan was there to keep an eye on things, but the way he kept sneaking looks at my best friend, Kim, I was beginning to believe he was really there to keep an eye on her. Riley must have blabbed that Kim would be there. I knew I hadn't told him and I couldn't think of anyone else Kim or I would have told.

Was Sutton planning on asking her out on a date? Here, at this god-awful hour and in front of all these people? Maybe Dan Sutton's nerves were more steely than I'd given him credit for.

"I'm tired of standing." Kim grabbed the thick navy-blue wool blanket I'd brought from the apartment and spread it out on the damp grass. John and I joined her; John in the middle and me on the opposite side.

"Where are those cookies you promised?" John asked.

I pulled a plastic container from my satchel purse and handed it over to John. "They're homemade," I explained. "Mom and her friend Anita have been experimenting. Mom made these herself."

John popped open the lid. "They smell good." He pressed his nose closer.

"Hey." I turned toward the aroma. "They do."

John extended the container to me and then Kim. He reached in and took one for himself.

I took a bite. Each cookie was the circumference of a hockey puck. And, though I'd never tasted one, there was not a doubt in my mind that a hockey puck would taste better. This thing tasted like feet. "Hmm." I turned the cookie over in my hand. "I just remembered that I'm not hungry."

John spat his out in the grass. "Sorry," he said, dusting crumbs off his shirt as he looked at me. "But I think Barbara needs to do more experimenting."

"I don't know what the two of you are going on

about." Kim stretched forward past John to see me. "These aren't bad at all." She held up her half-eaten cookie. "Am I tasting hazelnut? And bacon?"

I pulled out my Widow in the Lake chocolate bar from Otelia's and unwrapped it. "Want some?"

Both John and Kim declined. I polished it off in three bites and washed it down with a refill of coffee. I listened to the idle chatter of the watchers and the sloshing of the waves against the shore and waited. And waited. And waited.

This whole thing was probably a complete waste of time. Finally, I leaned back on my elbows, stared at the lake a few moments, then closed my eyes, figuring that at the very least I could get a catnap out of this.

"See anything?" and "No, you?" I heard repeatedly from voices in the crowd.

I opened my eyes to the sounds of throat clearing. Officer Sutton had inched closer to our blanket. I saw he'd been unable to restrain himself and was now holding his very own Widow in the Lake snow globe. "Morning, Miss Simms, Miss Christy."

"What, no hello for John?" I couldn't resist saying.

Sutton reddened. "Good morning, John."

"Hi, Dan." John saluted. "Here to keep the peace or nab a ghost?"

The officer shrugged. "Just curious, is all."

To make up for giving the officer a hard time, I scooted over and offered him a spot on the blanket. John and Kim moved over, too, and Dan appeared quite happy to take a seat beside my best friend.

He had his own coffee, bought at the Coffee and Tea House on the square. I recognized the logo—a sprig of tea leaves and four coffee beans. I didn't offer him one of Mom's breakfast cookies. He was a police officer, after all. I didn't want to become known as Amy Simms, Cop Killer.

Twenty more long minutes went by. We'd all but given up on Mary McKutcheon showing herself. The sun was coming up stronger now and the layer of fog on the surface of the lake was slowly rising, as if an invisible hand was pulling back a blanket. It looked like it was going to be a beautiful Carolina-blue day. Several people had already turned to leave. The word *breakfast* was mentioned and hunger pangs promptly rose in my gut. A chocolate bar can only go so far and I'd left the fudge in the apartment.

"Wait a second." I held out my arm and extended a finger. "What's that?"

"You see something, Amy?" John sat taller, eyes scanning the water.

"There." I wiggled my finger. "What is that?"

The susurrus of suddenly curious voices disturbed the near hypnotic sound the water made as it lapped against the beach.

A strong, cool wind was in our faces. A blurry, wet, white shape drifted sluggishly toward us.

"Dead fish?" someone asked.

"Don't think so," replied another.

"Looks like someone threw a bag of trash in the lake," I heard one of Amy the Ex's friends remark.

"Slobs," Amy the Ex said with an air of disdain.

Could it have been nothing more than a few bags of trash floating in Ruby Lake, our town's very own miniature version of the Great Pacific Garbage Patch?

Then I realized I was seeing a body. A human body. "That's a person!" I leaped into the lake, ignoring the harsh cold.

I heard splashing behind me. Officer Sutton grabbed my shoulder and held me back. "Let me." He sloshed forward through the water and muck.

Two of Amy the Ex's companions fell out of their chairs in their haste to retreat.

The body was draped in sopping, white cloth that wrapped tightly to the flesh. A large, rounded hump was visible along the back of the body, though equally shrouded. Several bits of what I thought might be sago pondweed clung to the bobbing form. The pondweed is a submergent species of plant and a favorite food source for waterfowl, which dive beneath the water's surface to reach the nutrient-rich plant. Only the reproductive stalk peeks above the water during the plant's summer flowering phase.

Sutton carefully pulled a tendril of the drooping green weed from the figure's face. It was a woman. Her half-submerged face was white and puffy. Nonetheless, I recognized Lana Potter behind that diving mask. "It's Lana." My voice came out a shrill whisper.

"Who?" John asked.

"She works at the diner." At least she did.

The officer grabbed Lana Potter under her flaccid arms and pulled her to shore with John's assistance. A long, black hose trailed behind her. Sutton removed her dive mask. Harsh red gouges outlined where the mask's border had pressed against her face. I saw now through the wet, semitranslucent material that the cylindrical shape on her back was a scuba tank. Sutton turned his head toward the group of us hovering near the edge of the lake like a bunch of skittish ducks. "She's dead."

There were gasps and screams. A crow cawed in response.

Kim idly held her phone in her hand. She'd joked that

she was going to get a shot of the widow in the lake rising from Ruby Lake and post it on YouTube. "We'll be famous!" she'd quipped earlier.

Officer Sutton looked at her. "I'd better call the chief," he said, his face set, his tone grim.

26

The police and EMTs arrived within minutes. Jerry now hovered over Lana Potter's body while Officer Reynolds snapped pictures of the scene. Wearing nitrile gloves, Jerry carefully pulled back the volumes of fabric covering Lana's form. A sci-fi looking contraption was strapped to her back along with the air tank. Curved PVC thrusters, their nozzles aiming toward her feet, were positioned along the side of each shoulder, attached with a stiff harness. Aluminum arms with controls on the ends were designed for steering, as I understood them.

As the day came into focus and under the sun's dominion, the small fishing boat I'd been watching earlier came toward us, moving fast. I recognized the *Sunset Sally* by her distinctive orange roof. Captain Harrow was at the helm.

Moments later, the boat came to a stop and a younger man, who I now recognized as Jean Rabin, dropped an anchor over the side. Ethan Harrow unstrapped a rubber dingy from the stern and lowered it into the water. Both climbed aboard and Jean picked up the oars and rowed them ashore.

Chief Kennedy intercepted them. "Stop right there." Both men stopped. "What are you doing here, Harrow?"

The big man looked pained. "I—we came to see."

Jerry narrowed his eyes at the two men. "You know anything about this?"

Harrow studied Lana from a distance. "Maybe." His voice a mere whisper.

Jerry pointed to the ground. "Don't move from this spot. Stay out of my way. I'll get to you two when I can."

Despite the chief's orders, I watched as Jean Rabin slinked away and took a seat some yards away on a fallen pine trunk. He held his head in his hands and stared silently out at the lake.

"What is that thing she's strapped into?" Kim asked.

"It appears to be a jet pack," Jerry said.

"A jet pack?" Kim's nose wrinkled up.

"One of those water jet packs, I believe," I replied.

Kim nodded in recognition. "I've seen people playing with those." Riding them had become a popular recreational activity at the lake in recent years.

"Stand back, please." Dan extended his arms and herded us away from the lake's edge. Everyone was ordered to stand back and wait to have their names and contact information taken by the police. They had come to see the widow in the lake and I wondered if some sort of weird cosmic joke had come to pass. I knew next to nothing about Lana Potter. Perhaps she had been a widow herself. That would be a very weird, very eerie coincidence if that proved to be the case.

Andrew Greeley, dressed in black, stooped stoically

over the body, watching the police do their work. An ambulance sat waiting to take her away.

"What was a waitress doing wearing scuba gear, a water jet pack and a white sheet?" Kim said.

Kim was clearly perplexed, but I wasn't. "Meet the widow in the lake," I replied.

Kim's eyes grew. "She was pretending to be Mary McKutcheon!"

The police looked at her with curious eyes.

"Why the hell would she do that?" demanded Jerry.

"My guess is that she was put up to it," I answered. "Lana was planning on rising up out of the lake."

"Just like we were all waiting for," Dan Sutton said.

"Why would a woman agree to a fool stunt like that?" Jerry asked. "And who might have put her up to it?"

I turned at the sound of plaintive howling. Gus McKutcheon came crashing through the woods from the direction of his house. "I think the answer to your question has arrived."

Jerry looked from me to Gus, who stood unsteadily in his bare feet, wearing black trousers and a white shirt with the tails hanging out.

Annika, Ross, and Dominik appeared at the edge of the trail and took in the scene. Annika and Dominik held hands. Ross separated from them and wandered over to where Jean was sitting.

"What happened?" Gus froze in place, his feet sinking in the soft grass. "Lana! Baby!"

Dan Sutton stepped forward to stop him but Gus broke past him and ran to Lana's side. He cradled her lifeless head in his hands. "Lana! Lana!" Tears ran down his face. "No, this can't be!" He turned to the chief, eyes afire. "She can't be dead! She can't be!"

Jerry barked a few words and Officers Sutton and Reynolds gently pulled Gus away from Lana's corpse.

Gus eyed them wildly, then spun on the skipper. "What happened? This wasn't supposed to happen!" Gus's hands were clamped around the fisherman's collar.

"I don't know," Ethan Harrow said, looking glum and not a little in shock himself. One end of the long hose, which had apparently been used to pump water to the jetpack, dangled limply in his hands.

"Looks to me like she got tangled up in this crazy contraption and drowned." Jerry jotted something in his notebook.

"She was supposed to rise up out of the water." The skipper wiped his brow with the back of his sleeve. "I checked her tank myself."

"So it was an accident?" Lance Jennings from the *Ruby Lake Weekender* had appeared from nowhere looking like he'd just been roused from bed.

Jerry turned. "What are you doing here, Lance?"

Lance explained that his father had demanded that he race over and get the story. "He heard about it on his police band radio."

"Fine," said the chief. "But get your story from over there with the rest of them."

"But, Chief, can't I get a statement?"

"I just gave you one!"

Lance reluctantly stepped back, snapping pictures from the camera around his neck as he did. I waved in Lance's direction. I was going to want a word with him later. I'd tasked him with looking into who else might have seen Bessie Hammond alive in the hours before her death and wanted to know if he'd come up with anything.

Amy the Ex and her friends were huddled tightly, away from the crowd, speaking in low whispers.

"Looks like a horrible accident, all right," agreed Officer Sutton, breaking into my thoughts. "A horrible, horrible accident."

Andrew Greeley, looking at Lana's limp form from two yards away through a pair of soda-bottle-thick glasses, agreed that appeared to be the case.

Chief Kennedy loomed over Gus McKutcheon. "It seems to me you've got some explaining to do. Was this damn fool stunt that got this young lady killed your idea, Mr. McKutcheon?"

Gus took a step back. "Well, I—"

"And you were a party to this?" The chief pointed his finger at Ethan Harrow.

The captain hung his head. His arms hung limp at his sides.

"This was all a hoax?" I heard the disgruntled widow-in-the-lake memorabilia salesman holler in our direction.

"You've got a lot of nerve spoiling things for everybody," added his wife, clinging to his arm. "Now the real widow in the lake may never appear!"

"You hear that, everybody?" bellowed the man. "This was nothing but a hoax!"

"It wasn't a hoax," Gus said. His eyes pleaded with the chief of police. "It was only meant to be a joke. A harmless prank."

"There was nothing harmless about it," I replied.

Gus sank to his knees and buried his face in his hands. "I am so sorry."

I wasn't so sure exactly who or what he was sorry for. But I was sorry that Lana Potter was dead. Especially since she was so insistent that we talk.

And now she'd never talk again.

27

As soon as Chief Kennedy was through with me, I backed away from the lingering crowd along the lakeshore. I pulled Kim aside. "Come on," I urged, taking her arm.

"Come on where?" Kim had wrapped herself in the blanket and looked tired.

"I want to take a look at that cemetery," I whispered. I couldn't risk anyone hearing. Especially the police or Lance, who was still sniffing around trying to flesh something more out of the story.

"Are you crazy?" Kim tugged the ends of the blanket tighter.

"Shh." I pressed my index finger to her lips. "No, I am not crazy. With everybody busy here, this is the perfect time to get a look." I took some satisfaction in knowing that philandering Gus McKutcheon's goose was cooked for sure now.

"This is the perfect time to go home and get a nap," Kim snapped. "I have no interest in getting a look at any dirty old graves. Not unless one holds a queen-size bed with a down comforter." She waved to Officer Sutton. "Oh, Dan!"

Dan jogged straight over, ignoring the ugly look his boss was aiming at his backside. "Yes, Ms. Christy?"

"Please, call me Kim."

He beamed. "What do you need?"

"Can I catch a ride back into town with you?"

Officer Sutton looked over his shoulder at the chief. "It might be a little while. But you can wait in the Bronco if you like." He fished out his car keys and handed them to Kim.

"Terrific." Kim turned and stuck her tongue out at me.

As Sutton returned to his duties and Kim headed for his truck, I marveled at my friend's ability to get men to bend to her will. Dan was so happy to oblige that he hadn't even asked her why she'd needed a ride. While Kim's breakup with Randy was still fresh, it was heartening to see the wound was showing signs of healing. Kim's a dear. Randy's an idiot.

To avoid drawing attention to myself, I worked my way in leisurely fashion away from the scene at the lake and toward the McKutcheon property. I knew my way around pretty well by this time. If I spent much more time out here, I might legally be entitled to file a homestead claim.

Treading lightly, I crept up on the forlorn and neglected-looking cemetery. It wasn't that I believed in ghosts or was particularly superstitious, but there was no sense taking chances of any kind.

Especially considering Bessie Hammond had met her end out here in this neck of the woods. A fact that, now that it had popped into my head, made me question the wisdom of my wandering around out here alone when her killer had still to be caught.

Then again, that killer could be Gus McKutcheon. And at the moment McKutcheon was otherwise occupied in the hands of police.

Though it was late morning, the heavy canopy of trees kept me in shadows. The forest was deadly still. Where were all the birds?

I wiped a bead of sweat from my forehead as I stood a dozen yards from the graveyard, taking it all in, before proceeding onward. The gate hung open on one broken hinge. The other hinge appeared to have rusted and come loose long ago. I counted eight tombstones. Half were simple stones partially sunken in the soil. The others were vertical sandstone grave markers whose names were now as illegible as those lying horizontally. No matter. The grave I was interested in was unmarked and far fresher than those that had stood here for a hundred years or more.

I exited the cemetery and turned to my right, toward the newer mound that had caught my eye the other day. Dirt and stones had been piled loosely a good foot or two above the surrounding ground. There was nothing to indicate what lay beneath. There was nary a weed, twig, or leaf on it.

The whole thing was rather odd. Why was the body buried here and not in the cemetery? Why had no effort been made to camouflage the site?

I knelt alongside the grave and ran my fingers through the cool earth. A woodpecker's tapping sounded far off, reminding me of Drummy, my wood-pecking friend-slash-alarm clock. I'd missed him that morning, having been out the door before his ritual hammering began.

I pulled my phone from my pants pocket and took a picture of the mound. "Here's some evidence for you, Jerry." I clicked a second picture for good measure. I typed in the message: *Fresh grave McKutcheon house—curious?* I then texted both pictures to Jerry Kennedy's personal cell phone along with my message. Let him dispute that hard evidence.

"Go ahead," an unwavering voice said. "Dig."

I gasped. In my haste to spin around, I got tangled up in my legs and fell to the ground sideways. I leapt to my feet, ready to fight or flee—preferably flee!

"D-Dominik!" The last time I'd seen him he'd been down at the lake with the others. Had he followed me? A chill crossed over me like an icy breeze.

"That is what you would like to do, no?" He swiveled his eyes toward the fresh grave. "You want to dig?" Dominik smiled now. "Maybe find your dead body?" His hands were deep in his pockets. "So. Dig."

I licked my lips and nodded. What choice did I have? I bent my knees and began plucking away tiny rocks, thinking that maybe I could hit him in the head with one and make my escape. The stones were so small though, and I'd never had good aim.

Feeling I had no alternative, I began digging earnestly with my fingers. The earth was soft and came up easily. While I dug, I kept one eye on Dominik. All the while, I wondered if I would get out of this alive or if I was digging to make room for me in that grave. "You mind telling me who he is?"

"I don't mind." Dominik stepped closer. "You want me to help you?" He knelt beside me and I caught a trace scent of bergamot.

"So, who is he?"

Dominik smiled, which only scared me all the more. Was he toying with me? "It is not a he. It is a she."

I paused, planting my hands in the ground to keep from tipping over again. "It?"

"The goat."

I shook my head. "The what?"

Dominik held out his hands and helped me to my feet. "Here, you seem to be tiring. Let me finish for you, Amy." He gently moved me aside. "Besides, I'm not certain you will enjoy the sight we are about to witness. To tell the truth, me either."

I stood in stunned silence as Dominik redoubled his efforts. In moments, he'd revealed a hairy, dirty white leg. I peered over his shoulder. "That's a—"

"Goat." Dominik took the word right out of my mouth. "Her name was Miss Kitty."

I wrinkled my nose. "Like from the old TV show?"

Dominik shrugged. "Channing named her. She did say it was a name in one of your American TV programs. The *Gunsmoke*?" He scraped some dirt from around the hoof. "Would you like to see more?"

I waved my hands at him to indicate he could stop. "I've seen too much already. Please, stop." I thought I'd gag seeing the tiny maggots silently crawling along the dead beast's leg.

"Good. To be honest, I'd rather not see more myself." He quickly covered the exposed portion of the goat.

"Miss Kitty was diseased," Dominik said as he wiped his hands on his trousers. "She died about a week ago. We have been having some illnesses with the goat herd."

"You should call a vet."

"Yes, we have suggested this to Mr. McKutcheon."

"So what is Miss Kitty doing out here?"

"We had discovered the cemetery in our wanderings in the forest. Channing is very fond of animals. A real animal lover, as you say. She wanted Miss Kitty to have a proper burial. She agreed that it would not be appropriate burying her in the McKutcheon family plot, but neither did she want us simply burying her in the field."

I nodded. It sort of made sense. "Are any of McKutcheon's remaining goats diseased?" I had been fed goat the night I'd come for dinner. Had I eaten diseased goat?

"Not that I have been made aware. At least, no others have died."

No, but I was thinking I might.

My stomach felt queasy. I had possibly eaten a goat with a deadly disease. I had been wrong about a human body being buried at the McKutcheon family plot.

Worse of all? I had texted the chief of police pictures of Miss Kitty the goat's final resting place.

I groaned. There'd be no living that down, not if I lived to be as old as Esther. And frankly, at that moment, I rather wished I was dead.

28

"Hey, careful!" I said, bending over to remove the empty bird-feeding tray that someone had carelessly left near the top step of the stairs leading to the second floor. I had returned to Birds & Bees, run upstairs to take a long hot shower and dress for work.

"What are you hollering about, Simms?" Esther shouted up.

I skipped downstairs carrying the tray with me. "This." I set it on the front counter beside her. "You left it on the stairs. I was coming down."

"So? You want me to thank you for bringing it? Thank you." Her voice was laced with sarcasm.

"No," I said, forcing myself to remain calm. "I want you not to leave things like this lying around. Especially on the stairs. I might have tripped."

"It wasn't me." Esther poked her nose under the counter. "Have you seen my feather duster?"

"Nope. Not me."

"Huh." She scratched her hips and started pulling open the drawers of the low cabinet against the wall. "Where could it be?"

I lifted the bird-feeding tray. I'd return it to the shelf where it belonged. "Just be more careful in the future, Esther. I could have been killed."

Esther yawned. "Were you?"

"Was I what?"

"Were you killed?"

I drew back my chin, rehearsing all the things I was going to say. Then I realized there was no sense arguing with the woman. Especially when I knew I couldn't win. I balanced the tray on the stack where it had come from, smiling as I watched Esther in her search for that feather duster. I glanced surreptitiously at the owl nesting box where I had sequestered that horrible feathered instrument. Esther could poke around all she wanted; her search was doomed to remain unsuccessful.

Channing came in followed by Riley, his hands filled with shopping bags. Cousin Riley lumbered over to the counter and dropped his load.

"What's in the bags?" I poked my nose in the first one.

"Esther sent me to the market for groceries."

"I thought Channing might need a hand." Riley thrust his hands in his pockets, looking like a puppy waiting to be given a pat on the head.

"How's everything here?" Channing ran a hand quickly through her locks as she began removing groceries. A lot of it looked like stuff that was probably going straight to Esther's apartment rather than the store's kitchen. I'd have to have a word with her about that. Store funds were not intended to be used to fill her pantry.

Channing pulled out a small can.

"I'll take that." Esther's hand shot out and her gnarled fingers wrapped around the can. She deposited it quickly in the pouch of her smock.

"Is that cat—" I turned in Pavlovian response to the tinkle of the front door chimes. It was Paul Anderson.

"Hey, Amy. I hear another one of your bird-watchers dropped dead," he said rather callously. "I'm sure glad I didn't decide to go on your little bird walk. I might have been next."

"You still could be," I couldn't help quipping.

"Ha-ha." Paul ran his fingers through his hair. "Seriously though, it's too bad about Lana Potter."

"You knew her?"

"We talked. Sometimes at the diner. Plus, she ate at Brewer's a time or two."

"Alone?"

"What do you mean?"

"Did she dine alone?"

Paul scratched the top of his head. "Well, once or twice. Yeah. Another time with that Gus McKutcheon. You know, the fellow who came to our Birds and Brews event." He chuckled. "The way that Gus was coming on to you, I thought Derek was going to blow a gasket."

I gave him my ugliest look. "Shouldn't you be at your beer garden doing beer stuff?"

Paul grinned. "I spilled a bucket of mash all over my pants." That explained the nasty stains all over his jeans and the strong smell. "I came home to change. See ya."

"Wait!" I called as Paul headed for the stairs.

He turned. "Yeah?"

My lips twitched. "Speaking of Derek . . ."

"What about him?"

"Have you seen him lately?"

Paul's hand gripped the banister. "He stopped in for a quick bite yesterday. Why? Trouble in Romanceville?"

I blushed. "Of course not."

"Right, of course not," Paul parroted insolently.

I pressed on. "Has Derek said anything to you about, you know, Amy—Amy the Ex, that is—and wedding gowns?"

"Oh, that." Paul waved a dismissive hand, then swatted at the lower half of his pant leg, leaving yeasty residue on the lower steps. "I'm sure it's only a phase. I mean, sure, right now she's all gung-ho, but from what Derek tells me about her, she'll be on to something or someone else before you know it. Well, gotta go."

Paul jogged upstairs, leaving me with a hundred unanswered questions. I'd read that the Egyptian plover dances around inside the open jaws of crocodiles, where it picks tiny bits of food from between their sharp teeth. The plover gets food and the croc gets free dental care. It seemed like a perfect arrangement, unless or until that crocodile yawned or simply decided to vary its diet with a little bird meat.

I was beginning to feel like that plover, dancing between the fangs of a crocodile, staying alive only through its whims.

I turned back, looking for Esther. I wasn't finished with her yet. But Esther was gone and Riley and Channing were putting things away in the corner kitchen. I walked over and told Riley that I wanted a word alone with Channing. I waited until he was out of hearing range, then waved for Channing to take a seat.

I sat beside her and folded my hands in my lap. "Did you hear what happened this morning?"

Channing smiled pleasantly. "No, what?"

"Lana Potter drowned in Ruby Lake."

The blood seemed to drain from Channing's face and she buried her face in her hands. "Are you sure?"

I nodded. "Yes, I was there." I explained how I and a group of others had been hoping for the widow-in-the-lake sighting.

"I don't get it," Channing said, lifting chin. Her eyes were filled with tears. "What was Lana doing there? I mean, how could she drown?"

I told her how it appeared that Lana had been part of an elaborate charade arranged for or with Channing's host, Gus McKutcheon. "She was planning to make an appearance as the ghost of Mary McKutcheon. When she floated to shore she was strapped into an intricate water jet-pack harness and wearing scuba gear."

Channing rose and paced across the small kitchen space. "I've seen the tourists flying in those things. I thought it would be fun and that I might try it one day. Now, you couldn't catch me doing that if my life depended on it!" She clamped her hand over her mouth as if to stop the words she'd just uttered. "Sorry."

"That's okay." I stood and draped an arm across her back. "So you didn't know that Gus and Lana were planning this little stunt?"

Channing shook her head vigorously even as she pulled back. "No!" She wiped at her damp eyes. "You're saying Mr. McKutcheon was part of this?"

"He's admitted as much to the police."

"The police?"

I told her how Gus had been asked to go down to the police station to explain his role in the hoax. "I expect he may be facing charges." It wasn't like you could go to jail for being stupid or lacking common sense, but a woman had died out there this morning.

"If Mr. McKutcheon goes to jail, what happens to us? We'll probably all get thrown out of the house. I know it sounds insensitive, but most of us have little money and nowhere else to go."

I told her not to worry. "I'm no lawyer, but I'm sure all of you will be able to stay. Nobody's going to throw you out. At worst, Ms. Potter's death was a terrible accident." Though I'd wait for the autopsy report before deciding one way or the other whether I really believed my words. Even if Gus McKutcheon had murdered Lana Potter, it might be difficult to prove.

I wasn't sure I was happy about that, but there was nothing to be done about it. "Besides, if you are forced to leave, you can stay here until you get back on your feet."

Channing embraced me. "I don't know how to thank you, Amy."

"No thanks necessary. We can make it the same arrangement that you have with Gus now, a little work in exchange for room and board. Deal?"

Channing rubbed the tears from her eyes and nodded. "I still don't understand how Ms. Potter drowned. Why would she agree to go in the lake if she could not swim?"

"Lana became tangled up in the equipment and drowned. Jerry thinks her air hose might have been blocked and maybe her legs got snarled up, too."

I explained how Lana had also been wearing yards and yards of white fabric. "Between the cloth, the jet pack, and the scuba gear, Jerry and the coroner think Lana probably got herself tangled up, ran out of air and . . ."

Channing's chest shook. I urged her to sit again and made her a glass of hot tea. "Thank you," she said softly.

"Did you know Lana well?" I asked, making myself a cup of Darjeeling, too. "Were you close?"

"No. She really kept to herself, you know?"

"Do you know where she came here from? I'm sure she wasn't local. Does she have any family?"

Channing frowned. "I don't know. You should ask Mr. McKutcheon."

"Speaking of Gus, Lana was living at the house with you all, wasn't she?"

Channing appeared to hesitate, the teacup balanced in her hand. "Yes."

"Were she and Gus lovers?"

The young woman smiled enigmatically. "You'll have to talk to Mr. McKutcheon about that, Amy. I stick to my own business. I am a guest in his house. It really isn't any of my business. Mr. McKutcheon would not be happy if I told stories about him."

"I get it." It sounded like Gus scared her a bit. "What about Dominik and Annika?" Her brow creased up and I pressed on. "What do you know about them?"

Her shoulders bobbed. "They seem nice."

"Did they know each other before coming to Ruby Lake?"

Channing giggled. "They should. They are brother and sister."

I sat back in the rocker. "I thought they were a couple. You know, boyfriend and girlfriend."

"Whatever gave you that idea?"

"I don't know. Silly of me." When I'd seen them together in the Italian Kitchen, I'd taken them for lovers having a spat. Instead they were brother and sister and I still didn't know what they'd been arguing about. "And Ross? What was his last name again?"

"O'Sullivan."

"Right, O'Sullivan." I hadn't known his surname at all. Now that I did, maybe I could do some digging and learn something more about him as well. "He told me he was from Ireland."

"That's right." Channing rubbed her nose. "Near Dublin, I believe."

I wracked my brain. Why had the word *Ireland* started bells ringing in my head? "Do you think he or any of the others, Gus, in particular, might have known Lana?"

"What do you mean?"

"Did you get the impression that any of your other roommates knew Lana before she came to Ruby Lake?"

The corner of Channing's lip turned down. "I don't know, Amy. As I said, I really didn't get to know Ms. Potter well." She stood and carried her cup to the sink, gave it a rinse, and set it on the towel to dry out. "Why all the questions?"

"Just curious, I guess." I smiled in an effort to hide my concern. Why had Lana Potter appeared in the Town of Ruby Lake at about the same time as Gus McKutcheon? Why had she been living in his house? Had it all been for the widow-in-the-lake ruse?

"You should talk to Mr. McKutcheon."

I would. If and when the police were through with him.

29

I hollered that I was going out.

And ran into Chief Kennedy coming in. The thought raced through my mind that I might duck out the back, but he had seen me. If he wanted me, he could hunt me down, sirens screaming.

So I held my ground as he marched up the walk. "Hello, Jerry." I held the door open for him and followed him back inside.

"You want to explain this?" Chief Kennedy thrust his cell phone in my face.

I was staring up close and personal at one of the pictures I'd taken of the goat's grave. "A joke?"

"A joke?" Jerry tilted his head. "What do you mean, a joke?" He planted his hands on his hips. "You think I got time for jokes, Simms?"

I opened my mouth but he wasn't ready for me to speak.

"I've got two dead people"—he held up two fingers—"clogging up my case files. I don't have time for your jokes." He was practically snorting like a bull.

"Now, calm down, Jerry. It was really an accident. I mean, not an accident exactly. But I thought I might have found the grave of that dead man—"

Jerry stamped his foot. "Listen to me, Simms. There is no dead man. I've got two dead women!"

Customers looked our way. I urged Jerry away from the front door. Channing, her face flushed and eyes red, watched from afar. Riley had disappeared.

"The man I saw, thought I saw, thrown out Gus McKutcheon's upstairs bedroom window."

Jerry looked down his nose at me. "And did you find him?"

"No." I slid back behind the sales counter, putting a little space and a big obstacle between us. "It was a goat," I said, eyes glued to the floor, voice barely audible.

Jerry loomed over the counter. "A what?"

I glared at him. "A goat." I crossed my arms over my chest. "A goat, Jerry. It was a dead goat. Are you happy?"

Jerry's eyes bugged out and he hooted. "That's rich, Simms. You go looking for a dead man only you can see, and instead you find a goat!"

I felt my face and chest turn crimson. The man was practically braying. "Oh, yeah?" I shot back, though I felt myself sinking back to middle-school mentality. "What about Lana Potter? What about Gus McKutcheon's stupid, and deadly, attempt to trick everyone?"

Jerry grimaced. "Stupid is right. But if stupid was criminal, I'd be locking up folks left and right." He pinned me with his eyes, leaving me no doubt who his first arrest would be. "Speaking of which." He looked at me hard.

"Yes?" I gulped.

"I ought to arrest you for being stupid and for obstruction of justice."

"What's that supposed to mean?" I demanded indignantly.

"It means Ed Quince dropped by the police station a short while ago and told me and Officer Reynolds how you'd found his knife in the vicinity of Bessie Hammond's corpse." Jerry drove his right fist into his left hand. "He said he couldn't sleep and was feeling guilty and wanted to let me know all about it and that he was innocent. He said he wanted to tell me himself before you told me."

"I really don't think Ed's guilty—"

"I don't give two hoots what you think!" Jerry's jaw flexed rapidly back and forth. "Stay out of police business!"

"I have every intention of doing just that. I'm simply saying that I do not believe Ed Quince killed Bessie any more than I believe Walter Kimmel did."

Jerry narrowed his eyes at me. "What's Kimmel got to do with Bessie Hammond's murder?"

"N-nothing," I said quickly. "That's what I'm saying. Mr. Kimmel's got nothing to do with Bessie's murder."

"You bet he doesn't. He and Quince both have ironclad alibis." He pulled off his cap and scratched his head. "Or should I say, nine-iron alibis."

"What's that supposed to mean?"

"It means Kimmel and Quince were playing golf at the time of Bessie Hammond's murder."

"So, there were witnesses?"

"Dozens of them," Jerry said firmly. "Including the other two fellas in their foursome."

That meant they'd all been lying about church. I

cleared my throat. "That's great, Jerry." And it was. I hated to think for a minute that either of the sweet old gentlemen had been mixed up in Bessie's murder. "Don't you see? That just proves what I've been saying. Gus McKutcheon is behind things." Jerry opened his mouth to retort but I cut him off. "The same as he was behind this whole widow-in-the-lake deadly fiasco."

"And the dead goat?" Jerry taunted me with his eyes.

That goat really was going to stay with me the rest of my life.

I took a step back, the wheels of my mind turning like the wheels of a NASCAR race car. "C'mon, Jerry. Gus McKutcheon may or may not be responsible for Lana Potter's death, but if you ask me, the man's guilty of something. Probably Bessie Hammond's death.

"Hey"—I snapped my fingers—"maybe Bessie stumbled onto Gus's plans to pull that widow-in-the-lake hoax!"

"So he broke her neck?" Jerry appeared dubious.

"Sure." I was pacing now. Surely the two deaths had to be related, being so similar in time and place. "McKutcheon comes back to town, insinuates himself into the local life—"

"And Moire Breeder's bed?"

"It appears that way." I waved my hand at him. "Let me continue."

"Go on." Jerry turned his back on me and walked across the small space to the self-serve birdseed bins.

I spun my tale. "McKutcheon has plans, big plans. He's going to take over the diner. He's got a bunch of innocent kids fixing up his house for him on the cheap. It costs him nothing but room and board.

"Then he hatches this whole widow-in-the-lake scheme. Or maybe he hatched the scheme first and came down here to set things in motion. It's quite a coincidence that he shows up just in time for her scheduled appearance, don't you think?"

Jerry frowned. "Mary McKutcheon has never showed up, not even once. She didn't this time either."

I didn't let Jerry's negativity deter me. "Creating a buzz about the widow in the lake could lead to him lining his pockets. Look how popular the Loch Ness Monster is. It could lead to a whole cottage industry."

"Oh, brother," Jerry said, reaching for a handful of peanuts straight from the bin.

I couldn't afford to have him eating up my merchandise nor my profits, but I could less afford having him stomp off without at least listening to my theory, so I let it go. "If the widow in the lake catches on, the diner will be busy, the house will fill up with paying guests, and McKutcheon will have it made."

"If," Jerry said, between mouthfuls, "the ghostie shows up."

I could smell his peanut breath from my side of the counter. "And he was determined to make sure that she did."

Jerry grinned. "Sounds to me like you just proved Gus McKutcheon had plenty of reason to want Lana Potter alive to perform her Mary McKutcheon imitation, not kill her."

I thumped down on my stool. "Shoot."

Jerry laughed. "Face it, Simms. You've got nothing."

I felt my foundation cracking and crumbling beneath me but asked anyway, "Where was Gus when Lana washed up?"

"Watching from a telescope in his house."

That explained why he'd come running. He had seen her wash ashore rather than rise from the lake as Mary

McKutcheon's spirit. My fingers wrapped around an ink pen. "So he couldn't have murdered Lana." I caught myself. "What am I saying? Lana drowned. It was an accident and I blame Gus for that, but still . . ."

Jerry fidgeted.

"What is it, Jerry?" I knew that move. Something was up.

"Greely says the Potter woman might have had some help."

"Help?"

"Could have been sabotage." Jerry rubbed his ear. "Leastways, that's what Mr. Foster over at the dive shop says."

"Do you suspect Ethan Harrow?"

Jerry rolled his eyes. "Ethan's a good ole boy. He wouldn't hurt a fly. And what reason would he have to want the woman dead? It's only caused trouble for him, too.

"Besides, Foster loaded the diving gear onboard himself at the dock. Of course, he didn't know what they were planning to use it for." He swallowed another fifty cents' worth of nuts. "Might be sabotage, might be a malfunction. Who knows? I've asked the state boys to look into it."

"What about the jet pack?"

"Ethan says Lana brought that aboard herself. Gus told me he ordered it off the internet."

"So Ethan's role in this whole thing was simply to provide the boat?"

"That's what he got paid to do." Jerry rested his hands on the sales counter and licked his lips. "You know, Simms, I never had this much work before you got to town. Now I've got dead people and missing people practically falling out of the sky.

"To top it off, I've got Lance Jennings harping on me for a story. Why doesn't that boy stick to covering super-market openings and birthday parties?"

"Don't blame me!" I threw up my hands. I saw no reason to point out to Jerry that the Town of Ruby Lake only has one market and it was far from supersized. "What about the missing guy? He ever turn up?"

Chief Kennedy shook his head no. "I just met up with the Garfinkles over at Ruby's Diner. They haven't heard a word. Not that I'm concerned. Fella's probably in Florida, soaking up the sun." His chest rose and fell. "I know that's where I'd be if I didn't have all this mess to deal with."

"It's not my fault, Jerry." I pushed back a lock of hair. "Where's Kim, by the way?" Last I'd seen of her, she was comfortably ensconced in Dan Sutton's Bronco, waiting for a ride back to town.

"Off corrupting one of my deputies." Jerry turned on his heels and left. He'd made that sound like my fault, too. I hurled a couple of the peanuts he'd dropped on the counter toward the door.

"You okay?" Channing asked, coming toward me with an open case of dried mealworms in eight-ounce plastic tubs. Mealworms are a particular favorite of the bluebird. Mealworms aren't actual worms at all. The small creatures are the larval form of the darkling bee-tle, which has a yellow-white body and an orange-black head. Bluebirds prefer live mealworms to the freeze-dried sort, but I'm too squeamish by nature to have wriggly larvae in my refrigerator case.

"Can you handle things on your own a bit?" I went to the door and picked up the peanuts I'd thrown.

"Sure," replied Channing, though she didn't look so sure. "I guess."

"I have to run over to Ruby's Diner." I gave her my cell number and told her to call if anything came up. I only hoped Moire Leora didn't throw me out of Ruby's Diner the way I'd thrown those peanuts at the door. Out on the porch, I tossed the nuts into the flowerbed. Something would eat them, bird or beast, and I jaywalked to the other side of Lake Shore Drive.

The parking lot was nearly half full but, as I entered the diner, the change in mood hit me immediately. There was a cheerless, subdued pall to the place rather than its usual breezy and welcoming ambience. The wait staff and kitchen crew alike seemed dispirited and distracted.

"Is Moire here?" I asked, pulling Tiffany aside.

"Upstairs. In her apartment."

I laid a gentle hand on Tiffany's shoulder. "Have you been crying?" Her eyes were streaked with red.

Tiffany sniffed and wiped her nose with a balled-up tissue. "Sorry," she said. "I barely knew Lana, I know, but still, I can't quite get over the fact that she's gone." Her head turned in the direction of the lake.

"I know how you feel." I looked toward the kitchen. "Is Gus here?"

Tiffany shook her head. "I haven't seen him. He never showed up for work at all today."

No surprise there. "Did Moire know Lana well?"

"I don't think so. She came in one morning looking for a job and Moire hired her on the spot."

"Just like that?" I snapped my fingers. "No background check? No references?"

Tiffany shrugged. "You know how it is. Wait staff come and go. Moire can't afford to be picky. Or nosy."

"You said Moire's in her apartment?"

"Once the lunch rush was over, she went upstairs for a little lie-down. Lana's death has taken its toll on her.

She's upset. And confused." Someone in the kitchen bellowed Tiffany's name. Tiffany shuffled through her order book as she talked. "We all are."

I nodded. "Would you say Gus is good at his job?"

"What can I say?" Tiffany waved goodbye to a customer heading out the door. "Working in a diner isn't rocket science. I'm not saying he is or isn't a great cook." She smiled suggestively. "But the way Moire has been walking around here on a cloud for the past few weeks, he must be good at something."

I wasn't so sure Moire would be walking on clouds anymore after today. Gus was going to have a lot of explaining to do concerning his relationship with the now deceased Lana Potter. "Did Lana ever mention any family?"

"Not to me." Tiffany looked past me. "Excuse me, table twelve's waiting on their order."

I stepped aside and watched Tiffany move expertly behind the counter to pick up her waiting dishes. As she passed by me again on her way to the customers, I tugged at the edge of her sleeve. "What's he doing here?" Ross O'Sullivan was moving behind the counter. In his arms, he bore a battered cardboard box. A diner apron hung over the side.

"Who?" Tiffany followed my gaze. "His name is Ross. He's here picking up Lana's things. Apparently, Gus sent him over."

I kept my eyes on Ross as he weaved through the diner with Lana Potter's personal belongings. What was his hurry? Why had Gus sent him to retrieve Lana's things so quickly? The body was barely cold yet.

Not a minute later, the cardboard box was in the back of Gus's pickup truck and Ross was gone.

30

My head was throbbing as I left Ruby's Diner. I was playing an impossible game of connect the dots. Bessie Hammond and Lana Potter. One death by broken neck. One death by drowning. The two women, at least their deaths, had to be connected. But I couldn't figure out how.

I hesitated, one hand on the wood rail leading to Moire's upstairs living quarters. What if Gus McKutcheon was up there, too?

Before I gave myself time to chicken out, I marched up the steps and knocked on Moire's door.

"Yes?" Moire said tentatively as she pulled open the door. "Oh, it's you." Her hand gripped the knob. She was in her diner uniform.

"Hi. How are you doing?"

"This hasn't been the best of days," Moire said. "What do you want, Amy?"

"Can I come in?"

Moire hesitated, then stepped aside. "For a minute. I need to get back to the diner."

Moire's small apartment was simply furnished with a

Southern flair. The cozy space was tastefully done up with weathered antiques and what appeared to be heirloom collectibles. The color palette was all golds, reds, and greens. Eclectic pieces of folk art decorated the four walls. A framed American flag hung behind glass over the farm table adjacent to the kitchen.

Moire invited me to have a seat on the sofa and took up a chair opposite. She folded her hands in her lap.

I could have used a drink, but Moire wasn't offering and I wasn't asking. "First, I wanted to offer my condolences about Lana." Moire made no reply. "Have you heard from Gus?"

"What's your fascination with Gus, Amy? Can't you stay out of things? Mind your own business?"

"Forgive me," I said hurriedly. "I meant no offense. I only wondered if—"

My ears caught a light tinkling sound. A moment later, a chubby beagle came prancing from the bedroom, its nails clattering across the hardwood floor. The dog laid itself at Moire's feet.

Her hand fell mechanically and she idly scratched the top of its head. "Gus makes me happy, Amy. Whatever it is you think, whatever it is you are trying to do: Let it go." Her eyes bored into me and I pressed my back deeper into the sofa cushion.

"I only want to help."

"You can help by leaving me alone."

"Did you know that Lana was living with Gus?"

Moire jumped up and the dog bounced to its feet and barked. "I think you'd better leave, Amy."

I hesitated, then stood. "How did he explain that?" How did I tell Moire that I had seen Gus and Lana making out in his pickup truck?

Moire threw open the front door. "Gus told me all about Lana. She was new to town and needed a place to stay. He helped her out. He wasn't even charging her rent." She motioned for me to leave. "The same way he isn't charging anyone else staying at his house."

I stepped onto the landing, the beagle nipping at my heels.

Moire clapped her hands and told her dog to stay. "He does things for people because he's a nice man. He's asked me to marry him and I intend to do just that!"

With that, she slammed the door in my face. I stared at the door a moment, then started down. Was I wrong about Gus? Was he really the nice man Moire believed him to be?

Did he do things for people? Or did he do things to people?

I skirted across the diner parking lot in the direction of Lake Shore Drive. A vaguely familiar couple stepped from Otelia's Chocolates and stood hand in hand on the sidewalk. It was the man and woman I'd run into at the police station. The visitors looking for the man's brother.

Feeling bad for them, I ambled over. "Any luck finding your brother?"

"Not yet," said the man. He extended his hand. "Bert Garfinkle. This is my wife, Danielle."

I introduced myself. Bert and Danielle Garfinkle were about my age, perhaps several years my junior. "We've been asking around some." He jerked his thumb at the chocolate shop window. "The lady who runs the store said she might have seen him, but she couldn't be sure." He sighed.

"It is the height of tourist season," I said. "We get a

lot of visitors." Though I noticed the couple selling widow-in-the-lake merchandise seemed to have packed up and moved on to their next venture.

"I simply don't understand," said his wife. "It isn't like JJ and his wife, Cece, to disappear without a trace."

Her husband nodded. "We made plans. My little brother knew we were coming. It was his idea really."

"We were looking forward to meeting his wife," added Danielle. "We'd been hoping to meet them when they flew into New York. Then we all agreed to meet here instead."

"What did your brother do?" I said with a sudden smile. "Elope?" It was beginning to seem to me that Bert's brother was of an impetuous nature.

"Nah." Bert stepped aside as a woman pushing a baby carriage jostled past. "They got married over in Austria. We were supposed to meet up here, then drive back to Cleveland together."

Danielle took up the story. "JJ finally decided to settle down and join Bert there in business."

I asked him what he did for a living and he explained that he was a plumber. JJ would be apprenticing under him.

"I suppose you tried all the hotels?"

"Yep. We even showed them this picture. It was the only one I had on my phone. I had it printed." Bert Garfinkle extracted a folded sheet of unlined paper from his pocket. "I don't suppose you've seen JJ?"

I studied the photo of Bert's brother. The shot was a little fuzzy and showed only his upper torso and head. The man in the photo wore sunglasses and a baseball cap. I chewed my cheek. "I can't be sure." To tell the truth, the man in the photograph looked like one of a hundred such tourists walking around the Town of Ruby

Lake on a daily basis. The only thing distinctive about the man in the picture was the thin silver nose ring piercing his left nostril.

"We're heading home tomorrow," said Danielle. She tugged her husband's sleeve. "We'd better get going, honey."

He nodded.

I wished them luck and went back home.

I was upstairs alone in my apartment wondering where I'd gone wrong. Here it was, Saturday night. I had no date, it seemed half my friends were mad at me, and I was no closer to figuring out Bessie Hammond's murder when Lana Potter turned up dead, practically at my feet, to complicate things even more.

Mom was spending the next few nights with her sister because Aunt Betty's husband was out of town for a few days. Aunt Betty doesn't like to be alone. Maybe that explained why she was never long between husbands.

I telephoned Lance and got his voicemail at the *Weekender*. I left a message asking him to call me so we could compare notes. He may have learned something further about Bessie Hammond or even Lana Potter.

Feeling lonely, fragile, and frustrated, I dialed Karl Vogel's number next. As our former chief of police, with an inside track to Jerry Kennedy, he'd be the man with answers. If there were any answers to be had. "Hi, Karl."

"Hello, Amy." I could hear a country tune playing in the background. "Have you heard the latest?" Karl hadn't waited for me to grill him and didn't wait for an answer to his question. "Lana Potter was pregnant."

"No!" I stared at the phone. "Who was the father?"

"Who's to say? Nobody's come forward so far."

"My money is on Gus McKutcheon."

"You really don't like that man, do you?"

"Not even a little bit. Maybe it's silly, but my intuition tells me that McKutcheon is bad news."

"Well, in this case your intuition isn't wrong."

I asked Karl what he meant.

"The man has been in trouble with the law on more than one occasion. No arrests, mind, but a man gets himself in that much mischief, some of it's bound to be true." Karl chuckled. "It's all a matter of proving it."

"Like what?"

"Jerry tells me your Mr. McKutcheon was married once before. About ten years back."

"Divorced?" I thought about what Moire had said about her and Gus getting married.

"Nope. His wife slipped in the bath and cracked her head wide open. Left Gus a widower. A well-to-do widower."

"How well-to-do?"

"One hundred thousand well-to-dos."

I whistled. "He doesn't seem to be well-off now. I wonder what happened to all the money."

"In my experience, a man like Gus goes through his money like he goes through his women."

"Do you know if Lana Potter was one of those women?"

"It's hard to say. Both Gus and Ms. Potter had been living in Portland, Maine, prior to showing up in Ruby Lake. But Portland's a fair-sized city. The police haven't found anything linking the two of them so far."

"So far," I repeated, pointedly.

The poignant twang of Hank Williams's "Your Cheatin' Heart" came through softly in the background as Karl filled me in on Gus's ne'er-do-well past. "McKutcheon left Portland behind in a wake of failed businesses and disgruntled investors."

"Do you think he killed his first wife?"

"If he did, he did a good job of it. You can bet the police and the insurance company dug as deep as they could."

I thanked Karl for the inside information and rang off when he said his dinner date was at the door. Far be it from me to interfere in the man's love life. Somebody deserved to have one. If it wasn't going to be me, it might as well be Karl.

I replayed Karl's words, but it only added to my confusion. So far, every road I took seemed to be a dead end.

I was about to heat up some rice and chicken when the home phone rang. It was Kim. "What happened to you?" I asked. "You disappeared."

"I hung out with Dan." There was a lightness to her tone that had been missing earlier.

I smiled while I banged a bag of frozen chicken tenders against the counter to loosen them up. "Glad to hear it. Any sparks?"

"What's that banging?"

I explained about the chicken. "You didn't answer my question. Are you being evasive?"

"No," Kim said. "It's too early to talk about sparks. I'm in no hurry this time. In fact, I—"

"Hold on a sec," I said. "My cell phone is ringing." I set down the home phone and ran to the bedroom where I'd set my purse. I extracted the phone. It was Derek. "Hello?" I said hurriedly.

"Hi, Amy. It's Derek."

"Yes, hello! Can I put you on hold for a second?"

"Sure," he replied.

I ran to the kitchen and picked up the home phone. "Kim? Derek's calling on my cell," I whispered. "Can I call you back?"

"Oooh," teased Kim. "Talk about sparks!"

"I'm not so sure about sparks," I replied. I'd half convinced myself that our relationship was about to go down in flames. It seemed Derek might soon be remarrying Amy the Ex.

I agreed to catch up with Kim the next day and snatched up my cell phone. "Hi, Derek. How are you?" Could he hear my heart thumping in my chest?

"I was hoping I could see you."

"Of course," I said. Was he about to break up with me? Was this the big kiss-off? "When?"

"How about now?"

"I guess so. Sure." I calculated the amount of time I'd need to wash and change clothes. "How soon can you get here?"

"That depends on how long it takes to get you to come open the front door."

"Huh?"

"Look out your window."

I did. Derek stood on the walkway. He was clutching a cell phone in one hand and balancing a pizza box with a DVD case atop it in the other.

He grinned up at me. "I hope you've got wine."

"Be right there!" I flew down the stairs to let Derek in.

I threw on the store lights and unlocked the door. "Smells heavenly," I said, catching the hunger-inducing aroma of pizza as Derek entered. I read the title of the DVD sitting on the pizza box. "*The Postman Always Rings Twice*?"

"Have you seen it? It's the original version. Not the remake."

I admitted that I had seen the film before. "But it's been years." My last boyfriend, Craig, had been more into *Star Wars* than stars of the Golden Age of Hollywood. "It's a favorite of mine. I could watch it again and again."

We went up to the apartment. Derek set the warm pizza on the coffee table in front of the sofa. The pizza was from Brewer's. I fetched plates and glasses and returned for a bottle of red wine.

"You do know this version stars John Garfield and *Lana* Turner?"

"I only realized while I was on my way here." Derek popped open the DVD case and slipped the disc into the player. "I heard about Ms. Potter, of course. The whole town has. Too weird?"

"No, I guess not." I settled into the sofa and tucked a pillow against my ribs.

Derek handed me a slice of pizza on a plate, then took one for himself.

As the movie ran through the opening materials, including an old black-and-white trailer for the film, I said, "Was there any special reason that you dropped by tonight, Derek?" I'd set another sofa pillow between us and put my plate on it.

"Can't a man simply want to spend time with a friend?"

Friend?! Was that what I was to the man, a friend? Not even a girlfriend, just a friend? "Derek," I said, looking him directly in the eye, "I know about the bridal dress." In fact, I was beginning to think half the town knew.

"You do?"

I nodded.

He chuckled, revealing a row of even white teeth. "Isn't that wild?" A bit of cheese stuck to his lower lip. I handed him a paper napkin, which he used to wipe it away. "I don't think Amy, my Amy"--Derek looked appalled and blushed—"I mean, my ex-wife," he said sternly, "knows a thing about the bridal business. If you ask me," he continued, grabbing a second slice of pizza from the box, "I think it was all her friend Nan's idea." He glanced at the TV screen, then back at me. "Do you know Nan? Nan Cooper, I think?"

I was feeling confused and dizzy. And I hadn't even started on the wine yet. "What's this Nan got to do with it?"

"Like I said," Derek explained, "I believe the shop was her idea."

"Shop?"

"The all-things-bridal shop." He grabbed for the wine but I reached out a hand and stopped him.

"All-things-bridal shop?"

"Sure, you know, a few gowns, some veils, some of those runner things you walk down the aisle on."

I leaned over and kissed him.

"Hey!" My plate slid to the floor and Derek reached out to stop it. "What was that for?" He set the plate on the pizza box.

"Does it matter?" I grabbed the pillow between us and tossed it at the nearest chair.

"Not at all." Derek pulled me closer and smothered my lips with his.

After we came up for air, Derek went on to explain that Amy the Ex and some of her gal pals had decided it might be amusing to open a wedding shop. They had found a space for rent along the town square. "She talked me into investing." He shook his head. "I don't know what

I was thinking." He rubbed the back of his neck. "I may never get my money back."

"I don't know. As much as I hate to admit it, it could be a good idea. Plenty of couples come to the area to get married. The business might do okay."

"I suppose." Derek appeared thoughtful. "How did you find out, anyway?"

I pressed my finger to his lips. "Let's just say a little birdie told me."

"Listen, Amy," Derek said, snatching my finger and pulling my hand toward his chest. "Amy, the other Amy, is my ex-wife and Maeve's mother. I can't exactly shut her out of my life."

"I know that. I would never want that." I laced my fingers with his. "But couldn't you at least ask her to change her name?"

He smiled. "Sure, I'll ask her. What name do you suggest?"

I opened my mouth and, in turnabout, he put a finger to my lips. "Never mind. Don't answer that."

"It's probably best if I don't. It could cost me my lady-like image." We both laughed.

The film started with a stranger coming to town, and my mind immediately drew similarities between the film character and Gus McKutcheon. By the end of the film, my brain was a tangle of dead-end possibilities to explain the deaths of Bessie Hammond and Lana Potter.

My eyes were drooping and I yawned.

Derek leaned forward, picked up the remote, and switched off the movie as the end credits rolled. "Call it a night?"

I glanced at the clock in the kitchen. "It's only ten. How about a double feature?"

"Sure. I can do that. I had Maeve last night because

her mom wanted to go down to the lake this morning, but she's staying with her tonight."

"I know. I saw her down there." I crossed to the bookshelf and looked through the library of DVD titles. I was in the mood for something lighter. "How about a Doris Day musical?"

"Perfect," agreed Derek, though I was sure he was only being gentlemanly.

I held up the DVD case of *Tea for Two*. "I believe it's Doris Day's first musical and the first time she danced on screen." The film, set in the Roaring Twenties, was an adaptation of the popular Broadway musical *No, No, Nanette*.

Derek was holding his copy of *The Postman Always Rings Twice* in his right hand and slapping it against his left palm. "People and things aren't always what they seem, are they?" he said thoughtfully. "And when you mix two different personalities, you never know what the results will be."

"How do you mean?"

Derek stretched his arms before answering. "Take Frank and Cora from the movie. Maybe not two of the nicest people on the planet, but if their paths had never crossed, would either of them have committed murder?"

I gave his question some thought. In *The Postman Always Rings Twice*, would Cora ever have murdered her husband, Nick, if Frank hadn't come along? "It's hard to say. Maybe not." Derek's point was certainly food for thought. Movies sometimes, oftentimes, did imitate life, and life sometimes imitated the movies.

I popped in the new film and rejoined him on the couch, tucking my feet up beneath me. I ran him through what I knew about Lana Potter's death, which wasn't much, except that it might or might not have been an accident. Then I told him all I'd learned about Bessie Hammond's murder since last I'd seen him.

"I hate to say it"—Derek said it anyway—"but there's not much to go on." He reached for his wineglass. "I think the police are going to have a tough time solving this one."

I rested my head against Derek's shoulder. Maybe it was the film we'd just finished watching, but I was getting some ideas. "What if Gus was going to marry Moire, kill her, and take up with Lana?" I speculated. I had explained to him earlier how Moire had said Gus asked her to marry him and she'd said yes.

"Are you forgetting that it's Lana who's dead, not Moire?" countered Derek. "Are you trying to say Moire killed Lana to keep Gus for herself?"

"No, of course not." Was it impossible though? My fingers drummed my knee. I don't know. Maybe. What did I really know about Moire Leora Breeder? When it came down to it, not much more than I knew about Gus McKutcheon. "Karl Vogel told me that Lana Potter was pregnant at the time of her death. He also had some rather unflattering information about Gus. Possibly Lana, too."

"Such as?"

I explained about his various business ventures gone sour, run-ins with the law, and, saving the best for last, his previous wife's own mysterious demise.

"All rumor and innuendo."

I pouted. "Sometimes you are such a lawyer."

"Sorry," he said with a smile.

"Don't be." I refilled his glass, then paused.

"What is it?" asked Derek, seeing the sudden look in my eyes.

I shook my head. "I'm probably being silly. But I wonder if Moire recently took out any big life insurance policy."

In *The Postman Always Rings Twice*, the husband of Cora, Lana Turner's film character, had recently taken out a big insurance policy on himself. "It always comes down to money, doesn't it?"

Derek paused the film as the opening credits to *Tea for Two* began to roll across the screen. "Money and emotion."

"That's the only thing I can think of. McKutcheon comes back to town and starts thinking about how he can capitalize on his property."

"And what better way than to generate interest in the old widow-in-the-lake tale?"

"Yeah. And what better way to do that than to have the widow in the lake, Mary McKutcheon herself, appear?" I gulped my wine.

"So he decided to make sure that happened."

I nodded. "But something went wrong."

"More than wrong," said Derek. "Deadly wrong." He brushed his fingers along the underside of my chin. "So where does that leave us?"

I thought a minute, but I could have thought a thousand minutes and wouldn't have been any closer to an answer. My cell phone chirped. I ignored it and snuggled up against him. "I need some Doris."

Derek smiled and hit the Play button on the remote.

31

I woke with a cramp in my side and another in my left leg. The TV screen displayed a sea of bright blue. I could feel Derek breathing deeply beside me on the sofa. The warmth of his body sent a soothing current through my skin.

I smiled, taking in his calm, rugged face. It would be a shame to wake him.

Rat-a-tat-tat-brrr!

I stifled a groan. So that's what had awakened me. Drummy.

I gently extricated myself from Derek's arm and stood. I switched off the TV and the living room fell into darkness.

Rat-a-tat-tat-brrr!

A cool breeze hit me in the face. I looked across the room. The faint light of a street lamp spilled into my bedroom. I'd left my bedroom window open. If I didn't shut it, between the woodpecker and the cold air, Derek would wake for sure and I was certain the dear man could use his sleep.

I tiptoed to my bedroom. A gentle breeze shook the curtains.

Rat-a-tat.

I thrust my head out the window. "Well?" I whispered. "Let's hear the rest of it."

Brrr! Brrr!

I couldn't help chuckling. "Silly woodpecker. Haven't you ever read a guidebook to birds? You're not supposed to be up this early."

I gripped the window ledge and watched by the light of the moon as Drummy skittered up and down the tree in search of insects that most likely were still lying in bed, chitinous heads on tiny goose-feather pillows, fast asleep. Like all of us should have been.

I placed my hands on the rail of the lower sash, determined to close the window before the woodpecker started up again. But I paused, something tickling at the recesses of my mind. Woodpeckers. What was it that someone had said about woodpeckers, and why did it now make me uneasy?

I found my eye drifting out across the street, across Ruby Lake, toward the McKutcheon house.

Stars twinkled above. Mary McKutcheon was in her watery grave. At least, there was no sign of her dancing atop the water.

What had Derek said? People and things weren't always what they seemed.

I picked up my binoculars and studied the house. There was no sign of activity.

I thought about the grave I had dug up. I thought about the goat. Had somebody made a goat out of me?

Call it curiosity or call it stupid, but I was going to take another look around the McKutcheon property.

And what better time to do it than when everyone was fast asleep?

Besides, I was feeling restless. I needed to move. I set the binoculars down on the window ledge. Next, I changed into a comfortable pair of jeans and a heavy sweater. A chill had swept in overnight. I grabbed my sneakers, gave a quietly snoring Derek a gentle kiss on the forehead, and shut the door as quietly as possible behind me.

I'd be back in an hour at most. Then I'd make us both breakfast and tell him what I'd been up to. He'd probably laugh, but we all need a good laugh once in a while. I'd make him French toast with real maple syrup.

I stole across the street. The diner was open but nearly deserted at this hour. I couldn't tell if Gus McKutcheon or Moire were inside or not, so I let it go. I didn't want to be seen spying in the windows. The two of them would only wonder what I was up to.

Not that I was so sure what I was up to myself. Things were swirling around my brain, indiscernible and indecipherable things. Things I had seen and things I had heard. If only I could tie them all together. Maybe a good, long walk would bring some of those unknowns into focus.

I crossed the murky marina parking lot and headed inland through the woods toward the McKutcheon house. First, I revisited the spot near the shore where Lana Potter's body had washed in. No trace remained beyond the trampled grass and a few bits of trash and several cigarette butts. There were no boats out on the lake as of yet.

I started inland, retracing the path I'd taken the day before. I swung past the tree where I'd discovered Bessie

Hammond's dead body. How in the world had there come to be so much death in one place?

I followed the narrow trail toward the house. Behind my back, the sun was rising slowly over the mountains. In a matter of minutes, I was creeping up on the old cemetery plot. Not that it mattered. What I wanted was a look inside some of the outbuildings near the house, starting with the barn. Who knew what secrets it might be holding?

I couldn't resist taking a look at the graveyard as I passed. My eyes were drawn to the stones and the mounds like magnets to iron.

I halted suddenly. Something about the area around the old cemetery seemed different somehow. There wasn't yet enough sunlight reaching this far back in the woods, so I inched closer. Then I realized what was different.

The burial mound that held the goat was different. Smaller, lower. I neared the mound. It was definitely smaller and the whole of it looked to have been redone. Why?

I bent to the ground and ran a hand along the cold earth. The mound was nothing more than a small rise with a shallow depression in its center. I glanced over my shoulder with a feeling of unease. It felt as if unseen eyes were watching me.

But looking around, I saw no one.

I grabbed a nearby fallen branch and scraped at the dirt mound. "Ugh!" I fell backward at the sight of decaying flesh. It was the goat.

But why had it been rearranged? I picked myself up and dusted myself off, tossing the limb aside. A yellowish glitter caught my eye near the edge of the earth I had scraped away.

I reached down. It was a slender gold chain. I held it

suspended before me at arm's length. A four-leaf clover dangled from the chain.

I'd seen a chain identical to this one before. It had belonged to Ross O'Sullivan.

I started thinking, my mind turning over and over. What if there had been a body buried here? What better way to hide one body than to cover it with another?

I fingered the chain and noticed my hand was trembling. What I'd seen last week must have been real. I hadn't been crazy at all. A man *had* been murdered at the McKutcheon house. Then that man was hastily buried out here in the woods. The goat had probably been slaughtered to cover up that murder. It might not have been diseased at all. That thought, at least, gave me a sense of relief.

The hypothetical body might have been removed after the last time I was here. That would explain the smaller mound. But why move the body now? And whose body was it?

I turned at the sound of running footsteps.

"Amy?"

I clutched my chest. "Channing! What are you doing here?" I shoved the gold chain in my jeans pocket.

"I thought I'd get in a morning jog down by the lake. You've got me scheduled to open the store this morning, remember?" I did. Channing adjusted the white sweatband wrapped across her forehead. She had on sneakers and a loose two-piece jogging suit. Her nose pinched up as she asked, "Why are you all dirty?"

"Where's Ross?" I asked. "Have you seen him?"

"Not this morning. Why?"

"There's no time to explain," I replied. "We need to get to the house. I have to use your phone." I hadn't thought to bring my phone or my purse.

"Follow me." Channing turned quickly and started up the path. Along the way, I told her my suspicions about Ross. "I only met him when he arrived here. He always seemed so quiet, shy even," she said.

I repeated what Derek had said to me. "People aren't always what they seem."

Channing veered to the left. "You really think he murdered some man and buried him out here and then killed Mrs. Hammond?"

"My guess is that Bessie came snooping around out here and Ross found her. Who knows? Maybe she saw something she shouldn't have. I don't know who the other man he killed might be." I rubbed my hands along my pants. "I'll let the police figure that one out."

We reached the house. Gus's pickup truck was nowhere in sight. "Where's Gus?" I whispered.

"He's at the diner. Moire gave him a lift."

Channing pushed open the front door and motioned for me to come inside.

"Where is everybody?" The house seemed so empty, devoid of presence and sounds of any kind. Though Channing switched on the light in the entry, it was one of those weird Edison-type bulbs and gave off little useful light.

"Like I said, Gus went to work at the diner. Jean is crewing with Captain Harrow. The others are having a ceremony for Lana," explained Channing.

"Oh?"

She tossed her headband on the table beside the stairs and shook out her hair. "Annika is all into that Wicca stuff. She's got the others down at the far end of the lake. She swears there's a black willow there that's sacred or something."

"Why didn't you go?"

"It seemed sort of sacrilegious to me. I don't go much for all that magic stuff."

"Like widows in the lake?" I said.

"Exactly," replied Channing. "I was raised Church of England. Mummy would be appalled by all this business. She considers it witchery, and if there is a widow in the lake, it seems to be more a curse than a magical blessing."

I told her I was beginning to agree.

"I don't have a cell phone. We can use the telephone in the kitchen." Channing started back.

I glanced up the steps. "You say Ross is with Annika and your other roommates?"

Channing paused in the doorway. "Yes. Why?"

I gnawed at my lower lip. "I'd really like a look at his room. Which one is his?"

"Top of the stairs to the left."

"Dial 911," I said. "That will get the local emergency operator. Tell them to contact Chief Kennedy and get him out to the McKutcheon house right away. Tell them it's an emergency."

Channing promised and I climbed the stairs.

The room Channing had indicated as Ross's was the room where the mysterious murder had occurred. Coincidence? I didn't think so.

I stepped inside. With the morning sun coming in, there was no need to turn on the lamp that still sat on the floor as it had the first time I'd been in the room. A single twin mattress rested beside it, covered with a tangle of bedclothes.

The telescope I had previously seen in Gus's room stood against the window. I pressed my eye to the glass. I could see all the way to Birds & Bees from here.

Had Ross been watching me? The thought made me feel uncomfortable and dirty.

A small, battered red suitcase rested against the wall. I opened it and peered inside. A couple pairs of jeans and several T-shirts, socks, and underwear. He seemed to live a simple existence.

There was little more to see in the sparse room. I moved across the hall. This was Annika and Dominik's room. Two separate beds with a crooked nightstand between them. Channing had said they were brother and sister.

Through the house's thin walls, I could hear Channing on the phone down in the kitchen. Sounds of a cat mewling mingled with the sound of her voice. Was she having trouble convincing the police to come investigate? Maybe I should have telephoned them myself. I should go talk to whomever she was speaking with.

First, however, I wanted a better look at Gus's room. Nobody's perfect. There had to be something incriminating to be found—if not linking him to Bessie Hammond's or Lana Potter's death, then something related to his nefarious business dealings or the death of his wife. I wasn't asking for much. A signed confession would do.

Moving up the narrow hall, I stopped outside a door I thought might lead to the attic. I was pretty sure Lana had been living there, or at least using the room in some fashion. That had to have been her that I'd seen peering out at me the night I'd come for dinner. Definitely worth a look.

But it wasn't a doorway to the attic, only another bedroom. I stepped inside. The curtains were drawn and the room was dark. I flicked on the lamp atop the six-drawer dresser. A brush, comb, and mirror had been laid out on the dresser as well. There were also several makeup bottles. A double bed sat angled in the corner. A white shirt hung over a chair that matched those in the dining room. This had to be Channing's room.

I turned to go. I didn't want her to think I'd been spying on her, too. Turning to leave, I spotted a tweed suitcase tucked behind the door.

My mouth went dry. The luggage tag attached to the handle read: CC. I fingered the tag. A barely legible London address was handwritten between the lines.

CC were Channing Chalmers's initials. But was Channing Chalmers Cece? Had I misunderstood the Garfinkles when they'd mentioned JJ and his wife, Cece? Had she really meant the initials CC?

Quietly, I slid the suitcase from behind the door. I unlatched the suitcase and opened it. The contents consisted of nothing more than an assortment of clothing, mostly heavier outerwear, including a scarf, a beanie, and a pair of black leather boots.

I discovered a slim, burgundy-colored British passport beneath a stack of frilly undies. I sucked in a quick breath. Drummy! I remembered now. Channing had told me that she had been raised in Australia and loved woodpeckers. There were no woodpeckers in Australia. She'd also mentioned being raised in the Church of England faith. I was reasonably sure the Church of England no longer existed in Australia, having changed its name to the Anglican Church of Australia, or something like that. I flipped through the passport's pages. There wasn't a single entry for Australia. Not only was Channing not a resident of Australia, but she had likely never been there.

I covered the passport back up and I was about to shut the suitcase and return it to its place, when I noticed a small photo album tucked into the side pocket. Printed on the cover in scrolling gold lettering were the words *Wedding Album*.

I removed the album carefully and flipped through it. There were several photos of castles and some foreign-looking town that I didn't recognize but that appeared to be Germanic. There were several other photographs as well. These showed Channing and a man, locked closely together and smiling for the camera. One had clearly been taken in a municipal building and showed a smiling official, the man in a brown sports coat, and Channing, CC, dressed in a simple A-line white dress and a delicate shoulder-length veil on her head. A wedding ceremony.

I thought I recognized that man beside her or at least his nose. If I was right, this was JJ Garfinkle.

The Garfinkles had told me that JJ had gotten married somewhere in Europe—Austria, if I remembered correctly.

I thought hard. Maybe it hadn't been a smaller man whom I had seen fighting with a larger man. Maybe, just maybe, it had been a woman. I squeezed my eyes shut, trying to picture what I'd seen that day. It might have been Channing fighting with JJ Garfinkle.

It would explain so much. Like Channing's mentioning a woodpecker in Australia, and how she happened to be jogging by the old cemetery just as I was poking around.

Was Ross O'Sullivan her accomplice? Someone had to have helped her move the body. She couldn't have done it alone. Unless she'd carried him in a wheelbarrow maybe . . .

Channing had been in Birds & Bees when I was talking to Chief Kennedy about digging up the goat at the cemetery. I suddenly realized she had also been present the time I'd asked what had happened to Bessie's camera.

At the time, he hadn't found it. But not long after my very public conversation with him, he told me he found the camera down at the lake. Why hadn't he found it earlier?

My guess was that Channing had kept the camera for some purpose. Who knew? Maybe she intended to pawn it for a few bucks. It was an expensive-looking camera. Then Channing heard me mention to the police that it was missing. She must have decided it would be better that the camera be found than to allow its disappearance to raise questions.

Channing as the killer also explained why the body was suddenly moved. She heard me tell Jerry I'd been digging at the cemetery. Maybe she, perhaps with the collusion of Gus and Ross, decided to move JJ's body in case I got curious again. Had Dominik been in on the murder, too? Had he goaded me into digging up the grave, knowing I'd stop once I came upon the dead goat?

Were all those men so enraptured of Channing that they'd do her every bidding? Including murder? The way Frank had agreed to murder Cora's husband, Nick, in *The Postman Always Rings Twice*?

Channing Chalmers was beginning to look like a very determined and very dangerous woman. She was right downstairs.

And we were alone in the house.

I tucked the album back where I'd found it. As I did, my eyes fell on the beanie tangled up with her clothes. If there had been any doubt in my mind as to the girl's guilt, this blew it away. One of the two people I'd seen fighting in the window that day had worn a gray beanie. I'd bet my life on it. And maybe I just had.

The skin on the back of my neck bristled. I had to get out of the house. I closed the suitcase and slid it back behind the door. I took a breath to steel my nerves, then tiptoed from the bedroom and headed for the stairs. Once outside, I'd jog to civilization and get help. I inched down the stairs, not wanting to alarm Channing.

I heard her voice drift up. "Say you have an emergency." There was a pause. "That's enough. Stop talking and get here. Now. I don't know how long I can keep her from getting suspicious. She thinks I'm calling the police."

I heard the sound of the phone being placed back on the hook and started back up the steps.

"Amy?"

I froze, my hands on the railing. "Hi, Channing." I looked over my shoulder at her, trying desperately not to show my emotions. "Did you manage to get through to the police?"

Channing tilted her head. "I think we both know the answer to that." She pulled her right hand from behind her back. It held a steak knife.

This was not the time for words. Looking madly about, my eyes landed on a heavy painting near where I stood, halfway up the stairs. I grabbed it and threw it down at her.

The painting crashed into her head and I scrambled up the steps as she tumbled down. Glancing left, then right, I realized I had limited options. I decided to take a gamble. I could hear Channing screaming bloody murder.

I slammed the door to Ross's room, as loudly as I could. Then I crept behind the door to Annika and Dominik's room and held my breath.

Channing screamed like a banshee and I heard the sound of her heavy steps as she raced upward. I didn't dare look. I squeezed myself against the wall.

Channing threw open the door to Ross's room and ran inside. "Aha! What?"

I eased from behind the bedroom door where I'd been hiding and took the stairs two at a time. Not a good idea. I fell and tumbled head over heels to the ground. My shoulder slammed against the floor and I cried out in pain. Looking up, I saw Channing practically flying down the stairs toward me!

What was the woman? Part witch?

I was in trouble and I knew it. There would be no cavalry to the rescue. I had to figure a way out of this myself.

I scrambled to my knees and ran blindly to the big sitting room with the fireplace at the opposite end. As Channing burst through the entryway, I gripped the iron poker from the brass stand and waved it wildly through the air.

Channing shouted. She came at me on the left and I moved to the right. Unfortunately, I didn't move far enough. She lunged across a wingback chair and I felt the tip of the blade tug at my sweater. Channing cursed like a fishwife.

More to scare her than with any expectation of producing results, I flailed the poker wildly in the air. I didn't know how long I'd be able to keep it up. I was already winded and in no little pain from my bounce down the stairs.

Channing lunged and I watched as the serrated blade darted toward my abdomen. I jumped and swung at her arm with every ounce of energy I had left.

I missed her arm but hit her a good shot on the shoulder. Channing cried out and tumbled. The knife flew from her hands. We both watched as it skidded across the floor.

Out of harm's way.

Channing looked up at me, eyes filled with hatred and hurt. She shrieked and I flinched. But instead of attacking me, she scurried to her feet and ran for the door.

After watching in shock for a moment, I found myself chasing after her, and I wasn't sure why. It definitely was not a good thing, but I couldn't seem to help myself.

I ran out the front door, tripping over the cat that had come to see what all the commotion was. The cat yelped and took off toward the woods. Channing was out in the yard and jogging down the rutted drive.

I caught the rumble of an engine racing closer. Channing ran toward the sound. I kept running, too, but Channing was younger and faster.

A second later, the white pickup shot around the blind corner, its backend slipping out as its rear wheels fought for traction. Before I could open my mouth to shout out a warning, the pickup slammed headfirst into Channing.

The poker I'd been clinging to for life, fell to my feet as Channing's body went hurtling a good twenty feet or more. The driver of the pickup slammed on the brakes mere yards from me.

I drew back, expecting Gus to come and finish me off. But it was Jean Rabin who flew from the pickup. He ran across the uneven ground and threw himself on Channing. *"Ma bichette! Ma bichette!"* Tears rolled down his cheeks.

I didn't know what the words meant, but I knew the sentiment. Then I noticed the sound of another vehicle. I reached for the poker once more, determined to defend myself.

A small car sped noisily into the clearing and stopped inches from my feet. I closed my eyes and dropped the poker.

It was Derek.

32

"How did you find me?"

Derek smiled and pulled a pair of binoculars from the passenger seat. "Your binoculars. You left them on the window ledge. When I woke up and you weren't there, I went looking for you in your bedroom. That's where I found the binoculars pointed across the lake. I couldn't help looking." He kissed me. "And I couldn't believe what I was seeing."

Derek explained how he'd sensed some commotion in Ross's room and decided to come see what I was up to. "And I'm glad I did. I figured you might be getting yourself into trouble."

I couldn't resist a small smile. "Trouble doesn't begin to describe it." My ears perked up. "Is that police sirens I hear?"

Derek nodded. "I called them on the way. Knowing you, I had a feeling we might need them."

I fell onto his chest and sobbed.

Derek lightly lifted my chin and looked into my eyes. "Are you okay?"

I nodded yes. He looked over his shoulder. The

sounds of Jean's distraught cries pierced the air. "I'll be right back." He pushed his car door open wide. "Sit. Wait for me."

I slumped behind the wheel and watched in stunned silence as Derek crossed over to where Jean sat cradling Channing's limp body in his arms. Derek placed two fingers on her neck and shook his head once. He patted Jean on the shoulder as Chief Kennedy came screaming up in one police car and Officers Sutton and Reynolds in another. An ambulance appeared moments later and squeezed past them.

Derek walked back to the car and rested his arms on the roof with an accompanying sigh.

My eyes were filled with tears. "Is she—"

"Yes," Derek said, his voice heavy. "She's dead."

The rest of the day was a blur that included a trip to the emergency room. Derek had noticed the blood on my sweater first. I hadn't even realized I'd been stabbed. It was really nothing more than a prick between the ribs, but he, and even Jerry, had insisted that I have it looked at. That and a few bruises.

I had a few stitches and was good as new, though the scar may stay with me the rest of my life. At least I was alive.

Derek stayed with me the entire time and drove me back to Birds & Bees in his car. He lifted me across the store's threshold. "Shall I carry you upstairs to your bed?"

Mom cleared her throat and I blushed at the sight of her. "Please," I whispered, "not with my mother watching."

Derek nodded and set me down in my chair. "Hello, Mrs. Simms."

I pressed my lips to his ear. "I'll take a rain check."

Kim and my mother smothered me with kisses and attention. Kim had even bought a bouquet. "Floyd and Karl called to say they'd be stopping by later, if that's okay?" announced Kim.

I said that it was. I still had nearly a pound of banana rum bonbons to deliver to Floyd. The longer I held on to them, the less of them there'd be to give him.

"Derek has been on the phone with the police," I said in answer to the questions that started coming fast and furious. "Let's let him tell us himself." He'd already told me part of the story, both in the hospital and on the car ride home, but I knew there was much more to the tale.

"I'd be happy to." Derek filled us in on what he'd learned that the police had pieced together so far, which was plenty. Mom, Kim, and I were sitting up near the store entrance.

"Did Gus do it?" inquired Kim.

"Anita told me this French boy was involved." Mom wrung her hands. "Is that true?"

Derek paced like a lawyer in front of the bench. "Jean is singing like a stool pigeon."

"Is that a thing?"

"Do you want to hear this or not?"

"I'm listening." I tugged at the push ring of my wheelchair. I'd also badly sprained my ankle in my skirmish with Channing, so the doctor and Derek had insisted I use a wheelchair for a day or two. By the time I got the hang of the thing, I'd be out of it.

"Do you need a hand, dear?" asked Mom rather solicitously.

"No, Mom. I'm fine, thanks."

"Let me get you a glass of water or maybe a cup of tea." Mom rose and headed to the store kitchen. I didn't have the heart to dissuade her. She wanted to take care of her baby, and this was one time I was going to let her.

I was so hungry that I reached for one of the breakfast bars neatly stacked on a silver serving platter near the front door. A handmade sign said: Free Samples.

"Continue, Derek." Kim looked refreshed and relaxed, kicking back in one of the rockers Derek had moved up to the front. Esther was fiddling around in the background.

"Bessie Hammond had returned to the McKutcheon property the day after your walk. Don't ask me why."

"Bessie must have got it into her head to find out what, if anything, had happened after Karl and Floyd mentioned what I'd claimed to have seen."

"That makes sense," Derek agreed. "Jean said that when Channing and he discovered her poking around, taking pictures, Channing insisted that he get rid of her."

"So he did." I shuddered at the thought of Channing so cold-bloodedly ordering Bessie's execution and Jean so cold-bloodedly carrying out those orders.

"They deleted all the pictures she'd taken of the cemetery and house."

"Leaving nothing but innocent shots of birds and flowers." I'd heard about them from Chief Kennedy. "And Lana?"

"Jean and Channing overheard Lana telling Gus about her suspicions concerning JJ's disappearance. It seemed she wasn't above pulling a little stunt like the ruse she and Gus had planned for the town doing their widow-in-the-lake act, but she balked at being a party to murder."

"So it was Jean who rigged Lana's diving gear?" That made sense. He would have been on the *Sunset Sally* with Captain Harrow and had the perfect opportunity.

"That's right," said Derek. "Jean wasn't much help leading the police to the first victim's body. He was too distraught over his girlfriend's death at his own hands. But Chief Kennedy borrowed some bloodhounds from a Mr. Jessup."

"Jessup owns a dog kennel," Mom put in. "Nice man."

Derek continued. "The police found JJ buried in a shallow grave not a hundred yards from where Channing and Jean had disposed of the body previously." Derek explained that Jean had been Channing's accomplice from the beginning. He and Channing were lovers. She had known Jean for many years before meeting JJ. It seemed Jean Rabin had lived in London and the two of them met at university.

According to Jean, Channing regretted her marriage to JJ the minute she'd spoken her vows. She'd only married him on the spur of the moment because she'd had a big fight with Jean and wanted to get back at him. Channing came to the States to meet up with Jean, assumed her maiden name, and told everyone she was from Australia. But JJ, Joseph James, somehow figured out where she'd gone and he was determined to win her back.

So when she came to the Town of Ruby Lake to hook up with Jean, JJ followed. The two of them fought and JJ met his end—I hadn't been imagining things at all. While the others were out, Jean and Channing hid the body, hoping to convince the others staying at the house that JJ had simply given up on his marriage and run off.

Jean and Channing believed Gus had his suspicions about what had happened to Channing's ex, but he hadn't confronted them. The deadly pair knew that if they killed him, they'd be forced to leave the house.

But Annika, for one, wasn't buying it. Neither was Lana, as it turned out. That had to be why she'd wanted to talk to me. Funny, because I still had a hunch that murder was the end game in Gus and Lana's plans for Moire.

Derek continued. "There's no doubt in my mind or Chief Kennedy's that Gus and Lana were con artists. The way Jean told it to Chief Kennedy, Gus and Lana had planned for Gus to marry Moire. Then, after an appropriate period of time, Moire would die."

"Die?" Kim's eyes grew wide.

Derek nodded. "Probably a quote-unquote *accident* of some sort."

"Lovely," I murmured. "So that after another suitable period of time, the two of them could get married."

"And run Ruby's Diner together." Derek's eyes drifted across the street toward the diner.

"What horrible, horrible people," Kim said with a sigh.

"I still wonder if Moire's taken out any new life insurance policies lately."

"Good question," Derek replied. "You might ask her that."

I would. If she would even speak to me again.

Channing and Jean weren't taking chances, so they'd decided to rig Lana's gear. End of problem. The only problem remaining was me, and they weren't quite sure what to do about me, short of murder, which might raise a whole lot more eyebrows than the deaths of Lana and Bessie had already raised.

Jean claimed that Channing had placed the tray on

the stairs that I'd accused Esther of negligently placing there. I suppose she hoped I'd fall and break my leg or my neck. I'd either end up dead or significantly slowed down. Funny how I was now sitting here in a wheelchair.

I shivered as I remembered how innocent and friendly the young woman had seemed and how I'd invited her into my life and business. "What about Ross O'Sullivan? How is he mixed up in all this?"

"He wasn't, according to Jean," answered Derek. "Just another patsy. They stole Ross's chain and planted it near the grave. That way, if anybody did start snooping around there again . . ." Derek paused and looked straight at me.

"We'd think Ross was involved," I concluded.

"At the very least," said Kim, "it would add to the confusion." She giggled. "I know I'm confused."

"Channing was a smart young woman," I said. "She was covering all her bases." And now she was dead.

"And Jean?" That was Kim.

"Jean Rabin is down in the county lockup," Derek replied.

"And Gus McKutcheon?"

"Still being interviewed by the police."

"Will he be charged?" asked Kim.

Derek could only shrug. "We'll see. I'm confident that if the police dig deep enough, they'll find a thing or two to charge him with. And get this," he added. "Gus broke down and admitted that he was the father of Lana Potter's child."

"No surprise there," I replied.

"I suppose not," said Kim, crumbling under the *I told you so* look I beamed her way.

Maybe now Moire Leora would forgive me for interfering. Not that I hadn't learned my lesson. I was never, ever going to interfere in anything ever, ever again. Not murder, not relationships, not woodpeckers hammering away outside my window at five in the morning.

My stomach called for my attention. I took a healthy bite of my breakfast bar and chewed. "Yuck-yuck!" I jumped from my wheelchair and instantly regretted the move, howling in pain.

Derek leapt forward and pushed me back into my seat. "Careful, Amy."

I spit madly, not caring how I must look to Derek. Gooey chunks of breakfast cookie crumbled down my blouse, leaving yellow-brown stains. I wiped my shirt, which only made the spit and cookie mess all the worse. "What is in those things?!" I eyeballed the breakfast bars of death.

"Amy!"

My eyes bounced up. My mother stood in the middle of the aisle, a shocked expression on her face, a glass of water sloshing in her hand. "What were you thinking?"

"Me? You made these things." I spat some more. I couldn't get the horrid taste out of my mouth. Maybe a swig of kerosene would do the trick. I could roll down to the hardware store later for a pint.

"I was thinking those were for the customers." Mom crossed the room and thrust the glass of water out at me.

I took it and swigged gratefully. "I'm not sure that's a good idea, Mom."

Mom planted her hands on her hips. "What's wrong with them?"

"They taste like . . . like . . ." I couldn't think of a single thing to compare the horrible bars to.

"Suet?" asked Mom.

"Yes! Suet!" That was precisely what they tasted

like, not that I'd ever tasted any of the stuff, but I'd smelled enough of it. Birds were fortunate to have such an underdeveloped sense of smell.

"That's because they are suet." Mom reached over and started picking bits of suet off my chest.

My mouth hung open. Derek and Kim were laughing, Derek loudest of all. "S-suet?"

"That's right," said Mom. "Suet cakes." She ran to the side of the counter and picked up the dustpan and broom. "All natural too. Peanut butter, cornmeal, lard—"

The laughter from the peanut gallery was coming harder and stronger. I glared at Kim and Derek and they stopped. Sort of.

When Mom stared at them, they shut up completely and suddenly the two of them found something very interesting about their feet. "I thought the customers might like them." Mom finished sweeping up and dumped the debris in the trash. "For their birds." She thrust the dustpan and broom back in the corner.

"What's so funny?" Cousin Riley stepped in from the back room, covered in fine black dust. I'd been barely tolerating the sounds of banging and scraping coming from the storeroom. His eyes fell on me. "Hey, welcome back, Amy!" He leaned over and gave me a big hug. "Glad to see you're okay."

With his shirt pressed against my nose, I caught a strong whiff of smoke. "What are you up to back there?" I refrained from snapping at him for the black smudge now transferred to my blouse, which Mom had had sent over to the hospital for me.

"A little repair work." He smiled broadly. "Almost done. It's going to be good as new."

I narrowed my eyes at him. "What's going to be good as new?"

Riley shot a troubled glance at Esther, who'd come hurrying over. Her lips were pressed tightly shut.

I started pushing myself toward the storeroom. "I want to see."

"Now, now," said Riley, putting his hands up as stop signs. "There's nothing to see."

"Nothing at all." Esther jumped in front of the wheelchair.

"Move," I insisted.

Esther frowned but stepped aside as I rolled to the back of the store. I instantly wished I hadn't. One entire wall was scorched floor to ceiling. "What happened?" I swiveled my head so I could see Riley and Esther. "What did you do?"

"I didn't do anything," snapped Esther. "Now get out of here and let the man finish his work."

"Don't worry, Amy." Cousin Riley clapped me on the back, ignorant of the bruises I'd suffered. I winced. "It's nothing a good coat of paint won't fix." Two gallons of paint, a brush, a roller, and a tarp blocked the rear door.

"Let me give you a hand," Derek said, rolling up his shirt sleeves. "You go get some rest, Amy." He instructed Esther to take charge of me.

Against my protests, Esther grabbed the handles of the wheelchair and rolled me back out front. "Put me in front of the window," I said. I could sit in the sun, watch the birds.

Esther obediently rolled me past Mom and Kim, who were now double-teaming a customer, to the front window. I closed my eyes, determined not to let Esther, Riley, or little things like fire get the best of me. My eyelids suddenly felt like there were twenty-pound weights sitting on each of them. A little nap would do me a world of good . . .

Rat-a-tat-tat-brrr!

I lifted a heavy eyelid. Drummy was going to work. In the middle of the day, no less. Didn't that woodpecker know it was siesta time?

I let my eye close again, determined not to let the bird get the best of me.

A sudden tickling shook me from my stupor. "What the—" Esther the Pester was looming over me. She ran the feather duster over the bridge of my nose.

I batted the feather duster away. "How did you?" I stared at the feather duster in my face. "Where did you?" I looked across the store to the tall pole with the owl nesting box atop it. The box was gone. "What happened to the owl nesting box?"

"A customer bought it." Esther hit me in the face with the feather duster once more. "And guess what he found inside."

I let my head sink back and closed my eyes. They say it's the early bird that gets the worm—but this time it was the old bird who'd gotten me.

Please turn the page for an exciting

sneak peek of the next

Bird Lover's mystery

To Kill a Hummingbird

now on sale!

1

"Amy, what are you doing up on that ladder?" asked Kim.

I jolted and the ladder's legs wobbled precariously. "Don't do that!" I had a hummingbird nectar feeder dangling from my index finger by the ring at the end of the metal rod attached to the round base. The rod was for hanging the feeder from a tree or hook.

Kim scratched her head. "Do what?"

"Scare me like that. I could fall." I looked down at the ladder's feet to make sure I was safe. "And to answer your question, what I'm doing up here is hanging a hummingbird feeder."

"Why?" Kim's my best friend and partner in Birds & Bees, my bird-feeding and bird-watching supply store in Ruby Lake, North Carolina. She only works in the business part-time. She's employed as a Realtor the remainder of her working hours. Still, for all her time spent in the store, she's far from an expert on bird feeding or bird-watching.

"To feed the hummingbirds, for one thing."

I hung the distinctive red plastic hummingbird feeder

on the steel hook my cousin Riley had attached to the porch eave. The red-topped feeders each have a clear shallow base that holds the sugar water they favor. "How does it look?"

"Okay, I guess." Kim didn't look impressed. She isn't as into birds as I am.

Esther poked her head out the front window of the shop. "Her ex-professor, Mason something, is coming and Amy's trying to impress him."

"Thank you, Esther." I frowned at her and climbed down. Ladders make me nervous. People sticking their faces out windows while I'm teetering at the top of one downright scare me. "And that's Mason Livingston." I dusted off my khaki shorts, part of the Birds & Bees uniform. That and the red tee I was wearing with our store's name and logo embroidered on it.

Kim removed a hummingbird feeder from the cardboard box on the front porch. I saw her lips moving as she counted the rest of the feeders in the carton. "Yeah, but *six* hummingbird feeders?"

I laughed and pushed a curl of hair behind my ear. "I want to impress him *a lot!*" I grabbed the feeder from Kim's hand. "Help me with the rest of these, would you?"

"Sure thing." Kim grabbed a suction-cup hanger and stuck it to the front door.

"Not the door." I pulled it down and moved it to one of the front windows opposite the cash register inside. That way we could watch the hummingbirds come and go while ringing up sales. "The nectar will spill. Besides, the hummingbirds may not like the door opening and closing all the time."

"Okay," said Kim, snatching another from the box. "What about the rest of these?"

I looked around the porch. "Let's put another on that side of the door." I pointed to the window Esther had stuck her head through. The rest can go in the garden."

"You must really like this guy." Esther stepped out on the porch. She had balked at the idea of wearing shorts around the shop, but had finally agreed to wear a pair of khaki slacks and had opted for a robin's-egg blue tee for herself.

I'd ordered her several colors of the shirts and made her promise to wear them. I was tired of seeing her around the store during business hours in her raggedy old housedresses that smelled of cigarettes and looked like a cat had been snoozing on them—both of which were forbidden in my business-slash-home.

The policy was no reflection on cats. I'm a big fan of the felines. Unfortunately, I have a strong allergic reaction to them. Esther Pilaster, aka Esther the Pester or Esther Pester, as I was wont to call her on days when she was especially pestering and I was especially short of patience, wasn't much for following my rules about either. Not that I had caught her smoking or frolicking with a cat, but all evidence pointed to the existence of both. One of these days, I was determined to prove it.

Since my mom had unilaterally given Esther a job in my store and she was already renting an apartment here, I could only make do until her lease was up.

"Mason Livingston was one of my college professors." I had attended the University of North Carolina at Chapel Hill on the other side of the state. "I admire him."

"I thought you were an English major. Not an ornithologist." Kim hung a feeder in a small Japanese maple just inside the white picket fence that hugged the sidewalk. "This okay?"

"Yes, fine. In answer to your question—yes, I was an English major. But I took a Birds of North America class from Mason as an elective. You know birds have always been my passion." Now they were my job.

"Esther, would you mind running over to Otelia's Chocolates and picking up a pound? I remember Mason was a fanatic about chocolate," I called as I carefully maneuvered the wooden ladder between the flowers. Otelia's chocolate shop sits catercorner to Birds & Bees and is within shouting distance of Ruby Lake and the marina.

"Sure. Anything special?" she asked with peppermint-scented breath. I was sure she sucked on the hard candies to cover the smell of tobacco.

"Something fun. Use your best judgment." I'd give Mason the chocolates later at the book signing. "My purse is behind the counter."

Esther went inside and returned with my credit card. "I'll be right back. Either of you ladies want anything for yourselves?"

"I wouldn't say no to a half pound of maple fudge," Kim answered quickly.

"What about you, Amy?" Esther hollered as she started down the brick path to the sidewalk. Bright yellow and red flowers, red salvia and yellow coreopsis, bordered the edges and were alive with bees. I was hoping to attract at least one hummingbird to my yard while Mason was in town.

"I wouldn't say no to some maple fudge either," I said. I laid the ladder down along the edge of the sidewalk and moved to a feeder pole I had earlier asked Cousin Riley to place in the center of a bed of hummingbird sage, formally known as *Salvia spathacea*.

"That's my problem." I ran my fingers over my

tummy. "A half pound of fudge seems to equal about four pounds of body fat. So nothing for me, thanks."

"How is that even possible?" Kim chuckled as Esther crossed the street, ignoring the crosswalk and the moving vehicles and their blaring horns. Like I said, Esther is not big on rules. Even rules of the road.

"Must be my metabolism."

I left Kim to finish hanging the last couple of hummingbird feeders while I went upstairs to get the sugar water I had prepared earlier for the birds.

"Okay, I'll top off the regular bird feeders while I'm at it," Kim answered. We have several bird feeders outside the shop. We keep them filled mostly with unshelled black oil sunflower seeds with occasional treats like peanuts or safflower seeds. The idea was to attract the birds to the feeders and the customers to the birds and then Birds & Bees. So far, it seemed to be working fairly well. Business had picked up since opening several months back. With summer in full swing, I was hoping that upward trend would continue.

I climbed up to the third level of the old Queen Anne Victorian-era house where I lived with my mother. The second floor was occupied by my current renters, Esther Pilaster and Paul Anderson. The business occupied the entire ground floor.

Some say the old house is haunted. I like to joke that it will cease being haunted once Esther moves out. She was on the last year of her legacy lease and I, for one, was looking forward to her moving on.

"Hi, Amy," said my mother, looking up from the English-countryside mystery novel she was reading. "Everything okay in the store?"

"Fine, Mom." I crossed the apartment to the kitchen on the other side of the small flat. We shared a two-bedroom, open concept apartment. Open concept because there was one bathroom, two bedrooms, and the living-area-slash-kitchen; we lived our lives in the open, like it or not. I pulled the plastic jug from the fridge and set it on the counter. "I came back for the hummingbird nectar."

"Anything I can do to help?"

"No, thanks. I've got it." I yanked open the freezer. "Thanks for boiling it up for me though." Hummingbird-feeder food is easy to make at home: four parts water to one part sugar. We dissolved the sugar in a saucepan of boiling water, let it cool, then stored it in a plastic jug in the fridge. Mom had prepared a batch for me the night before while I'd been out on a date.

I pulled the ice tray from the freezer and stabbed a cube with my finger. "Solid as a rock." I grinned with satisfaction. Mom had made up such a big batch of sugar water that I'd had the idea to try to freeze the extra in an ice-cube tray.

Mom looked up from her book. She appeared tired. Mom suffers from muscular dystrophy. She'd been getting worse there for a while, but the disease seemed to be in check now, which was a great thing. Still, she wears out easily and I do my best not to be a source of stress or worry for her. Sometimes I succeed. "How did it turn out?"

"Perfect. I'll use the liquid now and the frozen cubes will be ready next time our little friends need their feeders refilled."

The sugar water only lasted in the feeders for about three days tops. That wasn't necessarily because the birds drank it all up, but the liquid tends to get a bit funky out there in the hot sun, not to mention the effects of the insects that sometimes drown in the water and decompose therein. For the health of the hummingbirds, it was always best to clean the feeders and refill them every third day.

"Do hummingbirds really live on sugar water?" Mom asked. "It doesn't seem possible."

"It isn't. The sugar water is a nectar substitute. Hummingbirds also eat a lot of spiders and other insects. Sometimes when you see a hummingbird hovering over a flower it isn't because it's about to feed on nectar—it could very well be that the bird has spotted a tasty spider or even an insect trapped in a spider's web."

"I never knew that."

"It's quite common. They also perform hover-hawking and what's called sally-hawking."

Hawking? Yep. I grabbed a bowl from a shelf, set it on the kitchen counter, and twisted the frozen sugar cubes free of the ice-cube tray, then dumped them in the bowl. "Hummingbirds might fly through a swarm of insects, like gnats, and snatch them as they pass. Kind of like swifts do. That's called hover-hawking. Or they might sit on a branch, spot their prey, and make a beeline for it. That's sally-hawking." I jiggled the bowl of cubes.

"I don't think I'll ever learn everything there is to know about birds," sighed Mom.

I started to smile. "That makes two of us!"

Hoo-hoo-hoo-hoo!

The distinctive doglike hooting of a barred owl sounded from outside the house. But there was something funny about this call, it sounded a bit . . . metallic. Not to mention, I'd never seen a barred owl hanging around the Town of Ruby Lake in the middle of the day.

Mom turned her head toward the front window. "What on earth is that?"

"I don't know. It sounded like it came from the street."

I refilled the ice-cube tray and slid it back in the freezer. "I'll take a look." I crossed to my bedroom, from which I have a great view of Lake Shore Drive, the main road that sweeps along the lake and into town. The busy street is home to much of the tourist industry and shopping in our fair burg. It was the perfect location for Birds & Bees.

"What is that thing?" Mom had come to my room and she peered over my shoulder to the street below.

I cocked my head. "If I didn't know better, I'd say that was a giant birdhouse!"

ABOUT THE AUTHOR

J.R. Ripley is the pen name of Glenn Meganck, the critically acclaimed author of the Tony Kozol mystery series, the Maggie Miller Mysteries, and the Kitty Karlyle Pet Chef Mysteries (written as Marie Celine), among other novels. For more information about him, visit www.glenn meganck.com.

Connect with U(s)

Visit us online at
KensingtonBooks.com
to read more from your favorite authors, see books
by series, view reading group guides, and more.

for sneak peeks, chances to win books and prize packs,
and to share your thoughts with other readers.

f 🐦

facebook.com/kensingtonpublishing
twitter.com/kensingtonbooks

Tell us what you think!

To share your thoughts, submit a review,
or sign up for our eNewsletters, please visit:
KensingtonBooks.com/TellUs.